RECEIVE GOD'S FIVEFOLD BLESSING

It's Waiting for You

By
Rod Parsley

RESULTS
PUBLISHING

Receive God's Fivefold Blessing

By Rod Parsley
Published by Results Publishing
World Harvest Church
PO Box 100
Columbus, OH 43216-0100, USA
www.rodparsley.com

ISBN: 978-1-935794-03-5

CONTENTS

Introduction

What Are You Waiting For?

What are you waiting for? A breakthrough? A miracle? An answer to prayer?

Are you weary of waiting? Are you tired of that problem, that habit, that relational struggle, that debilitating sickness, that debt? I see multitudes of Christians waiting for a financial turnaround. Perhaps you're one of them, in need of an end to your need.

Friend, I believe today is your day. Your waiting period is over! Today can begin a whole new era in your life. God has spoken to me clearly, and revealed to me that He has five blessings ready for you.

How do I know? Because of the Word.

I remember the day God showed me this more clearly and more dramatically than ever in my life. In that moment, He gave me one of the most transformational truths I've ever experienced.

It was almost three decades ago. I was sitting with my Bible, asking God for the key to financial victory in His kingdom so that I could unlock the blessings I knew He had in reserve for me and everyone who would believe.

The gift God gave me that day changed my life. What God imparted then has changed the lives of multitudes of people who have embraced it and lived by it ever since.

It was a prayer-answering, destiny-altering revelation beyond anything I could ever have hoped or imagined.

On that day, 27 years ago, God pointed me to Easter Sunday—Resurrection Sunday—the commemoration of God giving His best on Calvary. And in that moment God spoke this word into my spirit:

"Declare to the people: On this one day a year, commemorate how I gave My best by giving your best to Me."

I obeyed. I called our people together and gave them this word from the Lord. I called on them to give, on Resurrection Sunday, not just the normal 10 percent tithe, but a best seed—one week's income—to honor God's greatest Seed, Jesus Christ, who suffered and died for you and me.

It seemed outrageous, but I could not deny what God had spoken so clearly to my heart.

And the Holy Spirit moved. Even though not one person in our congregation at that time could possibly give a full week's income, they began stepping out in faith, saving, sacrificing and selling possessions. They took on second jobs and did extra work.

They did whatever they had to do to sow an extraordinary "Resurrection Seed."

Their Easter Sunday offering was so anointed, so blessed, so miraculous that they catapulted our ministry to a new level of faith. It was their sowing that day that enabled our ministry to reach you, all these years later.

But this is the amazing side effect of that first Resurrection Seed being sown: God began blessing those people on a level we could never have dreamed. Miracles happened. Lifelong prayers were answered. The sick were healed. Marriages were restored. Businesses prospered.

Why? Because of the Word. God gave me the Word. I gave them the Word. We obeyed the Word. It worked for us in a powerful way.

This same supernatural level of blessing can be yours, as you obey the same Word today in sowing your own Resurrection Seed. Today you can unleash this same miracle-working power. Your wait is over.

Look at what Jesus did in John 5. A man lame for 38 years was lying by the public pool at Bethesda. He was blind to the possibility of his healing. He was halt, withered, impotent. He was waiting.

But then Jesus arrived. And what He gave to that man, He can give to you. He administered and offered him a fivefold blessing. It's summed up in five power-packed principles: **Receive. Release. Rain. Reproduce. Rise up.**

God gave His best to that man who was waiting. And now He wants to impart to you that same blessing.

I'm here today to proclaim: your wait is over. As you activate these principles in your life, you will see possibilities becoming realities like you've never known.

But this little book doesn't end there. The things God has revealed to me about this year, 2012, will take you to unprecedented levels of faith and blessing.

It's time for your harvest. 2011 was a year of chaos and struggle; that's what 11 signifies. But now it's 2012—and 12 is the number of order, of structure, of fulfillment. This is your due date for blessing. I believe God will accelerate your season of harvest, because of your step of faith today.

So I ask again, "What are you waiting for?"

Turn the page. Your fivefold blessing is coming. Your season of chaos, your season of burden, your season of struggle can be over.

Together, let's move forward into a new breakthrough.

Chapter One

The Fivefold Blessing Expanded

In 450 B.C., the king's cupbearer came before King Artaxerxes I, the great emperor of Persia. This man held a most important position in the empire, since he alone had the responsibility of certifying that none of the wine the king drank had been poisoned.

On this day, however, the man who protected an earthly king was now more concerned about our heavenly King. He had a very special request. The walls of Jerusalem, the city of his ancestors, had been destroyed. He wanted to rebuild its walls and gates.

The man's name was Nehemiah.

Because Nehemiah had been such a trustworthy servant, Artaxerxes granted his request. Nehemiah then led a team of skilled and hard-working craftsmen who left Persia and went back to Israel.

When Nehemiah first arrived, he inspected the damage. The walls were mostly rubble. They were so badly broken down that he couldn't even pass through some of the gates. He finally told the Jewish leaders and officials in the city:

> Then I said to them, "You see the distress that we are in, how Jerusalem lies waste, and its gates are burned with fire. Come and let us build the wall of Jerusalem, that we may no longer be a reproach." And I told them of the hand of my God which had been good upon me, and also of the king's words that he had spoken to me. So they said, "Let us rise up and build." Then they set their hands to this good work (Nehemiah 2:17-18).

They joined together and re-laid the foundations. The walls of Jerusalem—the holy city—were rebuilt. The Jews

9

as a nation were revitalized. Most importantly, the gates were cleared and opened.

One of those gates was called the Sheep Gate. Little did Nehemiah know that nearly 500 years later Jesus Christ would walk through this same gate. What He would do there would radically change not just one desperately hurting person's life, but it would also set the stage for each of us to partake in a blessing that God desires for everyone.

It's my prayer that the words I'm about to share will rebuild and revitalize your faith. If there are gates in your life that are burned, broken down and filled with rubble, I believe they will be cleared and opened.

The Lamb's Gateway

Flash forward to 28 A.D. Jesus has just come to Jerusalem. He first enters the city through the very first gate Nehemiah restored: The Sheep Gate. This passageway into the city had been given that name because it was where the sheep and lambs were brought through that were to be sacrificed in the temple.

There were many gates leading into the city, and Jesus could have gone through any one of them. But he did not go through the Horse Gate where the Roman soldiers and their horses would come and go. He did not enter through the Dung Gate where the refuse from the city was carried away. No, The Lamb of God came into Jerusalem through the Sheep Gate.

Once these sacrificial animals were taken into the city, they never came back out. They had to die. They were sacrificed for the sins of the people.

This gate was a passageway to death, yet Jesus identified Himself as the gate for the sheep.

This had tremendous significance for the people in Jesus' day:

10

Most assuredly, I say to you, I am the door [or gate] *of the sheep. All who ever came before Me are thieves and robbers, but the sheep did not hear them. I am the door* [or gate]. *If anyone enters by Me, he will be saved, and will go in and out and find pasture* (John 10:7-9, NKJV).

Jesus was signifying that He was the gateway through which the sacrificial lambs were led. But even more importantly, He was saying, "I'm the only way out for those lambs who are destined to die."

And unless we can find someone willing to take our place, we are destined to die for our sins.

Thank God, we no longer need to rely on the blood of sheep and lambs to take away those sins. Jesus Christ would become that offering Himself. He would become our sacrifice and our escape from the penalty of sin.

All of this symbolism at that one gate has tremendous importance, especially in light of what was about to happen.

A Pool Called Mercy

Jesus had just come through the Sheep Gate when He stopped at a place called the Pool of Bethesda.

Here is the apostle's John's firsthand account of what happened next:

Now there is at Jerusalem by the sheep market a pool, which is called in the Hebrew tongue Bethesda, having five porches. In these lay a great multitude of impotent folk, of blind, halt, withered, waiting for the moving of the water. For an angel went down at a certain season into the pool, and troubled the water: whosoever then first after the troubling of the water stepped in was made whole of whatsoever disease he had. And a certain man was there, which had an infirmity thirty and eight years. When Jesus saw him lie, and knew that he had been now a long time in that case, he saith unto him, Wilt thou be made whole? The impotent man answered him, Sir, I have no man, when the water is troubled, to put me into the pool: but while I am coming, another steppeth down before me. Jesus saith unto him, Rise, take up thy bed, and walk. And immediately the man was made whole, and took up his bed, and walked (John 5:2-9).

The name Bethesda means house of mercy. Please don't miss the importance of that designation. The Lamb of God, who had just entered through the Sheep Gate which was reserved for sacrificial lambs was now extending mercy to a man who badly needed it. This man had been paralyzed for 38 years. His condition was so debilitating that he couldn't even roll over and fall into a pool of water. Jesus not only healed him, He strengthened and restored all of those atrophied muscles to the point the man could carry his bed and walk.

All of these principles still apply to us today.

First and foremost, when we make Jesus Christ the first gate in our life, like Nehemiah, He clears that gate of all rubble so we can freely walk through. He then takes on our sin so that we don't have to offer any sacrificial lambs. He actually becomes for us the Gate, the Lamb and the Good Shepherd all at once.

He also becomes our house of mercy. In so doing He repairs, replenishes and restores us. He not only heals our infirmities, His mercy extends to all of our trials and troubles. Our finances, our emotional health and our relationships all are reestablished. Like Nehemiah of old, our walls and gates are rebuilt. And through those very gates comes the divine grace of the Lord Jesus Christ.

Five Porches: The Entranceway to the Fivefold Blessing

There's a very small fact within this story that appears so insignificant you might just miss it. But this little detail has huge implications.

Around the pool of Bethesda were five porches or porticoes. That's where the sick were lying.

This tidbit of information is not just an interesting architectural or even archaeological piece of evidence. It has tremendous importance within God's kingdom.

The number five in the Bible signifies grace, favor or blessing. These five porches representing blessing were situated around the pool known as the "house of mercy."

As we receive God's mercy, through Christ, we, like the lame man, will receive His favor and blessing. Consider this: The man was on one of five porches waiting on the Lamb of God to be his sacrifice, heal his infirmities and extend to him His blessing.

But let's go one step further. These five porches of blessing serve as an entrance, if you will, to five very specific principles that Jesus Christ demonstrated. I call them God's fivefold blessing.

Blessing #1: Receive

We can find ourselves just like the blind who sat on those porches. It's so easy to live in darkness. Of course, Satan is the prince of darkness and it's his plan to keep us in the dark. The ultimate obscurity is never to know the Light of the World, Jesus Christ, as Savior and Lord. But even after we're saved we can stumble around, living in the shadows, never fully thriving in the light and life that God has for us.

But praise be to God! The Bible says that in Jesus Christ ... *was life, and the life was the light of men* (John 1:4). He can light up our pathway, illuminate our purposes and enlighten our possibilities.

How do we fully activate this?

We must **RECEIVE**. When we embrace God's vision of our success, we are no longer blind to our potential for abundance. For instance, if you need a financial breakthrough, you need to see yourself as God sees you. God created you to be blessed. And the step to that abundance—that porch of plenty—is receiving.

Blessing #2: Release

The second blessing begins when we overcome a lack of motion. You might be thinking, "Pastor, I'm busy all the time. I work hard. I try and try. But nothing seems to be happening."

The kind of activity I'm referring to is not dissipated effort. It is moving in time with the rhythms of God's kingdom. David said:

> O Lord, my heart is not proud, nor my eyes haughty; Nor do
> I involve myself in great matters, Or in things too difficult for
> me (Psalm 131:1, NASB).

King David is speaking here—the one who defeated Goliath and conquered great armies. He did not involve himself in things too difficult! He knew that within his own strength he was useless. His efforts would all be for naught if he didn't simply rest and recognize how the Lord was moving. His labors would release nothing. In fact, how could a mere shepherd boy release the stone in his slingshot and have it hit the mark, if God weren't in the equation?

Jesus underscored this same real power principle. He said:

> Come to Me, all you who labor and are heavy laden, and I
> will give you rest. Take My yoke upon you and learn from

Me, for I am gentle and lowly in heart, and you will find rest for your souls. For My yoke is easy and My burden is light (Matthew 11:28-30, NKJV).

When we try in our own strength, under our own steam, we can actually become just like those found at the pool of Bethesda: the halt, or paralyzed. Our activity is actually immobilizing. Yet when we wait upon the Lord His power **is released** unto us. It is then that we become fully functioning, as Isaiah proclaimed:

But those who wait on the Lord shall renew their strength; They shall mount up with wings like eagles, they shall run and not be weary, they shall walk and not faint (Isaiah 40:31, NKJV).

As we receive God's light, He also releases His fully illuminated provision. God is about to **RELEASE** the full harvest from your previously sown seed. You will no longer be halt. You may have been paralyzed like the man by the pool—going nowhere. But Jesus Christ says, "You don't have to stay in that condition anymore!"

Blessing #3: Rain

God is about to **RAIN** down the power of His Word on your seed. If your finances and other resources (family, health, job, etc.) have been under attack or shrinking back—if they have shriveled and withered—it's time for them to grow exponentially.

Rain is a symbol of God refreshing and revitalizing. Rain replenishes the earth. Spiritual rain replenishes the spirit. And through the power of prayer, rain can pour forth.

James writes that:

Elijah was a man with a nature like ours, and he prayed earnestly that it would not rain; and it did not rain on the land for three years and six months. And he prayed again, and the heaven gave rain, and the earth produced its fruit (James 5:17-18, NKJV).

Of course, this is referring to actual raindrops falling from the sky. But as we apply this principle, we'll also see God's spiritual rain from heaven in innumerable ways. You may suddenly find that troublesome job has been rained upon. What was a source of worry becomes watered. That difficult situation with a child, grandchild, or in-law receives showers of blessing and there comes a divine refreshing. The windows of heaven open and new supply is poured out upon that desperate financial problem.

The storm clouds may seem ominous, but I'm here to tell, you raise your hands to heaven and welcome—ask for—the rain that is coming. It will bring forth new growth in your life.

Blessing #4: Reproduce

It is the nature of a seed to **REPRODUCE**. If you have received and God has released and rained on your life, then you can fully expect your seed to multiply. In fact, the first command that God gave to Adam and Eve in the garden had to do with reproducing abundantly.

Then God blessed them, and God said to them, "Be fruitful and multiply; fill the earth and subdue it; have dominion over the fish of the sea, over the birds of the air, and over every living thing that moves on the earth." And God said, "See, I have given you every herb that yields seed which is on the face of all the earth, and every tree whose fruit yields seed; to you it shall be for food" (Genesis 1:28-29, NKJV).

He was certainly alluding to the physical seeds that you put in the ground to grow crops. But God was also establishing the spiritual concept of seed planting, of reproducing, of being fruitful and multiplying every capacity and opportunity in our lives.

You may say, "But Pastor, all I see is barrenness and fallow ground. Nothing's growing!"

Look no further than the nearest farmland. The Bible says, *To everything there is a season* (Ecclesiastes 3:1, NKJV). You may be in winter right now, but springtime is coming. The crops from previous years may have grown and been harvested, but there is new ground to till and new seed to plant. The leaves may have fallen off the trees and the sap retreated back into the roots. But trust the Lord, because the spring sunshine is coming.

Be ready. The season of plowing and sowing is about to come upon you. Do what farmers do during the winter months. They consider how they'll plant their fields. They acquire the seed they'll need to sow.

Brothers and sisters, God is about to multiply your seed. Gather it up, and be ready to sow it and grow it!

Blessing #5: Rise Up

RISE UP. God can't do this for you. You've got to obey His Word and take responsibility for your blessing. You must be just like the man by the pool, when Jesus told him to rise up. His 38 years of waiting were over, but only when he obeyed and arose. God will do His part, and the seed will do its part. Now be ready to do yours.

James said, *But do you want to know, O foolish man, that faith without works is dead?* (2:20) It's vitally important that you activate the gifts God has given. God never intended for us to sit idly by—to be so heavenly minded that we're no earthly good.

You might be asking, "But you just asserted that I'm to rest, to wait, not to attempt things too difficult for me. Now, Pastor, you seem to be saying work, strive, put forth effort."

We have to go back to the root of our faith—our very personhood—to rightly divide this truth. Rising up, responding to God's Word, being obedient is not an external, fleshly thing. It is a matter of the heart. The apostle Paul completely understood the dilemma when he wrote:

> *For the good that I will to do, I do not do; but the evil I will not to do, that I practice. Now if I do what I will not to do, it is no longer I who do it, but sin that dwells in me. I find then a law, that evil is present with me, the one who wills to do good. For I delight in the law of God according to the inward man. But I see another law in my members, warring against the law of my mind, and bringing me into captivity to the law of sin which is in my members* (Romans 7:19-23, NKJV).

The power of obedience does not come and will never come in my members. The power to activate the Word of God, the strength to rise up, comes from the heart. We move because we believe. We go forth because the Spirit has come forth within us. The Spirit controls the mind and the mind controls the actions. If you want to see actions change, then focus on the things of the Spirit. As it—or rather, He—rises up in you, you will rise up and change your world.

Chapter Two

The Power of 12

In the Bible, numbers have a divine design. But the power of all Biblical numbers isn't based on some magical numerology. No, they are simply a confirming core reality in God's economy. In other words, these aren't God's "lucky" numbers. This has nothing to do with superstition or chance. God isn't revealing special ordinals that will then allow us to hit a lottery jackpot.

But God does use numbers to confirm His plan and even His personhood. They are profound signals, if you will, that point to His purposes. To those who seek Him, they indicate a deeper kingdom intent. They serve as signs to His wonders. And when you see them in scripture and even in life, you need to know they will result in new revelation.

God and His Word are accurate and confirming. In many non-biblical, ancient stories and even histories there often is a dubious quality to them—an "I'm not so sure about that" aspect. That's not true with the Bible. Scriptures written hundreds and even thousands of years before are precisely confirmed in passages that come later. To say it another way, it is simply beyond coincidence how the numbers add up in the Bible.

Consider these facts about the number 12. In God's kingdom it has vast implications and significance.

These divine digits represent order. It signifies that a thing has come to where God intended. If it were a symphony it would be the final resolution, the denouement. If it were a building, it would be the capstone. Ribbons are cut when the things in God's world add up to 12.

This inspired integer gives us that wonderful feeling of, "Ahh... we've finally arrived. This is what life always was meant to be. This is how God ordained things to function."

The special purpose in this sacred number is quite simply this: *order always brings the opportunity for abundance.* When things are in line, they perform as they should. When all the parts are present and in working order, the mechanism operates at maximum capacity.

In God's economy, the number 12 signifies that He doesn't need one thing more. In fact, if there is one thing less, the whole thing falters. It's not just a little less than, it is completely and utterly dysfunctional. Incomplete in God's world means out of order, unfinished, imperfect.

Think of it this way. If a tire is perfectly weighted, it turns flawlessly. Yet if you took weight off of just one part of the wheel, it would throw the entire rotation off. Your wheels would be out of balance. You may be able to drive at a very slow speed and you might not notice. But we all know that feeling of driving down the freeway when a wheel is out of kilter. The car shakes violently. You just have to stop.

The same is true in God's kingdom. If your spiritual wheels are out of balance, you might be able to go through life at a very slow speed with minimal blessings, seeing marginal opportunities and mixed results. But if you want to move at high speed, fluidly, gracefully, powerfully, then you need all the wheels poised in perfect equilibrium.

In the revolutions of God's universe, 12 means balanced order and perfection.

The number 12 is mentioned throughout scripture. Jacob had 12 sons and they became the 12 tribes of Israel. In the book of Revelation, the New Jerusalem—the heavenly city that Christ is preparing for His people—has 12 gates and each is one of 12 pearls. There are 12 angels guarding those gates. The foundation stones of that city in paradise are adorned with 12 precious stones: jasper, sapphire, chalcedony, emerald, sardonyx, sardius, chrysolite, beryl, topaz, chrysoprase, jacinth and amethyst.

Of course, there were 12 disciples and 12 baskets left over when Jesus finished feeding the 5,000. The woman had the issue of blood for 12 years (and in that 12th year came her healing). There were 12 stones that God asked the people of Israel to put up as a memorial after they crossed the Jordan river. (More on this in Chapter Five.)

All of these groups of 12 demonstrate God's divine and corporate order—His completion. His chosen people, the nation of Israel, were organized in 12 tribes. Each served a specific purpose. But as a group, they bespoke the masterful plan of God.

The New Jerusalem in the book of Revelation IS the final fulfillment, the highest heaven signifying God's purposes since time began. It will be the home of the saints for all eternity. It's where Christ will reign supreme forever. It is the city of completion, the sanctuary of the sacred, the expression of eternal excellence.

Christ chose 12 disciples. Yes, multitudes would follow Him. But these 12 served a pivotal purpose. He didn't need a million, a thousand, even one hundred to carry out this leadership role. No, He tapped into the taproot of God's corporate order of 12. Then Christ poured Himself into them, knowing the fruit that would come.

The Number 11 Falls Short

Perhaps one of the best ways to understand the power in 12 is to examine the lack of potential in the number 11. This number, 11, signifies chaos and confusion. If 12 is completion, then 11 is imperfection. If 12 is whole and perfect, 11 is limited and less than. If 12 is fully realized, then 11 is half-done and half-baked. It's fractional, marginal, partial. God uses this number to demonstrate what shouldn't be and hasn't been.

The power and purpose of these two numbers—12 and 11—is demonstrated clearly in the story of Joseph and his brothers. If you remember, Joseph has been sold by his brethren. Joseph was, in fact, the 11th son of the 12 sons of Jacob, who became Israel.

But what happened to Joseph? He was despised, rejected and humiliated because of the favor that his father had shown him. His father gave him a coat of many colors. His brothers became enraged. They became so jealous of him that they mistreated him terribly. They rejected him. They mocked him. They spoke of killing him. They cast him into a pit, and then when a caravan came by on its way to Egypt, they sold him into slavery.

You remember that according to Isaiah 53:3-5, the same thing was said about Jesus. He was despised, smitten of God. We did not esteem Him.

He was despised.
Who was?
Jesus.
He was rejected, a man of sorrows acquainted with grief.
We hid, as it were, our faces from Him.

He was despised, and we esteemed Him not. Surely, He hath borne our griefs and carried our sorrow; yet, we did esteem Him stricken, smitten of God and afflicted. He was wounded for our transgression, bruised for our iniquities. The chastisement of our peace was upon Him, and with His stripes, we are healed.

Joseph is a type of our Jesus. He, the 11th son, represents the incompletion, the lack of divine order, the not-quite-there-yet reality. That certainly doesn't mean Joseph wasn't important in God's plan. But he signified a greater thing that was coming. He was the chaos, the confusion, the out-of-balance incompletion.

And God's divinely ordained order then unfolded.

The Bible says in Genesis 43:1, *And the famine was sore in the land.*

Joseph was the 11th son of Jacob and he ended up in Egypt. A severe famine came, but God had uniquely positioned Joseph to be over the granaries—the very storehouses—of Egypt.

The famine was so bad that Jacob said to ten of his sons, "I want you to leave here, go to Egypt, and buy grain there."

Now the fact is Jacob actually had 11 sons still with him. But Benjamin was the baby, and he didn't want to risk him. So he said to him, "Benjamin, I want you to stay here. I've already lost Joseph." You see, Benjamin was the only remaining son of Jacob's beloved wife Rachel.

So off the ten brothers went to Egypt. Joseph immediately recognized them, and he asked them, "Do you have a father? Do you have any more brothers?"

And they said, "Yeah, we've got a father. He's still alive at home. We're all the brothers of one father, and we have a brother there."

So Joseph said, "I want you to go back to your father, and when you get there, I want you to get that other brother, and bring him here to me. And when you do, I'll make provision for you; but until then, I'm going to keep your brother Simeon here in Egypt, because I need some assurance."

The brothers went home. They stayed awhile. They used up all the grain that Joseph had sold them. Jacob told them they needed to go back to Egypt and get more provisions. The brothers responded, "We can't go to Egypt, because the man in charge there told us not to come without Benjamin."

In terms of birth order, where did Benjamin fall? He was the 12th son. Joseph, his brother now in Egypt, was the 11th son. So Joseph, the 11th son, is saying in essence, "Go get the 12th son."

Your Bible calls Jesus our elder brother in the faith. So if Joseph is a type of Jesus—because, like Christ, he was despised and rejected—that would make Benjamin a type of you and me. That would mean that God is waiting on us to come just like Joseph was waiting on Benjamin to come to him.

But something from our past is hindering us. Fear has entered, but there is a solution.

One of the other 12 sons of Jacob, named Judah, comes forth. Judah said, "Hold everything, Dad. You don't need to worry about this, because I'm going to take care of the boy."

Judah means *praise*. Judah means *a word given*. Here's what the Bible is telling you: "You might be afraid. But I have a way to overcome that fear. I'm going to send you a Word, and that Word is going to take you by the hand. Praise is going to come alongside and literally escort the Word!

Judah said unto Israel, his father, *Send the lad with me, and we will arise and go; that we may live and not die, but we and thou and also all our little ones* (Genesis 43:8).

Blessed Coming in and Going Out

So the brothers went back to Egypt. Judah was responsible for Benjamin. And when Joseph saw Benjamin, the 12th son, he said to the ruler of the house, *Bring these men home, and slay, and make ready; for these men shall dine with me* (Genesis 43:16).

The brothers were invited to Joseph's house for a meal, exactly at noon, or 12 o'clock.

The 12th son was coming at 12:00. And when he got there the Bible says, *And he took and sent messes unto them from before him: but Benjamin's mess was five times as much as any of theirs...* (Genesis 43:34).

Joseph blessed Benjamin upon his arrival with a fivefold blessing! His provision was five times as much as the other brothers.

But the blessing of the 12th son doesn't stop there.

Move forward in the story. In Genesis 45:22, when Benjamin and the brothers were getting ready to leave Egypt and go back to their father it states: *To all of them he gave each man changes of raiment; but to Benjamin he gave three hundred pieces of silver and five changes of raiment.*

Benjamin was blessed fivefold coming in and fivefold going out. Blessed coming in, blessed going out.

This fivefold, coming-in-going-out blessing is reserved for all those who are the 12th child. And who are those that are designated as the 12th child? All who call Jesus Christ their elder brother in the faith.

That would be you, if you claim Him as Lord.

God Almighty has saved, stored, and stockpiled this blessing just for His people.

Specifically, God revealed to me that this coming-in-and-going-out blessing applies as we transitioned from the year 2011 to 2012—as we moved from 11 to 12. The blessing of Joseph, the 11th son, was released on Benjamin, the 12th son. So too will it be poured out on us.

But wait a minute. It doesn't end there.

Please understand that the fivefold blessing—the coming-in-and-going-out blessing—can be activated and applied to all the areas of your life. As the 12th son, you are in a privileged position to receive it.

If you operate under this mantle of blessing, you will see your relationships revitalized, your finances fixed, your job situation solved, your health made whole whenever you are coming in and going out.

You say, "Pastor, what does that mean exactly—that I am coming in and going out? When does that occur?"

The Bible says that God is the Alpha and the Omega, the beginning and the end. And we are His children—specifically, His 12th child. So our coming-in-and-going-out blessing is available to us from start to finish, from beginning to end, through and through, inside out and above and beyond. The Almighty God desires to pour out His fivefold blessing and immerse you in abundance from the first to the last.

In fact, no matter what situation we find ourselves in, we can shout, "I'm blessed coming in, and I'm blessed going out!"

The Twelfth Man

LSU was playing Texas A&M in the Cotton Bowl. An LSU fan discovered that he was sitting right in the middle of a very wild and ecstatic Texas A&M cheering section. Everyone had a t-shirt that read: *The Twelfth Man.*

The LSU fan asked the meaning of about this curious moniker.

An exuberant Texas A&M fan said, "There are 11 men on the field. But all of us here in the stands complete them. We cheer. We shout. We encourage. It gives our guys an edge."

I thought about that little story. The number 12, of course, is quite prominent in the Bible. It is the number that represents order—corporate order—divine order. It signifies completion.

What these enthusiastic fans symbolized was a profound spiritual principle. Through Christ, our position in the kingdom of God is that of completion. He has completed us.

The work—the battle, if you will—was and has been done by the selfless sacrifice and work of Christ: the hard fought effort that went on out on the field. Our position is that of divine cheering section as we praise, exalt, and magnify the work that is in fact playing out before us.

We are God's enthusiastic witnesses. We play the role that Judah did with his brother Benjamin. Judah means *a word given* and *praise*. In the midst of fear, he stepped forward and brought a word, accompanied by praise.

We occupy this position as well. We cheer and celebrate when there are good things happening, points scored, and great plays made. In Psalm 52:9 it says, *I will praise You forever, because You have done it* (NKJV).

But we also shout when things aren't going well. As Paul wrote in Romans:

> *...We also glory in tribulations, knowing that tribulation produces perseverance; and perseverance, character; and character, hope. Now hope does not disappoint, because the love of God has been poured out in our hearts by the Holy Spirit who was given to us* (Romans 5:3-5, NKJV).

The Greek word for tribulation means *pressure*. Despite any pressure that presses in on us, we can glory in it. We can be just like those fans who cheer, shout, praise and encourage. In fact, you could even say that when things are going badly is exactly when we need to shout and praise even more.

This attribute and attitude of praise—of being a wildly ecstatic adoration advocate and cheer champion—is exactly where God desires us to be. It is actually the position of joy.

James said, ... *count it all joy*... even... *when you fall into various trials*. Why? ...*that you may be perfect and* **complete**, *lacking nothing* (1:2,4, NKJV).

As we fully take on that role of completion, we see and fully grasp the victories played out before us. We are transformed. We are filled with joy.

But there is so much more that's part of truly being a Twelfth Man—or Twelfth Woman within the kingdom of God. How can we realize our full capacity as the one who sits in the seat of completion? And what unfathomable, unmitigated and unbelievable opportunities appear for those who claim this position?

Chapter Three

Get Your Head on Straight

The fivefold blessing, the perfect 12 completion and even the chaos and confusion of 11 is demonstrated in many others ways in the Bible and throughout God's history.

Consider these fact about the number five which stands for favor, grace, and blessing.

- Five and its multiples are inscribed on almost every part of the tabernacle.
- The fifth phrase in the Lord's prayer is, *Give us this day our daily bread* (Matthew 6:11).
- The fifth commandment—honor your father and mother—has a specific blessing attached to it. *That your days may be long upon the land which the Lord your God is giving you* (Exodus 20:12, NKJV).
- Five kinds of animals were sacrificed under the old covenant: goats, sheep, cattle, pigeons, and doves.
- There are five books that form the Torah, the Pentateuch, or the first five books of the Old Testament.
- Daniel proclaimed the Fifth Kingdom to be an Everlasting Kingdom.

And how is this fivefold blessing to be administered? Again, the Bible is very clear: through the specific guidance and gifting of five distinct leadership positions. The apostle Paul writes:

And He Himself gave some to be apostles, some prophets, some evangelists, and some pastors and teachers, for the equipping of the saints for the work of ministry, for the edifying of the body of Christ, till we all come to the unity of the faith and of the knowledge of the Son of God, to a perfect man, to the measure of the stature of the fullness of Christ (Ephesians 4:11-13, NKJV).

The church will fully realize the fivefold blessing as each position does its work. The apostles are the kingdom's risk-takers and trailblazers. They are on the front line, boldly going where others haven't, forging new pathways. They are the entrepreneurs that energize new movements of faith. And they make great sacrifices for the church and the body.

The prophets speak the Word. They have one ear in heaven, yet their feet are firmly planted in the turmoil and trials of the earth. They are unprovoked by earthly power. They care really about only one thing: the truth. And they proclaim the divine message without deference to the audience. In other words, their message is the polar opposite of what is so popular today: being politically correct.

The evangelists call for repentance. They are like John the Baptist, preaching and baptizing. They live to tell others the Good News. The evangelists are the salespeople in God's divine business. They walk out to the world with open arms saying, "Come on in. You'll love it." They are the apologists, defending the faith, and the proclaimers, declaring the faith. They live that others might discover eternal life.

Pastors care for the flock. They are the shepherds here on earth and they know how to deal with all kinds of sheep. Whether the sheep wander and stray, are hungry and need fed, are thirsty and desire water, refuse to lie down in green pastures or run off to sow wild oats, the pastor is always there for the sheep. They offer words in season and out. They inspire and console, listen and compel God's people to experience the fullness of God.

The teachers open up the Word and the will of God. They don't just share facts, they dig much deeper. As they are illuminated, they shed light. They are the treasure-diggers and fortune-finders of the kingdom. But unlike greedy opportunists, their heart freely gives what they find that others might be blessed.

Do you see how these five together bless the church... **coming in and going out?**

The apostles push us forward. The pastors are there when we fall back. The prophets tell us about God's plans for the future. The teachers share His treasures from the past. And all the while the evangelists enlighten a darkened world bringing in more saints that can join us to take the Gospel into all the world.

These who occupy the five leadership positions, under the Almighty God's inspiration and direction, help discharge God's fivefold blessing. Five leaders freeing five blessings! Prophets RECEIVE the Words from God. Apostles, like those massive ice-breaker ships, RELEASE pioneering ministry in new unchartered areas. Pastors RAIN on their flocks and help them grow and flourish. Teachers REPRODUCE by discovering, collecting and dispersing new seed. Evangelists compel people to RISE UP and take hold of the gifts that God wants to give.

When Jesus fed the 5,000 He did so with five loaves and two fish. Loaves, bread, or feeding in the Bible symbolize the nourishment that comes through the Word, or scripture. Is it any wonder, then, that even as Christ used five distinct loaves to feed 5,000 people, the Apostle Paul, inspired by God, would designate five positions in the church to feed the entire church?

This hearkens back to another grouping of five. When David was about to confront Goliath, he went to a brook and chose five smooth stones. Even as these stones were instruments to defeat the Philistine enemy, so too the five leadership positions provide the church with the tools—indeed, weapons—to take on the battles we encounter.

It's Time to Get Your Head on Straight

We've already seen how the number 11 symbolizes chaos and confusion. Satan relishes this number; he loves to kill, steal, and destroy God's perfect and divine order of 12, reducing it to 11.

When he manages to do this, he's not taking away just an insignificant part. Take, for instance, the God-ordained institution of the 12 disciples. This is what God Almighty desired for the church. You could say they were the apple of God's eye. Yet Satan wanted to tip over that apple cart.

So he entered one of the twelve: Judas. The Devil wanted to do everything he could to make sure God, through Jesus Christ, did not establish divine order on the earth. By corrupting Judas, he thought he could obliterate what was ordained.

Of course, the actions of this corrupted disciple did set off the events that led to Christ's death. Judas not only betrayed the Lord, he betrayed God's order. Death resulted and with it came—at least for a time—chaos and confusion. The other disciples fled and went into hiding. You can only imagine how confused they were as they watched, to their horror, the brutal death of Jesus. Not only did He die, but the divine dream that Jesus Christ had instilled within them appeared to be destroyed as well.

Because Christ is the Lord and leader of the church, in essence, Judas' action had the effect of severing the head from the body. And without a head, the body of Christ would be in an utter state of confusion. To use a very graphic example, the church would be like a chicken with its head cut off.

The manner of Judas' death is a dramatic picture of what he did—or at least attempted to do. As you know, Judas committed suicide. But how did he choose to die? In a final act of chaos, he disconnected his head from his body. Judas didn't stab himself, jump off a cliff or cut his wrists. He hung himself. In essence, he disengaged the head from the body.

This is exactly what Satan was trying to do. By killing Christ, Satan wanted to disconnect the true Head and Lord of the universe from the body of Christ.

Of course, God had a glorious plan that Satan and Judas played into. The vacancy left by Judas who abandoned his position as the 12th disciple was reinstated before the day of Pentecost.

Divine order was restored. Satan's effort to disengage the head from body backfired. The chaos and confusion the forces of darkness tried to create were countered by the ultimate, divine, ordained order.

5,000 Fed. 12 Baskets of Blessing.

The Bible says in the Gospel of Luke:

But He said to them, "You give them something to eat." And they said, "We have no more than five loaves and two fish, unless we go and buy food for all these people." For there were about five thousand men. Then He said to His disciples, "Make them sit down in groups of fifty." And they did so, and made them all sit down. Then He took the five loaves and the two fish, and looking up to heaven, He blessed and broke them, and gave them to the disciples to set before the multitude. So they all ate and were filled, and twelve baskets of the leftover fragments were taken up by them (Luke 9:13-17, NKJV).

Do you see how the number five surfaces: 5,000 men, groups of fifty, five loaves? God's fivefold blessing runs throughout this passage. The number five stands for favor, grace, and blessing—and leadership order. Jesus was about to extend His grace and blessing on 5,000 hungry men (who actually represented 5,000 families). The leadership order is manifested when he asks them to get into groups of 50. And then Christ took only five loaves to feed all of these 5,000.

Five, five, five! Blessing, blessing, blessing! 5,000 coming in hungry, and 5,000 going out fed.

But Jesus goes one step further. He reestablishes and reaffirms God's divine order. His miracle of expansion—multiplying five loaves and two fish—had some remaining. When they collected this blessing, it resulted in 12 baskets of leftovers. There's that wonderful number 12 again!

By doing this Jesus is affirming, in no uncertain terms, this has been a miracle created by and resulting in God's divine order. It is complete. There weren't 11 baskets taken up. This miracle had nothing to do with chaos or confusion. In fact, Jesus went about it in an orderly, organized fashion, grouping the crowd into the divinely ordained, church leadership/organizational divisions of five.

It wasn't a "less than" miracle. It was fully realized according to the eternal plans and purposes of God. Those 12 baskets look back to the 12 sons and tribes of Israel. And they look forward to the 12 gates, angels, pearls, and gemstones in the New Jerusalem.

Coming and going, divinely ordered and ordained, fully realized and released, God's blessings were not only poured out that day, but they are available to each of us in the same manner and fullness every day.

Chapter Four

Look Back. Leap Forward.

First Chronicles 16:12 says, *Remember his marvelous works that he hath done, his wonders and the judgments of his mouth.* It is essential in the exercise of our faith to look back. In order to receive, release, rain, reproduce, and rise up—in other words, to realize fully the fivefold blessing—we need to remember and look back.

But when we do, we will leap forward!

We're not to look back like Lot's wife did. God had rescued her from an evil city. But even as she fled from Sodom and Gomorrah—literally spared from death—she still couldn't help gazing back with regret and longing. She possessed a sad nostalgia for the things she wished she still had even though they were wrong and could hurt her. This is not the kind of looking back that God desires.

No, the Lord Almighty asks us to look back lest we leap forward in the wrong direction.

We look back because we're lining up a true trajectory for our future. The touchstones and touchpoints of God's purposes from the past are so very important for us, because He doesn't want what's coming to be polluted by the mistakes of what's already been.

God continuously asks us to remember.

Remember that it is the Lord thy God that giveth thee the power to get wealth (Deuteronomy 8:18).

…This do in remembrance of me (1 Corinthians 11:24).

Remember me when you come into Your kingdom (Luke 23:42).

Remember, remember, remember His marvelous works. This command is important because our memory can prove to be a very treacherous beast.

In the physical world, Sir Isaac Newton established that a body in motion tends to stay in motion, but a body at rest tends to stay at rest. That is not only true in the natural universe, but in the spiritual realm as well. The longer folks have been "in the way," the more "in the way" they seem to become. People remain fixed, as it were, despite strong admonitions to the contrary.

The Bible says, "Clap your hands."

We say, "Why?"

The Bible says, "Shout."

"Why?"

"Move."

"Why?"

God knows that the older we get, naturally and spiritually, the more our memory tends to betray us. But that still does not excuse us.

Newton's law goes on to say that a body in motion tends to stay in motion **unless acted on by an outside force**. We all know that the ultimate outside force is the Lord God and His precepts and principles. That's another reason why He admonishes us to remember. These actions and activities from the past serve as rods and staffs provoking and prodding us forward. They are the most significant outside forces that can and will make a difference in our spiritual walk.

King David knew this principle. That's one of the reasons why he sent for the Ark. He knew it served as a reminder to memory. And this prompt would remind, restore and revitalize the children of Israel. The Ark of the Covenant was overlaid within and without with gold. All of this adornment represented the tabernacling presence of the

Almighty God. David was setting before the people a brilliant, resplendent reminder of the living God!

However, there are two aspects of this Ark—its radiance or glory, and the actual Presence it contained. I don't need to tell you which is more important.

This is a very critical point. It wasn't enough just to behold God's glory. There are many people today who want to hang out in the glory. They want the manifestation. They don't want the doctrine, but they want the demonstration. They don't want the government, but they want the glory. They don't want the message, but they want the miracle. They don't want the logos, but they want the rhema. Yet I implore you to take a lesson from the Ark of the Covenant. Don't be blinded by its dazzling shininess. Open your eyes to the true Spirit within.

Three Ark Articles

David was about to be established as the king over the entire nation of Israel. He was about to set up the City of David just on the outskirts of what is now modern-day Jerusalem. That is where he brought back the Ark, which represented the indwelling presence of God in the earth. The only tangible presence of God to the entire nation of Israel and the world was that box.

The Ark of the Covenant housed three things.

First, it contained the Decalogue, or the Ten Commandments, given to Moses at Sinai. So what exactly was the first thing put in the box that represented the shekinah or the glory of God? It was the word of God—the Law.

God admonished, "Don't ever go anywhere without this box. In fact, it must go before you." Yahweh was making it very clear. He didn't say, "Run on out there and then get a Word." He said, "Don't move until you have a

Word. But when you get that Word—when the Lord has made it abundantly clear and has made you ready—then move!"

The second thing that was in that box was Aaron's rod that budded. Now this wasn't Moses' rod. Rather, this was Aaron's rod. There's quite a difference. Aaron's rod was the symbol of government. In fact, when the children of Israel began to murmur, they actually came against Moses. To solve the problem, Moses declared from the eternal God that the Levites would be the priests. God chose the tribe of Levi to be the priests, one of the 12 tribes which were the 12 sons of Jacob, who became Israel.

The reason that rod budded was so that God could display, through Aaron, that the priesthood belonged to the Levites. Moses delivered this as a direct message from the voice of the Eternal One to the people. In other words, they didn't vote. There were no caucuses. They didn't conduct primaries. God said, "The Levites will be the priests. And by the way, this box that I'm giving you will confirm that."

Please notice that He gave them the Ark of the Covenant after the golden calf incident, not before. This was another strong message and precept from God. During the golden calf rebellion, the people had melted down their gold, made for themselves a golden calf and began to worship it. In other words, they wanted the outward visible representation of divine glory. But they were completely misguided about this.

So God said, "If you want an outward visible representation of my glory, I'll give you one. But it starts with my command."

You want the glory? Get the command.

The commandment says, *You shall have no other gods before Me.* The Word says, *Husbands, love your wives.* Paul wrote that we're to submit ...*to one another in the fear of God.*

But you might be saying, "No, no, no. I just want to shout, buck, dance, and run. In fact I want to start my own ministry, get a TV show. But I'm submitted to no one. I'm going to start a church with no understanding of authority."

Yet God asserted, "I'll give you an outward representation of My glory. I will give you the Ark of the Covenant." It would be so mighty that when the Philistines stole it, and set it down in front of their idolatrous god, they came back in the morning, and that god, Dagon, had fallen on his face. And his head and his hands were broken off.

So is it any wonder that the first thing God said to put in the Ark was the Word—the authority—of God.

The preeminent thing in your life must be The Word, which is the Law.

The second thing that went in the Ark was Aaron's rod that budded. In fact, tradition tells us that that rod would continue to bud. It budded to show that the Levites, as God had said, were the priests. Those priests were to bear that Ark upon their shoulders. It was to proceed before the children of Israel, wherever they went. No one was to touch it.

And they certainly were not supposed to put it on a cart to make it easy. In other words, they were not supposed to make the commands and the understanding of spiritual leadership and authority easy.

The third thing that was to be placed in the Ark was the manna that came down from heaven. If there ever was something that would serve as a reminder of God's provision, it would be manna. It not only was His miracle and gift to the people, it represented His daily provision and His abiding sustenance. He would nourish them. He would sustain them. He would supply them with exactly what they needed each day. They would not be their own provider, Jehovah Jireh would.

These three articles were critical, and still are vital for us today. We can't move without and until we receive the Word. We can't function without the authority of God's government, the true priests. We certainly can't sustain ourselves without His provision.

God's Word, Aaron's rod, and the manna are all reminders—signature signposts if you will—of God's dealings and directives from the past.

When we look back on these glorious reminders and apply them to our lives, we will leap forward into fresh anointing and blessing.

Ignore at Your Peril

So now that David was king over Judah and king over Israel, he sent for the ark. It was the very Word, government and provision of Yahweh Himself.

Yet when they arrived with the Ark at Nachon's threshing floor, one of the oxen stumbled. A man named Uzzah reached out his hand and touched it. He was just trying to steady the ark and not let it fall. The Bible says,

> *Then the anger of the Lord was aroused against Uzzah, and God struck him there for his error; and he died there by the ark of God* (2 Samuel 6:7).

You might be saying, "Well that's incredibly harsh. Why would God react so strongly?"

God was indeed making a very clear and definitive point. The divine message was essential: It's imperative that each person hear, understand, and rightly apply the Word. God unmistakably established and mandated, "Don't touch the ark." But Uzzah glossed over that edict. He had good intentions. "I don't want the ark to fall off its cart. Here, I'll help. I'll jump in where angels fear to tread."

In essence Uzzah's "word" in his own mind or his own rationale usurped God's Word and authority. The fact is the Word had been given, and Uzzah was either oblivious or rebellious. Either way, he was in error.

Of course, everyone knows that it's wrong to violate the law. For instance, we are fully aware if a traffic light is red, and we go through, it's a violation of the law. When we know what the rules are and we break them anyway... that's rebellion.

But ignorance is every bit as bad, not only as far as a violation, but also in terms of consequence. There's a legal principle within our own U.S. law: *ignorantia legis neminem excusat.* This means, "ignorance of the law excuses no one." Quite simply, it purports that any person who is unaware of a law may not escape accountability and liability for violating that law merely because they were oblivious to it.

Brothers and sisters, we certainly shouldn't be rebellious, and we shouldn't be ignorant, either! We can't play the part of the proverbial ostrich with our heads in the sand. Ignorance is not bliss when it comes to engaging with a living God.

Uzzah represents a common misunderstanding today. People think, "Well, let the preacher really worry about the Word. I don't have to pay attention. I don't have to obey it and operate by it. In fact, I don't even have to know what it says."

And yet that very Word says loud and clear, *Study to shew thyself approved unto God, a workman that needeth not be ashamed, rightly dividing the word of truth* (2 Timothy 2:15). And ...*work out your own salvation with fear and trembling* (Philippians 2:12).

In other words, Bibles tend to disappear between Sunday mornings.

So, the problem was that the Israelites did not remember the specific instructions given, nor did they give any attention to detail. "Don't bother me with the facts.

Just bless me, God." That was their attitude. "I want the Ark—which is the ultimate blessing of God, His presence. But I don't want to take the time to know what that Presence requires."

Please let this soak down into your spirit. It's not "the devil is in the details." No, my friends, the living God is in the details. And He wants us to pay close attention to these spiritual specifics.

You say, "Well, that's just not my responsibility... that's just not my personality to pay attention to detail. Pastor Parsley, you drive us out of our mind, because you notice this little thing, and that little thing."

Let me tell you why.

I don't have a passion for the Word of God that is any different than any other living human being, except that I refuse to die by not paying attention to the specifics.

If God says ten percent, He doesn't mean eight.

If He says, *Not forsaking the assembling of yourselves together, as is the manner of some... and so much the more as you see the Day approaching* (Hebrews 10:25, NKJV), He didn't mean come when you want to.

When He says, "Shout!" He doesn't mean when you feel like it, if you feel like it, how you feel like it.

When He says, "Study," He doesn't mean give a cursory glance. He means study, dig in.

When He says, *Speaking to one another in psalms and hymns and spiritual songs, singing and making melody with your heart to the Lord* (Ephesians 5:19, NASB) He meant share with all through ecstatic praise, singing, and worship.

So brothers and sisters, when He says "Remember," He surely didn't mean "Forget!"

"Remember" is a command that produces present faith from past experiences... present faith from past victories. In 1 Samuel 17:37, David declared,

42

*The Lord that delivered me out of the paw of the lion, and
out of the paw of the bear, he will deliver me out of the hand
of this Philistine…*

That brave shepherd boy remembered what God had
done, and that same God certainly wasn't going to deny His
power in the face of a giant. As you remember what God
has done—and do it—you will overcome the "giants" in
your life.

God desires—and this preacher certainly proclaims—
that God wants to pour forth the fivefold blessings into
your life. You can receive, release, rain, reproduce, and rise
up to the fullest, but you first must be attentive to the
details of His Word and will.

God and His ways are sure not sloppy, they are clear
and not compromised, perfect and not imprecise. Hebrews
4:12 says,

*For the word of God is living and powerful, and sharper than
any two-edged sword, piercing even to the division of soul and
spirit, and of joints and marrow, and is a discerner of the
thoughts and intents of the heart* (NKJV).

There's a fine line between soul and spirit and joints
and marrow. God's Word allows us to accurately divide it.
Is He holding us to this exacting standard because He is
some nit-picking, fault-finding disciplinarian? No, He wants
us to wield the weapon of His Word skillfully and
powerfully that we may be victorious in His kingdom.

Remembering His statutes increases our stature. Paying
attention to His precepts leads to promotion. Applying His
divine doctrines delivers results. Does that mean we're
opportunists? No, but it does mean as fully functioning
believers we can make the most of—indeed increase—
every opening and possibility life offers.

As we look back, remember, and respond, we will leap forward into abounding treasures of His goodness and grace.

Chapter Five

Stones of Promise

Stones represent many things in scripture: the past and the future; the pain and the promise; breakdowns and breakthroughs. Most of all they signify God's transforming power!

They can signal lack. When Jacob fled from his brother Esau who wanted to kill him, he literally had nothing to lay his head on, no pillow or even an extra article of clothing. The Bible says, *And he took one of the stones of that place and put it at his head, and he lay down in that place to sleep.*

Yet despite having nothing, God revealed to him everything.

The account goes on to say,

Then he dreamed, and behold, a ladder was set up on the earth, and its top reached to heaven; and there the angels of God were ascending and descending on it. And behold, the Lord stood above it and said: "I am the Lord God of Abraham your father and the God of Isaac; the land on which you lie I will give to you and your descendants. Also your descendants shall be as the dust of the earth; you shall spread abroad to the west and the east, to the north and the south; and in you and in your seed all the families of the earth shall be blessed. Behold, I am with you and will keep you wherever you go, and will bring you back to this land; for I will not leave you until I have done what I have spoken to you" (Genesis 28:12-15, NKJV).

As Jacob slept on that stone representing impoverishment, God showed him His pathway of inspired empowerment.

In fact Jacob declared, *"This is the gate of heaven!"* He knew that this was such a sacred place, and more importantly a sacred promise, that the Bible says,

> *Then Jacob rose early in the morning, and took the stone that he had put at his head, set it up as a pillar, and poured oil on top of it. And he called the name of that place Bethel; but the name of that city had been Luz previously. Then Jacob made a vow, saying, "If God will be with me, and keep me in this way that I am going, and give me bread to eat and clothing to put on, so that I come back to my father's house in peace, then the Lord shall be my God. And this stone which I have set as a pillar shall be God's house, and of all that You give me I will surely give a tenth to You"*
> (Genesis 28:18-22, NKJV).

Jacob—through the power of the revelation and the mighty presence of Jehovah God—was moved to transform that rock of discomfort and poverty into a stone of remembrance and blessing. It would be a pillar—a cornerstone if you will—to remind Jacob of God's authority and pledge. He was setting an anointed marker that signified where he had been and where God was taking him.

That stone symbolized the death and loss of Jacob's past way of life, and even his limited identity. Yet it was transformed to signify the new possibilities and expanded character that God had prepared for him.

Two Stone Tablets of Testimony

When Moses went up to Mt. Sinai, God gave him the ten commandments. He carved them on two tablets of stone.

> *And when He had made an end of speaking with him on Mount Sinai, He gave Moses two tablets of the Testimony,*

tablets of stone, written with the finger of God (Exodus 31:18, NKJV).

These keystone principles were carved in stone. The rock from which Moses carved those two stone tablets had been lying there, taking up space for years. This inert, immobile rock was totally insignificant. The stone tablets were simply lifeless natural rocks until the supernatural transformed them. And how were these rocks transformed? By the Word. In this case, it was the most profound collection of words in all of mankind's history. The Ten Commandments are the ten cornerstone principles that serve as the bedrock for our moral law.

But please notice the symbolism. God, once again, turned dead stones into a life-altering monument. These stones suddenly became two tablets of Testimony. They now proclaimed God's awesome power, His divine holiness and His eternal precepts.

Stones into Bread

What was Satan's first temptation of Jesus? The Bible records,

> *Then Jesus was led up by the Spirit into the wilderness to be tempted by the devil. And when He had fasted forty days and forty nights, afterward He was hungry. Now when the tempter came to Him, he said, "If You are the Son of God, command that these stones become bread"* (Matthew 4:1-3, NKJV).

Satan was tempting Jesus to create His own provision—to trust Himself rather than God for His food and sustenance. He could take care of that entirely on His own. In other words, Jesus could take a lifeless thing and create life out of it.

You can almost hear Satan's persuasive logic. "After all, Jesus, isn't this what God did with Jacob? He inspired Jacob to turn his stone pillow into a cornerstone promise. The stone of his poverty would be the very stone of his completion. After all, Jesus, isn't that what God did with Moses? He turned lifeless rock tablets into the very foundation stones for the entire Mosaic Law."

Turning stones into living testaments—creating life where there is none—was nothing new to Jesus. So why shouldn't He do it now and save Himself from starving?

Jesus certainly knew that He possessed that power. But He also operated by a higher principle. He wasn't about to use that supernatural strength outside of the eternal precepts of God. He wasn't going to usurp God's authority and appropriate His own.

In fact the Bible says,

> *But He answered and said, It is written, 'Man shall not live by bread alone, but by every word that proceeds from the mouth of God* (Matthew 4:4, NKJV).

Please see the point. Jesus used the Word of God to establish the true Word and contradict Satan's counterfeit. Yes, Jesus knew He had the power to turn the lifeless into the life-giving—stones into bread—but He wasn't about to do it in violation of God's specific Word.

The Last Impossibility and the First Miracle

In Joshua chapters 3 and 4, we read about the story of the children of Israel who were about to cross over the Jordan River into the Promised Land.

> *And they commanded the people, saying, "When ye see the ark of the covenant of the Lord your God, and the priests the*

Levites bearing it, then ye shall remove from your place, and you shall go after it" (Joshua 3:3).

It was the Word from the Lord that would take them into the Promised Land, and likewise, the Word will take you into a land of promises, to a place you've never been before.

A lot of people want to simply have a magic, "hocus pocus" laying on of hands and think they'll arrive at another level. But God's kingdom doesn't work that way. It's a power principle of the Lord Almighty's that *nothing happens unless it is by, through, and because of the Word.* We should consider ourselves paralyzed until we utterly understand and are fully filled and functioning by His Word. The fact is the Word will do exactly what it did with the Israelites. God was saying, "Don't just dream about the Promised Land." He was in essence urging, "Get up and get your feet on the ground."

The Jordan River represents a very critical boundary. It signifies the last impossibility. But at the same time, it also symbolizes the first miracle.

So often in life we stand on the brink of our own Promised Land or the land of promises, but we haven't inhabited it yet. It might be a job prospect, a healing, a restored relationship, a promised pregnancy or new life after the death of a loved one. There are so many potentials in life to move from pain to promise. But the manifestation, the materialization, indeed, the miracle hasn't happened yet.

I'd like you to take just one minute right now and say out loud or write down the thing you don't have. That's right. Tangibly express the thing you're holding on to and hoping for. What is that promise you're waiting for—and probably worrying about?

Yes, take a moment and stand where the Israelites stood on the eastern bank of your Jordan and peer with me into your Promised Land.

I know how badly you desire what perhaps you've only seen through the eyes of faith. I know exactly that feeling in the bottom of your soul. Most of the time, we are literally aching and in anguish over it. David even said, *I am poured out like water, and all My bones are out of joint; my heart is like wax; it has melted within Me* (Psalm 22:14, NKJV).

But there is a way—God's way—that you can pass over to your Promised Land. He showed Joshua and the Israelites His powerful pathway.

The passage goes on to say, *And Joshua said unto them, Pass over before the ark of the Lord your God into the midst of Jordan...* (Joshua 4:5).

Here's what He's saying to us: "When you see the Ark move, it's time to go." Many in the church have been trying to run out there and get into the land of promises, but they haven't seen the Ark move yet.

Remember, the Ark represents the shekinah or the glory. Inside are the Ten Commandments representing the Word; Aaron's rod representing God's priestly government; and the manna representing His provision. God is saying to us, "You can only move into the promise that is before you when you follow after these things. Don't get out ahead of them. They are a sword and shield for you. They are My lighted pathway and illuminated portal. If you go without them, you will be defeated. If you go with them, you will be triumphant."

Please remember that the Jordan represents the last impossibility before you step out of your wilderness—your prolonged season of difficulty, the struggle with struggles attached to it, the bondage, the hindrance, the sickness, the disease, the pain, the malady, the malfunction, the infirmity. It signifies whatever has been hindering you, whatever it is that has been holding you back from breaking into everything that God promised you in Deuteronomy 28:1-14.

We are at the brink of Jordan. The last bastion, the last representation of impossibility is standing in front of us. Yet if we will follow the scriptural precedent, we will pass over to the other side.

Hallelujah! We can exclaim, "I'm getting ready to move!" In fact, this principle is so potent, we can actually shout to others, "I'm passing over Jordan. Just as soon as I see the Ark move, I'm running. Just as soon as I get a Word, I'm running. Just as soon as I recognize the spiritual authority that God has placed and ordained in my life, I'm ready to move."

God had Joshua tell the priests, "Go get the ark and bring it to the Jordan." But please remember that the people were behind him. Your Bible says that when the priests that bore the ark touched the brink of Jordan it would be just like what God did for Moses at the Red Sea. God even told Joshua, ...*As I was with Moses, so I will be with thee* (Joshua 1:5).

So just like Moses, now Joshua stood with only the Jordan separating Israel from the Promised Land. He commanded the Ark to be taken, and the priests touched the edge of that water. The Bible said that the Jordan, *heaped up against itself.* As the Red Sea parted for Moses, so now the Jordan was parting for Joshua. He had the same anointing.

Then the priests went out into the middle of the Jordan. They stood in the middle of Jordan, but they were not standing on the water. They were standing on stones.

Now, my friends in California and other arid western states know what it's like when the streams and rivers dry up during the long, hot summers. The river bed is usually nothing but stones. The Israelites were walking over on stones. Under their feet were the very stones that served as reminders of their past impoverishment but also God's empowerment. Even as they walked, these stones served as a highway—a cobblestone thoroughfare if you will—to their future blessing.

Do you see how powerful the imagery of stones is in the Bible? They are useless things that are turned into uplifting things. Those stones represent our lives—scattered and strewn, hard and unforgiving. Yet when stacked up and anointed, stones are used to lay down pillars, to build foundations, to serve as anointed altars that pronounce the permeating Presence of God.

Having seen the ark of the covenant move out into the midst of Jordan, God said, "Everybody stop right here, because, Israel—in fact all believers—have a memory problem. There will not even be one single, solitary beginning of a miracle over there until you remember back there."

You might be saying to God, "I want to go into this next year, this next opportunity and I want it to be the best I've ever had. I need to increase in my finances. I need my relationships mended. I need my body healed. I need—and I want—and it's all over there in the Promised Land."

But God is saying, "Stop! Stop." He said to the children of Israel, "You complained about the mountains on one side and the desert on the other. You complained about the Red Sea. You fail to understand that those things were the escape route for you against your enemies. You forget that I buried them."

The Almighty is calling us to remember as we stand on the edge of our Jordan. He is saying, "Whoa, stop right here and talk to Me about what I just brought you through! If somebody needs a miracle tomorrow, start shouting about the one I gave you yesterday. You complained that you didn't have water, so I brought it out of a rock. You complained that you didn't have anything to eat, and I opened the heavens and manna came falling down. You

52

complained about your shoes, so I gave you shoes that showed no sign of wear for 40 years. You complained about being led by a man, so I gave you a pillar of cloud by day and a pillar of fire by night."

In fact, there won't be any future wonders until we remember a past Word. There won't be any future miracles until we remember a past message. We have to look back before we can leap forward.

12 Stones of Promise

The priests stood in the middle of the Jordan with the Ark, and the children of Israel passed over on dry ground. When they were all safe on the other side, Joshua said, "I want you to go get 12 stones from where the priests stood. Bring them over here, and we'll build a memorial."

Do you know what a memorial is? A memorial is erected so that you can remember something you received that you didn't pay for.

Take the Vietnam Memorial, for instance. You can actually see the names of the men and women who paid the ultimate price for our country. When a person considers those names or, even better, transfers that name onto a piece of paper with a pencil, they are giving thanks. They are saying, "I didn't do anything to earn what this soldier did for me. But I am going to bear it in mind. Their heroic sacrifice bolsters my spirit."

So you can see that in life it is very important the role that memorials play. In fact we've all got to lay down our own memorials, so that we can raise up our own future. We've got to look back to the cross. We've got to look back to the blood. We've got to look back to the fact that He saved us. We've got to look back at when He baptized us in the Holy Ghost. We've got to look back and remember that He healed us, delivered us, brought us out and broke the powers and principalities, the rulers of the darkness of this world.

Joshua erected just such a memorial in the middle of Jordan with those 12 stones. The Bible says:

> *Take for yourselves twelve men from the people, one man from every tribe, and command them, saying, "Take for yourselves twelve stones from here, out of the midst of the Jordan, from the place where the priests' feet stood firm"* (Joshua 4:2-3, NKJV).

God wanted one stone per tribe brought out from underneath the feet of the priests. Those stones were to be carried to the other side, the victory side of Jordan.

Those stones didn't come from the shore of the Jordan. They came out of the middle of the river. And the river represented the final barrier, the last hurdle. It also spoke of all their wilderness trials.

It represented the mess they'd been in. God was saying, "There will be a rock hewn out of—or simply collected from—that mess. I want you to build a memorial with it. I don't ever want you to forget that in the midst of your mess, I established you on a rock. And the Word that brought you in is the same one that brought you out!"

Then the Bible says,

> *And those twelve stones which they took out of the Jordan, Joshua set up in Gilgal. Then he spoke to the children of Israel, saying: "When your children ask their fathers in time to come, saying, 'What are these stones?' then you shall let your children know, saying, 'Israel crossed over this Jordan on dry land'; for the Lord your God dried up the waters of the Jordan before you until you had crossed over, as the Lord your God did to the Red Sea, which He dried up before us until we had crossed over, that all the peoples of the earth may know the hand of the Lord, that it is mighty, that you may*

fear the Lord your God forever" (Joshua 4:20-24, NKJV).

Why Gilgal? The word Gilgal is interpreted, "the axle." Do you know an axle is only good for putting on a wheel? Do you know the only thing a wheel is good for? A turnaround.

Here's what God is saying. "If you'll learn to praise me in the middle of the mess—if you'll embrace the true Word—I'm going to take you up to Gilgal. And when you get there, everything is about to turn around!"

No matter what you are facing, God intends to turn it around. You might be overwhelmed with insecurity, weariness, weakness or outright attack. It doesn't matter. When you stand in the middle of your Jordan and remember that God prevailed despite your problems, your current struggles will become things in your past.

And it all turns around on a rock: a rock of remembrance, a rock of memorial. We need to hold up that rock and shout, "I'm on my way to Gilgal. I've looked back, but God is going to have me leap forward."

How many rocks were they asked to acquire? Twelve rocks. Of course, there are 12 months in a year.

I'm declaring a Word unto you: Somewhere in the middle of every one of those months, you're going to come up against another Jordan. Yet God is going to ask, "Are you going to praise your way out of it? Will you build a memorial to My victories in the past. Do you want to go to Gilgal and see the promised fulfilled?"

You can shout, "God is indeed going to turn it around."

So rest in the Lord. Remember, the stones in your life might represent the poverty of your past. But more importantly, they represent the sufficiency of your future. When you place His Word first, He'll literally inscribe it on the stones of your life. This will transform those hard, unyielding positions—those stony circumstances—into abundant cornerstones of blessing and promise.

Chapter Six

Five Keys to Transition

God's fivefold blessing is waiting for us. It is His desire to open His arms wide and bestow it upon us. It is His eternal will that we receive, release, rain, reproduce, and rise up in all of the fullness and richness that is reserved for those He calls His beloved.

However, to experience these manifold blessings, there are a few critical gateways that are necessary to open these powerful pathways. I call them the five keys to transition. They are like keys turning a lock, and once those locks are opened we will be unshackled and realize a vibrant new freedom. As we step out in faith and fulfill these critical faith exercises, we will see God move us and in turn transform the world around us.

The five keys to transition can be found in the book of 1 Chronicles 16:8-12:

> Give thanks unto the Lord, call upon his name, make known his deeds among the people. Sing unto him, sing psalms unto him, talk ye of all his wondrous works. Glory ye in his holy name: let the heart of them rejoice that seek the Lord. Seek the Lord and his strength, seek his face continually. Remember his marvelous works that he hath done, his wonders, and the judgments of his mouth;

Transition Key #1: Give Thanks

The first key is simply to give thanks. I say "simply" but I know that it is not always so simple to give thanks. Our circumstances can be overwhelming. In fact, our situation can seem so utterly hopeless that we say in our spirit,

"There is absolutely nothing here worthy of giving thanks. How can I thank God for this dead end, this disaster, this death?"

We've all been there. The bottom has fallen out, the sky has fallen down, the earth beneath us has crumbled and the mountains in front of us appear impassable.

But here's the good news: operating in and by faith has nothing to do with our present circumstances. In fact, faith operates entirely on another plane that is outside of our situation. We're not moving in a fourth dimension—we're operating in the faith dimension!

The Bible says, *Now faith is the substance of things hoped for, the evidence of things not seen* (Hebrews 11:1).

Please see the critical words "things hoped for" and "things not seen." Operating by faith requires eyes that don't look at the things in front of you. Faith functions with eyes that see above and beyond that. The eyes of faith look into the very heart of God.

When we look into the heart of God, we find all of His attributes: hope, joy, patience, and love. These fruit of the Spirit will lift us above the hopeless, joyless, impatient, and unloving circumstances that bombard us.

Think of it this way. Night vision goggles allow someone to move from stumbling around in the dark to actually seeing in the dark. As we move out in faith, even though darkness may be all around, we suddenly can see our way through.

Operating by faith is a paradox. We have the reality of our circumstances, but we operate by another, greater reality. You might be thinking, "Pastor Parsley, that sounds like a person who is out of touch with reality." No, I'm asserting that the person who functions by faith is entirely in tune with the reality of the universe.

Moving by faith is not some ephemeral, loosey-goosey, head-in-the-clouds activity. We haven't checked out; we've dialed in. We don't live in denial; we live knowing He will deliver.

Faith is substance and evidence. The word for substance in Hebrews 11:1 is *hypostasis*. It literally means "a setting or placing under; a substructure or a foundation." We place God's will under us when we operate by faith. We are literally positioning the foundation of the universe beneath all of our activities.

The word for evidence is *elegchos*. This means, "a proof, that by which a thing is proved or tested." That has powerful repercussions when it comes to faith. It means that we have verification and corroboration that the thing we're believing in is not a fantasy. It isn't pie in the sky. Operating by faith is not something reserved for dreamers. We have the inerrant proof that is tried, true, and tested.

Please hear this: *Operating by our circumstances is actually the unsure course.* The Bible describes our life as *but a vapor.* We're like steam coming out of tea pot—it's here for a moment and then gone. We are like fog in the morning that burns off. That is our life. And I'm asserting to you, dear friend, that that is how we need to see our conflicts, our crises, and our situations.

The real substance and evidence of our life is fully realized in God who is rock solid, not the shifting sands of circumstance.

Being assured of this substance and evidence is how and why we give thanks. Our praise is not always because of our earthly circumstances. It is due to God's eternal reality. We can praise Him despite our dark and dreary situations because He, in the grand scope of His eternal purposes, has already fixed, filled, and brought to fruition His goodness. Through giving thanks we are literally reaching out using our faith muscles and grabbing hold of the thing that already exists in God's universe. His assets are ours. His attributes are ours. His actions are ours. His gifts are already given and we are simply grateful receivers.

"Hallelujah" comes easily to our lips because we already have what doesn't seem to be before us. "Praise God" bubbles up from our spirits because the Holy Spirit knows the beginning from the end and *makes intercession for us with groanings which cannot be uttered* (Romans 8:26). "Thank you, Lord" tumbles forth out of our mouths because we are utterly grateful in light of all that He has and will do for us.

Giving thanks is not meant to occur only in private. We're to *make known his deeds among the people.* We give away giving thanks. God has given to us. We give thanks back to Him. And in the process, we express that thanks before others. They in turn are energized and begin giving thanks as well.

In other words giving thanks is just one, big, continual, communal releasing. And isn't that the true nature of God? Give, give, give!

When you walk around before a church service, I would encourage you, don't just share your favorite recipe or the news of the week. Share something good about God. I think we ought to all be bragging on Him.

Through the eyes of faith everything is already completed. Our giving thanks is like a down payment on the things He says we already own. And as you give thanks—as you call the things that aren't as though they are—your attitude and outlook will spring to an entirely new altitude.

Transition Key #2: Sing

God asks us—indeed implores us—to sing. It's a command. *Sing unto him, sing psalms unto him. Talk ye of His wondrous works.*

Why is singing so important?

Singing or music has a profound purpose in God's kingdom. I'd like you to consider something. We all know how nervous people can get when they have to sing in front of others. Why is that? I suppose we don't want to sing off key and sound silly. But I think it runs much deeper than that.

There's an aspect to singing that involves letting go. Singing can be very humbling. You have to be transparent when you sing. Pretense must fade. In other words, you can't be puffed up when you sing—especially when you're singing praises to God.

Singing releases you. Some even say you release your inhibitions and your hang-ups. I would go one step further and say you liberate your anxieties. Your frail, finite self-consciousness fades, and it is replaced by God's greater, glorious self-consciousness.

Giving full voice is giving in to a greater goodness.

I submit to you that every human being on the planet desperately wants to let go like this. Even if a person doesn't know God, they still desire to be free of their inhibitions and let their inner being come out in singing. If you don't believe me, just watch a secular rock concert. People love to sing along with the musician up on stage. Sometimes it takes people getting drunk or high to let go of their self-consciousness. That's sad. But it does reveal the heart of man that God gave us, and that heart desires to sing.

So when God asks us to sing psalms unto Him, He's really reminding us of something we crave anyway. Of course, He's also challenging us to renounce and release those reservations that bind us. He's saying to us from heaven, "Why hold back? You know you want to."

My encouragement to you echoes that voice from eternity. Let go, my friend. Burst forth with singing. Allow the melody that God has placed within your heart to come forward in music. It will be an orchestra of the extraordinary, a symphony of the soul, a composition of conviction that will indeed reverberate throughout your life.

Transition Key #3: Glory in His Name

God also asks us to, *Glory in His holy name*. What is it about His name that is so vitally important?

Names, obviously, are very significant. Even Shakespeare asked the question with his famous line: *"What's in a name? That which we call a rose by any other name would smell as sweet."*

Interestingly, that line comes from his play *Romeo and Juliet*. Of course, in that play the two star-crossed lovers come from warring families. By this question Juliet is saying to Romeo, "It doesn't matter what your family name is, the true essence of who you are is wonderful." In other words, you could call a rose whatever you wanted, but the true character and nature of a rose will always be beautiful.

When we glory in God's holy name we are magnifying the true essence of who He is. We are reaffirming, reasserting, and recounting all that God stands for.

Satan's main goal is to condemn people before God and to condemn God before people. He is continuously besmirching, slandering, and defaming us to God, and God to us. The devil can't change who God is, but he certainly can change how we perceive Him. In fact we can think of Satan as a wicked "spin doctor." He is putting out outright lies about the nature and purpose of God.

Remember what he said when he tempted Eve in the garden?

Now the serpent was more cunning than any beast of the field which the Lord God had made. And he said to the woman, "Has God indeed said, 'You shall not eat of every tree of the garden'?" And the woman said to the serpent, "We may eat the fruit of the trees of the garden; but of the fruit of the tree which is in the midst of the garden, God has said, 'You shall not eat it, nor shall you touch it, lest you die.'" Then the serpent said to the woman, "You will not surely die. For God knows that in the day you eat of it your eyes will be opened, and you will be like God, knowing good and evil" (Genesis 3:1-5, NKJV).

Do you see how Satan twists the command and the character of God? "You surely won't die," he says. "That's not who God is. No, your eyes will be open."

Satan was lying to her about the very essence of God.

So, when we glory in His name we are reestablishing the true nature of God. We are saying to the devil, "You are a liar. God's not who you say He is." We are proclaiming the correct and accurate character of God when we reassert His name.

God's name is multi-dimensional. He has countless names that declare and affirm His genuine nature. God is like a multi-faceted diamond. Have you ever seen a diamond slowly turned in the sun? It refracts and reflects many different colors. Each name of God sparkles with yet another attribute of His true nature. These brilliant hues add up to a God with an infinitely diverse color spectrum.

So we can glory in the name that is King of Kings and Lord of Lords, Wonderful, Counselor, Mighty God, Everlasting Father, Prince of Peace. He is Jehovah Tsidkenu, my righteousness. He is Jehovah M'Kaddesh, my holiness. He is Jehovah Raah, the Lord God my shepherd. He is Jehovah Rapha, the Lord my God that healeth all my diseases.

We glory by saying thank you, Jesus, you are Jehovah Shalom, the God of my peace. You are Jehovah Shammah, the God who is present with me right now. You are Jehovah Yireh, the God that supplies all my needs. You are

El Shaddai, the God who reserves the right to alter His own law!

Oh, how we bless You for every name that You are, for those names renounce Satan's counterfeit and remind me whom I serve. They are holy, and by proclaiming them, I am pronouncing Your holiness and wholeness over my life.

Transition Key #4: Seek His Face

The next transition point is, *Let the heart of them rejoice that seek the Lord.*

Seeking is certainly not a vain exercise in the kingdom of God. Seeking leads to finding, and finding opens up untold blessings.

First and foremost God desires that we seek one thing above all else: His face. In Psalm 24:6 David proclaimed, *This is the generation of them that seek him, that seek thy face.*

When we become the generation of them that seek His face, what are we doing? First, we're seeking His mouth. And what comes from His mouth? His Word. We desire those precious Words that flow from His lips: His pronouncements and precepts; His proverbs of wisdom and His psalms of praise; His specific Words of knowledge and His bold prophecies.

What else comes out of His mouth? His breath. And the breath of God is in fact the Spirit of God. We're seeking His Spirit, because it takes the Spirit to interpret the Word. You get the Word, then immediately the Holy Spirit comes to illuminate that Word. You could even say that a word can't even be uttered without the spirit or breath pushing it through the vocal cords, across the tongue and out for the world to hear. This is how the relationship is between Word and Spirit. The Spirit of God breathes forth, activates, animates, and interprets the Word of God.

Third, when you seek His face you discover a smile. God spoke to me prophetically about this. He told me, "When we come face-to-face, you're going to be smiling." But He didn't stop there. He also said, "You're going to see Me smile right back at you."

Imagine what will happen when we have a generation that believes God is smiling at them. I don't know about you, but religion always taught me God is mad at me—that I couldn't ever do enough to please Him. In fact, I come from a generation of fathers who found it very difficult to express their love for their children. Very few men in my generation grew up with fathers that were comfortable enough to tell them, "Come here. Sit in my lap. Now look me in the eye. Have you ever lived a day that I didn't tell you I loved you? Do you know I love you? When you smile at me, do you know I will smile back at you?"

You might have felt this kind of fatherly rejection. But I'm asserting and proclaiming over you, God is smiling at you. God's not mad at you. I can go to Him and say, "God, I messed that up." He just stands there and smiles at me. All His smile does is make me want to run away from anything that displeases Him. The fact is God wants to draw you to Him through the hope of favor, not through the fear of wrath.

So when we seek His face we are in fact seeking His Word, seeking His Spirit, and seeking not only His smile, but the smile that will break across our faces. All this adds up to one thing: we are seeking His strength.

You might be saying, "Pastor, this all sounds like namby-pamby tenderness to me. Isn't that actually weakness? Where is the strength in that?"

In Psalm 18:35 David said, *Your gentleness has made me great.* David was a mighty warrior who won many battles in the name of the Lord. He was not only a commander of armies, he was victorious in hand-to-hand combat. In other words David was one tough guy. And he became a powerful king over many people.

Yet to what did he attribute his true strength and greatness? God's gentleness. It was the Almighty's loving-kindness that was the bedrock in David's life. As we seek God's face we will rediscover over and over again that His still small voice, His abiding Presence, His compassionate and affectionate Spirit, indeed the very face of God will light up our faces with His love.

Transition Key #5: Remember

The final key to transition is simply to remember. *Remember his marvelous works that he hath done, his wonders, and the judgments of his mouth.*

In an earlier chapter we looked at how God asked the Israelites to set up 12 stones as a remembrance and a monument to all that God had done. They had wandered in the wilderness for 40 years. They could just as well have sung the verse from the famous song "Amazing Grace": *Through many dangers, toils and snares I have already come.*

That's what the stones were all about. It's as if those voiceless rocks were saying, "Remember, God brought you out of the midst of all those dangers, toils and snares."

But memory in God's timetable isn't just to remain in the past. It illuminates our future. God is saying, "You'll recognize that there's nothing in front of you any bigger than what's behind you. You have already conquered all of that in My name, so you might just as well begin rejoicing. Because the same God that brought you out across the Jordan is going to bring you into the promise!"

In your life, you may have wandered, but consider His wonders. You may have suffered under the works of Satan, but consider the handiwork of God's overcoming. You may have felt the harsh judgment of condemnation, but reflect on His true judgments.

It is so easy to misappropriate God's judgments. In fact many well-meaning believers can become "judgmental." Jesus said, *Judge not, that ye not be judged* (Matthew 7:1). In other words, we're not to look down our nose at others. The Lord admonished us not to try to remove a speck in someone else's eye when we have a log in our own.

Yet Jesus also said we are to judge with righteous judgment (John 7:24).

Taken together those two admonitions might seem confusing, even contradictory. We are to judge not, yet we are to judge with righteous judgment. What does that mean?

The answer to this seeming conundrum lies in the little phrase "judgments of his mouth." What did we learn about the mouth of God? First, from that mouth comes His Word. So true judgment must first and foremost rest on the Word of God. We can't make up things about God that aren't true. We also are admonished to:

Study to shew thyself approved unto God, a workman that needeth not to be ashamed, rightly dividing the word of truth (2 Timothy 2:15).

The more we dig into His Word, the more treasures we will find. And those riches will accurately divide the Word of truth.

From His mouth comes the breath and that Spirit will quicken our spirits to know the true interpretation of the Word of God. And, of course, the judgments of his mouth are coming from a mouth that is smiling at us. Paul exclaimed,

There is therefore now no condemnation to those who are in Christ Jesus, who do not walk according to the flesh, but according to the Spirit (Romans 8:1, NKJV).

We can accurately assess and apply the judgments of His mouth because they are coming from a mouth that brings His Word, His breath, and His smile.

Chapter Seven

The Wait Is Over.
Your Breakthrough Has Come.

This ministry is called *Breakthrough* for a reason. God is continuously inspiring His people to move from dark to light, from sickness to health, from pain to promise, from despair to deliverance. In other words, we aren't held captive. We break through the walls of our imprisonment and move on out into His glorious liberty.

That's what the fivefold blessing is all about. Each power-packed blessing represents a breakthrough for you.

Receive. Everything may seem to have been taken from you. But Psalm 81:10 says, *Open your mouth wide, and I will fill it.*

Release. You may feel like the man who was paralyzed by the Pool of Bethesda. The problems of this life may have traumatized and immobilized you. But the Lord is about to release you, saying, "Get up and walk." You will move like Isaiah declared, *They shall run and not be weary, They shall walk and not faint* (Isaiah 40:31, NKJV).

Rain. The dry earth longs for refreshing. When there hasn't been rain, it literally opens up and cracks form, begging for water. As we let go and give, God pours out even more. Malachi 3:10 says,

> *Try Me now in this… if I will not open for you the windows of heaven And pour out for you such blessing That there will not be room enough to receive it.*

Reproduce. God's very first action was to create. *In the beginning God created the heavens and the earth* (Genesis 1:1). But He didn't just create a stagnant earth. No, that creation is continually recreating or reproducing. In other words, God's act of creation is still perpetually in play today. It is His abundant desire to create new, fresh things in your life—to reproduce His goodness and His grace over and over again.

Rise Up. In light of all that God has done and is doing, our response can only be one thing: to move onward, outward, and upward. Jesus did when He rose from the dead. That selfsame power is now ours and enables us to rise up and overcome every situation that may appear dead, difficult, or even destroyed.

So wait no more. Your breakthrough has come. The fivefold blessing is yours!

My Prayer for You

Lord, it's a new day! It's a new year! It's a new season filled with possibility! My tomorrow is filled with opportunity. Victory on the left hand. Victory on the right. Joy in front of me. Joy behind me. Peace above me. Peace beneath me.

Thank you, God, that You are in my coming and my going. Thank you that You surround me with every good thing. Thank you that You have filled me with joy unspeakable.

God, remind us where we were and where You brought us from, so that we can see where You want to take us. Move every obstacle out of the way. Let faith have her perfect work. Let faith be manifested. Bind every hindrance, every attitude, every worry, everything that is contrary to You and to your Word having preeminence. We will not step out of order. We will not move out of due season. We will stay. We will move. We will be enlightened. We will not go unless your Word goes before us.

Let your Word, mighty God, clear a path. Let us not walk in darkness because we have been contrary to or negligent of your Word.

God, may we be refocused. May we find true north. May You direct our thoughts, our passions, our heart, our desire, our impulses toward the heavens. From there and there alone we understand is our help.

Forgive us for leaning upon the arms of the flesh. Forgive us for these religious underpinnings, which are so contrary to that through which, by which, and in which You desire to lead us. Oh, God, we lay ourselves before You ready to hear from You.

I enthusiastically look back on Your mercies knowing that it's Your desire that I leap forward into all that you have for me.

God, this is the moment. This is the time. I agree, accept, and activate Your fivefold blessing in my life!

Breakthrough
Scriptural Principles

I will praise You forever, because You have done it (Psalm 52:9, NKJV).

You see the distress that we are in, how Jerusalem lies waste, and its gates are burned with fire. Come and let us build the wall of Jerusalem, that we may no longer be a reproach." 18 And I told them of the hand of my God which had been good upon me, and also of the king's words that he had spoken to me. So they said, "Let us rise up and build." Then they set their hands to this good work (Nehemiah 2:17-18).

Now there is at Jerusalem by the sheep market a pool, which is called in the Hebrew tongue Bethesda, having five porches. In these lay a great multitude of impotent folk, of blind, halt, withered, waiting for the moving of the water. For an angel went down at a certain season into the pool, and troubled the water: whosoever then first after the troubling of the water stepped in was made whole of whatsoever disease he had. And a certain man was there, which had an infirmity thirty and eight years. When Jesus saw him lie, and knew that he had been now a long time in that case, he saith unto him, Wilt thou be made whole? The impotent man answered him, Sir, I have no man, when the water is troubled, to put me into the pool: but while I am coming, another steppeth down before me. Jesus saith unto him, Rise, take up thy bed, and walk. And immediately the man was made whole, and took up his bed, and walked (John 5:2-9).

O Lord, my heart is not proud, nor my eyes haughty; Nor do I involve myself in great matters, Or in things too difficult for me (Psalm 131:1, NASB).

Come to Me, all you who labor and are heavy laden, and I will give you rest. Take My yoke upon you and learn from Me, for I am gentle and lowly in heart, and you will find rest for your souls. For My yoke is easy and My burden is light (Matthew 11:28-30, NKJV).

But those who wait on the Lord shall renew their strength; They shall mount up with wings like eagles, they shall run and not be weary, they shall walk and not faint (Isaiah 40:31, NKJV).

Elijah was a man with a nature like ours, and he prayed earnestly that it would not rain; and it did not rain on the land for three years and six months. And he prayed again, and the heaven gave rain, and the earth produced its fruit (James 5:17-18).

Then God blessed them, and God said to them, "Be fruitful and multiply; fill the earth and subdue it; have dominion over the fish of the sea, over the birds of the air, and over every living thing that moves on the earth." And God said, "See, I have given you every herb that yields seed which is on the face of all the earth, and every tree whose fruit yields seed; to you it shall be for food" (Genesis 1:28-29, NKJV)

For the good that I will to do, I do not do; but the evil I will not to do, that I practice. Now if I do what I will not to do, it is no longer I who do it, but sin that dwells in me. I find then a law, that evil is present with me, the one who wills to do good. For I delight in the law of God according to the inward man. But I see another law in my members, warring against the law of my mind, and bringing me into captivity to the law of sin which is in my members (Romans 7:19-23, NKJV).

...We also glory in tribulations, knowing that tribulation produces perseverance; and perseverance, character; and character, hope. Now hope does not disappoint, because the love of God has been poured out in our hearts by the Holy Spirit who was given to us (Romans 5:3-5, NKJV).

And He Himself gave some to be apostles, some prophets, some evangelists, and some pastors and teachers, for the equipping of the saints for the work of ministry, for the edifying of the body of Christ, till we all come to the unity of the faith and of the knowledge of the Son of God, to a perfect man, to the measure of the stature of the fullness of Christ (Ephesians 4:11-13, NKJV).

But He said to them, "You give them something to eat." And they said, "We have no more than five loaves and two fish, unless we go and buy food for all these people." For there were about five thousand men. Then He said to His disciples, "Make them sit down in groups of fifty." And they did so, and made them all sit down. Then He took the five loaves and the two fish, and looking up to heaven, He blessed and broke them, and gave them to the disciples to set before the multitude. So they all ate and were filled, and twelve baskets of the leftover fragments were taken up by them (Luke 9:13-17, NKJV).

Then the anger of the Lord was aroused against Uzzah, and God struck him there for his error; and he died there by the ark of God (2 Samuel 6:7).

...The Lord that delivered me out of the paw of the lion, and out of the paw of the bear, he will deliver me out of the hand of this Philistine... (1 Samuel 17:37).

For the word of God is living and powerful, and sharper than any two-edged sword, piercing even to the division of soul and spirit, and of joints and marrow, and is a discerner of the thoughts and intents of the heart (Hebrews 4:12, NKJV).

Then he dreamed, and behold, a ladder was set up on the earth, and its top reached to heaven; and there the angels of God were ascending and descending on it. And behold, the Lord stood above it and said: "I am the Lord God of Abraham your father and the God of Isaac; the land on which you lie I will give to you and your descendants. Also your descendants shall be as the dust of the earth; you shall spread abroad to the west and the east, to the north and the south; and in you and in your seed all the families of the earth shall be blessed. Behold, I am with you and will keep you wherever you go, and will bring you back to this land; for I will not leave you until I have done what I have spoken to you." Then Jacob awoke from his sleep and said, "Surely the Lord is in this place, and I did not know it." And he was afraid and said, "How awesome is this place! This is none other than the house of God, and this is the gate of heaven!" Then Jacob rose early in the morning, and took the stone that he had put at his head, set it up as a pillar, and poured oil on top of it. And he called the name of that place Bethel; but the name of that city had been Luz previously. Then Jacob made a vow, saying, "If God will be with me, and keep me in this way that I am going, and give me bread to eat and clothing to put on, so that I come back to my father's house in peace, then the Lord shall be my God. And this stone which I have set as a pillar shall be God's house, and of all that You give me I will surely give a tenth to You (Genesis 28:12-22, NKJV).

And when He had made an end of speaking with him on Mount Sinai, He gave Moses two tablets of the Testimony, tablets of stone, written with the finger of God (Exodus 31:18).

Then Jesus was led up by the Spirit into the wilderness to be tempted by the devil. And when He had fasted forty days and forty nights, afterward He was hungry. Now when the tempter came to

Him, he said, "If You are the Son of God, command that these stones become bread (Matthew 4:1-3, NKJV).

And they commanded the people, saying, "When ye see the ark of the covenant of the Lord your God, and the priests the Levites bearing it, then ye shall remove from your place, and you shall go after it" (Joshua 3:3).

Take for yourselves twelve men from the people, one man from every tribe, and command them, saying, 'Take for yourselves twelve stones from here, out of the midst of the Jordan, from the place where the priests' feet stood firm (Joshua 4:2-3, NKJV).

And those twelve stones which they took out of the Jordan, Joshua set up in Gilgal. Then he spoke to the children of Israel, saying: "When your children ask their fathers in time to come, saying, 'What are these stones?' then you shall let your children know, saying, 'Israel crossed over this Jordan on dry land'; for the Lord your God dried up the waters of the Jordan before you until you had crossed over, as the Lord your God did to the Red Sea, which He dried up before us until we had crossed over, that all the peoples of the earth may know the hand of the Lord, that it is mighty, that you may fear the Lord your God forever (Joshua 4:20-24, NKJV)

Give thanks unto the Lord, call upon his name, make known his deeds among the people. Sing unto him, sing psalms unto him, talk ye of all his wondrous works. Glory ye in his holy name: let the heart of them rejoice that seek the Lord. Seek the Lord and his strength, seek his face continually. Remember his marvelous works that he hath done, his wonders, and the judgments of his mouth; (1 Chronicles 16:8-12)

Now the serpent was more cunning than any beast of the field which the Lord God had made. And he said to the woman, "Has God indeed said, 'You shall not eat of every tree of the garden'?" And the woman said to the serpent, "We may eat the fruit of the trees of the garden; but of the fruit of the tree which is in the midst of the garden, God has said, 'You shall not eat it, nor shall you touch it, lest you die.'" Then the serpent said to the woman, "You will not surely die. For God knows that in the day you eat of it your eyes will be opened, and you will be like God, knowing good and evil" (Genesis 3:1-5, NKJV).

Study to shew thyself approved unto God, a workman that needeth not to be ashamed, rightly dividing the word of truth (2 Timothy 2:15).

There is therefore now no condemnation to those who are in Christ Jesus, who do not walk according to the flesh, but according to the Spirit (Romans 8:1, NKJV)

About the Author

ROD PARSLEY, bestselling author of more than sixty books, is the dynamic pastor of World Harvest Church in Columbus, Ohio, a church with ten worldwide ministries and a global outreach. As a highly sought-after crusade and conference speaker whom God has raised up as a prophetic voice to America and the world, Parsley is calling people to Jesus Christ through the good news of the Gospel.

He oversees Bridge of Hope Missions, Harvest Preparatory School, Valor Christian College, and the *Breakthrough* broadcast, a television and radio show seen by millions and broadcast to nearly 200 countries around the world. In addition, Parsley works as an integral part of other worldwide ministry outreaches and serves on the board of several local and international organizations.

Parsley's refreshingly direct style encourages Christians to examine and eradicate sin from their lives. A fearless champion of living God's way, Parsley follows the high standard set by Jesus Christ and compels his readers to do the same. He and his wife Joni have two children, Ashton and Austin.

BY THE SAME AUTHOR

There Was a Young Man from Cardiff

The sequel to *Ash on a Young Man's Sleeve*.

'In the immense splendour of a halcyon summer night, I should have felt awe and humility and gratitude for the gift of being alive. Instead, I experienced a sense of dread – but a dread of what?'

There Was a Young Man from Cardiff is Dannie Abse's memorable collection of fictional reminiscences about life in Wales. Here he combines warmth, subtle humour, and elegiac prose in a vivid evocation of Welsh-Jewish family life. His childhood escapades and adolescent experiences in wartime Cardiff, his rich, intriguing portraits of friends and relatives – including his Bolshevik Uncle Isidore, and the mysterious Welsh Red Indian Jack Evans – together with his marvellously offbeat memories of his experiences as a doctor, illuminate a prose work of Chekhovian skill and artistry – storytelling at its finest.

'Abse can . . . turn out a really subtle portrait, full of odd insights and sharp little glimpses into remote fretful lives' – D. J. Taylor in the *Sunday Times*

READ MORE IN PENGUIN

A SELECTION OF FICTION AND NON-FICTION

A Start in Life   Anita Brookner

Now forty, Dr Ruth Weiss looks back and tells the story of a life impassioned and seduced by literature. As she recalls her London childhood, her friendships and doomed Parisian love affairs, she knows that once again she must make a start in life.

The Shape of Love   Gelsey Kirkland and Greg Lawrence

In this compelling sequel to her bestselling *Dancing on My Grave,* Gelsey Kirkland takes up the story as she returns to the London stage to star as Juliet in *Romeo and Juliet* and Princess Aurora in *Sleeping Beauty*. 'Heart-rending ... the very image of passion' – *Observer*

The Life and Death of Mary Wollstonecraft   Claire Tomalin

'Wide, penetrating, sympathetic ... there is no better book on Mary Wollstonecraft, nor is there likely to be ... The author brings a deep understanding to a remarkably complex woman ... but it is more than a biography: it illuminates the radical world of the 1780s and 1790s as few others do' – *New Statesman*

Isabelle   Annette Kobak
The Life of Isabelle Eberhardt

'A European turned Arab, a Christian turned Muslim, a woman dressed as a man; a libertine who stilled profound mystical cravings by drink, hashish and innumerable Arab lovers ... All the intricate threads of her rebellious life are to be found in Annette Kobak's scrupulously researched book' – *Daily Telegraph*

Going Too Far   Caroline Lassalle

On the terrace of a Greek villa Bettina and her guests – malicious, unstable Johnny and dedicated but excessive Delia – pass the morning, afternoon and evening of one day in quarrels, reminiscences and the telling of classical myths and legends. 'A brilliant and emotionally satisfying book' – *Sunday Times*

READ MORE IN PENGUIN

A SELECTION OF FICTION AND NON-FICTION

Money for Nothing P. G. Wodehouse

Lester Carmody of Rudge Hall is not altogether a good egg. Rather the reverse, in fact. For his intention is to inherit a large sum from the family silver by arranging its theft... 'His whimsical, hilarious stories aimed to do nothing more than amuse' – *Sunday Express*

Lucky Jim Kingsley Amis

'Dixon makes little dents in the smug fabric of hypocritical, humbugging, classbound British society ... Amis caught the mood of post-war restiveness in a book which, though socially significant, was, and still is, extremely funny' – Anthony Burgess

The Day Gone By Richard Adams

'He is the best adventure-story-writer alive ... Answers to the literary and personal puzzles of the Mr Adams phenomenon lie buried like truffles in his admirable autobiography' – A. N. Wilson in the *Daily Telegraph*

Romancing Vietnam Justin Wintle

'Justin Wintle's journal is a memorable, often amusing, always interesting diary of a tour of duty in a land where sharp-end history pokes round every corner' – *Yorkshire Post*. 'Compelling reading' – *Sunday Telegraph*

Travelling the World Paul Theroux

Now, for the first time, Paul Theroux has authorized a book of his favourite travel writing, containing photographs taken by those who have followed in his footsteps. The exquisite pictures here brilliantly complement and illuminate the provocative, wry, witty commentaries of one of the world's greatest travellers.

READ MORE IN PENGUIN

A SELECTION OF FICTION AND NON-FICTION

Yours Etc. Graham Greene

'An entertaining celebration of Graham Greene's lesser-known career as a prolific author of letters to newspapers; you will find unarguable proof of his total addiction to everything about his time, from the greatest issues of the day to the humblest subjects imaginable' – Salman Rushdie in the *Observer*

Just Looking John Updike

'Mr Updike can be a very good art critic, and some of these essays are marvellous examples of critical explanation … A deep understanding of the art emerges' – *The New York Times Book Review*

As I Walked Out One Midsummer Morning Laurie Lee

As I Walked Out One Midsummer Morning tells of a young man's search for adventure as he leaves his Cotswolds home for London and Spain. 'A beautiful piece of writing' – *Observer*

The Secret Lemonade Drinker Guy Bellamy

Before Bobby met and married Caroline he believed in sex, drink and a good time. He still does… 'Sparkling … It cracks open a thousand jokes, some old, some new and some blue. As hideously addictive as drink' – *Sunday Times*

A Thief in the Night John Cornwell

A veil of suspicion and secrecy surrounds the final hours of John Paul I, who died of a reported heart attack in September 1978. Award-winning crime-writer John Cornwell was invited by the Vatican to conduct a full investigation and his extraordinary findings are revealed here.

For Good or Evil Clive Sinclair

'The stories are not only very finely poised but genuinely contemporary, stylistically serious… a striking collection' – *The Times Literary Supplement*

READ MORE IN PENGUIN

A SELECTION OF FICTION AND NON-FICTION

Brightside G. H. Morris

Stuffed with magic, coal grit and wayward, Rabelaisian humour, this wonderful trilogy chronicles the lives of three generations of the Brightsides – a family with an appetite for the extraordinary. 'We've just mined a seam of home-produced – and Northern – magic realism' – *Observer*

Chasing the Monsoon Alexander Frater

In 1987 Alexander Frater decided to pursue the astonishing phenomenon of the Indian summer monsoon and this fascinating account of his journey reveals the exotic, often startling discoveries of an ambitious and irresistibly romantic adventure.

Love in the Time of Cholera Gabriel García Márquez

'For fifty years a breath-taking beauty, now old and just widowed, has recoiled in pride and guilt from her secret lover. His desolate obsession has led him into an enigmatic existence in spite of his renown in business. One Pentecost, love found a new tongue with which to speak. Unique Márquez magic of the sadness and funniness of humanity' – *The Times*

The Invisible Woman Claire Tomalin

'Made visible is Nelly Ternan, and in the process, Tomalin gives us the world of a nineteenth-century actress and most importantly, the real world of Charles Dickens, whose passion for her … changed his life, his career and his work' – Melvyn Bragg in the *Independent*

Shots from the Hip Charles Shaar Murray

His classic encapsulation of the moment when rock stars turned junkies as the sixties died; his dissection of rock 'n' roll violence as citizens assaulted the Sex Pistols; his superstar encounters, from the decline of Paul McCartney to Mick Jagger's request that the author should leave – Charles Shaar Murray's *Shots from the Hip* is also rock history in the making.

READ MORE IN PENGUIN

In every corner of the world, on every subject under the sun, Penguin represents quality and variety – the very best in publishing today.

For complete information about books available from Penguin – including Puffins, Penguin Classics and Arkana – and how to order them, write to us at the appropriate address below. Please note that for copyright reasons the selection of books varies from country to country.

In the United Kingdom: Please write to *Dept. JC, Penguin Books Ltd, FREEPOST, West Drayton, Middlesex UB7 OBR*

If you have any difficulty in obtaining a title, please send your order with the correct money, plus ten per cent for postage and packaging, to *PO Box No. 11, West Drayton, Middlesex UB7 OBR*

In the United States: Please write to *Penguin USA Inc., 375 Hudson Street, New York, NY 10014*

In Canada: Please write to *Penguin Books Canada Ltd, 10 Alcorn Avenue, Suite 300, Toronto, Ontario M4V 3B2*

In Australia: Please write to *Penguin Books Australia Ltd, 487 Maroondah Highway, Ringwood, Victoria 3134*

In New Zealand: Please write to *Penguin Books (NZ) Ltd, 182–190 Wairau Road, Private Bag, Takapuna, Auckland 9*

In India: Please write to *Penguin Books India Pvt Ltd, 706 Eros Apartments, 56 Nehru Place, New Delhi 110 019*

In the Netherlands: Please write to *Penguin Books Netherlands B.V., Keizersgracht 231 NL–1016 DV Amsterdam*

In Germany: Please write to *Penguin Books Deutschland GmbH, Friedrichstrasse 10–12, W–6000 Frankfurt/Main 1*

In Spain: Please write to *Penguin Books S. A., C. San Bernardo 117–6° E–28015 Madrid*

In Italy: Please write to *Penguin Italia s.r.l., Via Felice Casati 20, I–20124 Milano*

In France: Please write to *Penguin France S. A., 17 rue Lejeune, F–31000 Toulouse*

In Japan: Please write to *Penguin Books Japan, Ishikiribashi Building, 2–5–4, Suido, Tokyo 112*

In Greece: Please write to *Penguin Hellas Ltd, Dimocritou 3, GR–106 71 Athens*

In South Africa: Please write to *Longman Penguin Southern Africa (Pty) Ltd, Private Bag X08, Bertsham 2013*

PENGUIN BOOKS

ASH ON A YOUNG MAN'S SLEEVE

Dannie Abse is a doctor as well as a poet and novelist. He has written three novels, including *There was a Young Man from Cardiff*, also published by Penguin, two autobiographical works (*A Poet in the Family* and *A Strong Dose of Myself*) and ten volumes of poetry, the most recent of which, *Remembrance of Crimes Past*, was published in 1990. His collected poems appeared in 1989 under the title *White Coat, Purple Coat*. In the same year he edited *The Hutchinson Book of Post-War British Poets*.

Dannie Abse is a Fellow of the Royal Society of Literature. He lives in London with his wife Joan Abse, the art historian.

DANNIE ABSE

ASH ON A
YOUNG MAN'S
SLEEVE

PENGUIN BOOKS

PENGUIN BOOKS

Published by the Penguin Group
Penguin Books Ltd, 27 Wrights Lane, London W8 5TZ, England
Penguin Books USA Inc., 375 Hudson Street, New York, New York 10014, USA
Penguin Books Australia Ltd, Ringwood, Victoria, Australia
Penguin Books Canada Ltd, 10 Alcorn Avenue, Toronto, Ontario, Canada M4V 3B2
Penguin Books (NZ) Ltd, 182–190 Wairau Road, Auckland 10, New Zealand

Penguin Books Ltd, Registered Offices: Harmondsworth, Middlesex, England

First published by Hutchinson 1954
Published by Vallentine, Mitchell and Co. 1971
Published in Penguin Books 1982
9 10

Copyright 1954 by Dannie Abse
All rights reserved

Printed in England by Clays Ltd, St Ives plc
Set in Monotype Times

To Joan

Acknowledgements are owed to *Forum*,
Encounter, *The Jewish Monthly* and to the
American periodical *Commentary* where
excerpts of this novel first appeared.
Acknowledgements are also due to the
following for permission to quote from the
songs mentioned:
Boosey & Hawkes Ltd ('Danny Boy');
Chappell & Co. Ltd ('Miss Otis Regrets' and
'Body and Soul'); Francis, Day & Hunter Ltd,
Williamson Music Inc. Publishers, and J. Albert
& Sons Pty Ltd ('I'll Be Seeing You'); Keith
Prowse & Co. Ltd ('Roll Out the Barrel');
Lawrence Wright Music Co. Ltd ('Lazybones').

Ash on an old man's sleeve
Is all the ash burnt roses leave.
Dust in the air suspended
Marks the place where a story ended.
Dust inbreathed was a house –

T. S. Eliot, *Little Gidding*

June the first was our agreement, our day of peace. It came in that year with all sunshine and the windows open and the neighbours' radio. It was tennis-players and the yellow seasick trams grinding down Cathedral Road. It was the end of a school day where we left our carved initials, hurt and momentous, in the wooden desk, and schoolteacher (old Knobble-knees) rubbing off chalk from the blackboard like a nasty day from the calendar. 'Mind how you cross the road,' she said. 'Please, Miss Morgan,' asked Philip, 'can I have my yo-yo back? I won't talk again during lessons.'

Keith had asked me to his house for tea, for it was our day of peace, an interlude in our constant campaign of being mean to each other, of masterful vilification. We walked hardly together for we were enemies. Suddenly Keith said, 'There'll be bananas and cream, so you can leave as soon as you've eaten 'em.' 'I like bananas and cream,' I said. Other people's houses have a strange smell. Keith Thomas's home was no exception and I was sniffing. 'What's the matter?' Keith's mother asked. 'Is there something burning?' I went very red when the others sniffed. They just stood there, Keith and his mother, heads cocked, drawing air through their nostrils. 'I can't smell anything,' she said. I could. Perhaps it was the odour of sin or the past remains of previous tenants. I ate bread and butter and jam and Welsh cakes, and Keith sniffed and sniffed louder and louder, quite ostentatiously I can tell you. 'Blow your nose, Keith,' said his mother. I tipped the tea over the tablecloth and grew redder . . .

This was all a long time ago: I was ten years high and I lived in South Wales. There everything was different, more alive some-how. The landscape and the voices were dramatic and argumenta-

tive. Already I knew the chapels and the pubs and the billiard halls and the singing.

'How old's your mother?'

'Thirty.'

'Mine's forty.'

'Mine's fifty.'

'Mine's sixty-three.'

'Mine's ninety.'

'Mine's hundred and ninety.'

Near the White Wall, I was born in a smoky house, boasting. I knew the paper flowers, the Sunday suits, the stuffed animals, the brass, the clocks, and the ferns. Always there was too much furniture in the room. Always there was too much noise and familiarity. Always there were visitors. Lovely it was.

But Porthcawl was the place with the long wind and the terror of the sea coming over the promenade with sloppy white paws. On Sundays, father would drive us down, plush and proud, scrubbed and avid, dodging in and out amongst the procession of cars that the seaside attracted like a magnet. And I would be in a race steering from the back seat. Over Tumble Down Dick and down Crack Hill. Past the Golden Mile and the green and green. Stop for Bull's-eyes. Stop for weewee. Porthcawl was the place. Posh. The Figure of Eight and the Ghost Train. The slowest Speedboats in the world and the thinnest Fat Lady. Come and See Minny, She Creeps and She Crawls, She Walks on Her Belly Like a Reptile – Hey, Hey – Tanner a Time. Not to mention Sandy Beach and the parents shouting at the deaf children: 'Don't swim out too far.' 'Stop that!' 'Dai, you'll get sick eating sand.'

I used to take two pebbles and throw them at each other. They were boxers fighting or two armies locked in a stony embrace. One was Wales, the other was England or France or Siam, or red-haired, freckle-faced Keith Thomas. My mother was born at Ystalyfera one rainy Tuesday, my father on Guy Fawkes night in Bridgend, so Wales always won, unless the inevitable cloud would interrupt the struggle with a lamentation of rain. Then the people, the lovely folk, would go scooting for the public shelters and wait for the rare Welsh sun or for the Western Welsh bus or for the

Welsh pubs to open. And they would sing whilst they waited. Oh, sing my beautiful, Sospan Fach, Cwm Rhondda. They would sing . . .

Keith's mother put a plate under the tablecloth.

'Never mind,' she said to me.

'What are you blushing for?' asked Keith. 'Look, Ma, he's as red as a beetroot.'

'Quiet darling,' said his mother.

'I thought we were going to have bananas and cream,' I said.

Later the man of the house came in, ate, and said no word. Grumpy he was. My mother used to say that he had whisky instead of blood running through his body. It was true too; I could smell it through his mouth. Besides, lunch-time yesterday, I heard him and saw him come out of *The Bull with One Leg*. Drunk he was and shouting: 'I am damned, we are damned. I know what sin is, so I know what God is. We're damned, damned, damned.' I stood in the street as the pub's doors swung behind a weeping Mr Thomas, who staggered tenderly into the sunlight. 'Darro,' he said, looking at me with spaniel eyes, 'you're damned too, little one.' And wobbly he walked down the road under the two o'clock sun. But now, in his own house, he said no word, looking at me without recognition, though only yesterday lunch-time it was that he confided to me the terrible, the most unspeakable truth. 'Come and sit down, Mr Thomas,' said his wife, so Keith and I went out into the garden. (Their garden is not as big as ours.)

'What's that?' I asked.

'Our washing machine,' Keith said.

'Does it work?' I asked.

'Put your finger by 'ere,' Keith said.

I did so and he turned the handle and my nail was crushed and I went home crying to mother. He was my enemy.

It was Friday night and we were Jewish. The two candles burning symbolized for me holiness and family unity. My mother could speak Welsh and Yiddish and English, and Dad knew swear words as well. One of my big brothers would say the prayer and we would eat. My brothers' names were Wilfred and Leo.

The meat was kosher. 'Wash your hands, wash your hands, wash your hands. Comb your hair.' I loved my brothers best.

In the schoolyard, too, they would dance around me:

> 'Dan, Dan, the dirty old man,
> Washed his face in a frying pan;
> Combed his hair with a leg of the chair,
> Dan, Dan, the dirty old man.'

'I'll do you in, Keith Thomas,' I said furiously. That settled it. Keith and I would lead a procession of whooping boys into the lane and we would threaten each other, spit at each other, and finally swing our fists against the air until, by chance, one of us would get our face in the way and the fight would end. Fierce it was. Afterwards I would go into our garage so that I could weep alone and not show the shame of my tears to the other boys.

I loved my brothers best. Leo was a revolutionary. I already knew the *Red Flag* and *the* Alphabet.

> 'A stands for Armaments, the Capitalists' pride,
> B stands for Bolshie, the thorn in their side . . .'

Oh, election day was a holiday. I would go over the town looking for a Labour car. I couldn't find any, so I chased the Liberals instead, and insulted the big slick cars that wore the blue colours.

> 'Vote, vote, vote for Johnny Williams,
> Kick old Whitey in the pants.'

'What are you shouting for?' said my enemy Keith Thomas, his eyes, poison blue, leering at me. 'Vote, vote, vote,' I shouted. Keith pulled a penknife out of his pocket, unclasped it and tested the edge with his thumb. 'It's sharp,' he said casually. 'You broke my fingernail,' I said. An election car passed by. 'Vote, vote, vote,' I shouted. 'Quiet,' ordered Keith, and he once more tested the edge of his knife ominously. 'You coward,' I said, 'fight like a Great Britain.' The street was empty. A cat slept on the sunlit doorway.

14

'Shut up, you podgy Jewboy,' said Keith.

'Podgy son of a whisky man,' I said.

'I'll slit your throat,' said Keith.

'I'll bash you on the nose,' I retaliated.

'I'll cut you into pieces,' said Keith.

'I'll split your lip,' I answered.

'I'll cut your ears off,' Keith said.

'I'll put your eyes out,' I said.

'Shut up, you podgy Jewboy,' said Keith.

'Podgy son of a whisky man,' I said.

Keith slowly came towards me with his penknife ready.

'Fight like a Great Britain,' I said.

Round the far corner ambled Dirty-face, pushing a pram, his dog following behind.

'Gosh,' I said, 'there's Dirty-face.'

We both hesitated. Then we ran away. We were both afraid of Dirty-face. In the Park I heard Keith shouting: 'Podgy Jewboy. Podgy Jewboy. Podgy Jewboy.' I walked home quickly to ask Wilfred to buy me a penknife.

This was all a long time ago. I was ten years high and I lived in South Wales. I was not to play with Dirty-face, or go down the Docks, or make noises in my belly when visitors came. I was to tie up my shoe-laces, be kind to the cat and wash. But there were more 'don'ts' than 'dos'.

And throughout all this my mother kissed me.

Cariad, clean heart, listen to me, this is my beginning. Let me start again.

We sat there, brown-headed, black-headed, fair-headed, red-headed, bowed over our books silently. In the next classroom a music lesson progressed and the piping unbroken voices sang out clear and true as water. 'The Minstrel Boy to the wars has gone, in the ranks of death you'll find him.' Outside, birds chattered and the traffic passed. Inside, on the window-shelf, tadpoles were black commas in the fish-and-chip water. On teacher's desk stood a vase of sweet peas that Tubby Taylor had brought her. Somebody passed me a note which read, 'Miss Morgan is in luv with

the Head.' I dipped the note in the inkpot and threw it at the back of Foureyes' neck. He looked up, startled, thinking he had been stung. I was gazing with great concentration at the electric bulb and counted four drunken flies. 'You wait,' whispered Foureyes. The sweet peas in their faded colours reminded me of old-fashioned young ladies frayed in cheap dresses. I giggled. Then the bell rang: it was the end of school. Brown heads, black heads, fair heads, red heads, looked up eagerly. The Minstrel Boy abruptly came to an end next door. 'Class dismiss,' said Miss Morgan.

I ran out of school with my arms horizontal (for I was an aero-plane) into the summer evening. In the Park it said PLEASE KEEP OFF THE GRASS and DOGS ALLOWED ONLY ON A LEASH. I kicked the notices over. In the distance, the park-keeper stabbed with his little iron spear, cigarette cartons, pieces of newspaper and other rubbish. Old men were playing bowls over on the West Side. Young men were taking off their tigerish blazers to play tennis on the red gravel court. Lol, the idiot boy, was fishing with a net for tiddlers in the brook whilst another lad repeatedly banged the chained metal cup against the fountain for no reason. Suddenly, as I was swooping and zooming over my terrestrial sky, I found my enemy before me, his face frenetic, insane, ridiculous. His small stones of fists stung my body and my face, whilst all the other boys who had come to watch exhorted him to further savagery. Then once again, I was alone, weeping, the pebbles in my knees bruised and the skin over them bleeding, for the gravel pathway had curiously risen to meet me. 'I'll kill you,' I said, 'I'll kill you.' Nobody was in earshot. One of the tennis-players shouted 'Thirty-forty.' From afar, I could hear the wooden click as the bowls cannoned off each other. Through my splintered glass tears Lol, the half-idiot boy, came towards me with his fishing net slung over his shoulder. He stood there gawking.

'Go away,' I said.

He smiled sadly.

'I cry too,' he said.

'Go away,' I shouted.

'I fell into the brook and drownded myself,' he said, and added, almost whispering, 'So I don't cry no more.'

'You wait,' I boasted, 'I'll get that Keith.'

But, later, Keith Thomas became my greatest friend, for he, with his parents, moved to the next street, the other side of the lane. Keith's father would pass our house at night after the pubs closed, and I would hear him shouting:

'We're damned, the whole world is damned.'

Mother used to say: 'His poor wife, what she has to put up with, and her with a weak heart and swelling of the ankles. All his doing, *his*. Thank God that's one thing your father doesn't do.'

'His wife's condition is nothing to do with the drink,' Wilfred would say, who was a medical student. 'Mrs Thomas had rheumatic fever when she was a child.'

'Don't tell me,' my mother would reply. 'If that's the sort of diagnosis you're going to make when you're a doctor your father is pouring money down the drain.' Why did Wilfred laugh, I wonder? Sometimes I call Wilfred Big Stiff. He likes that.

'What sort of a future has little Keith with a father like that?' mother would go on.

Later in the night I would wake up and listen to Mr Thomas swimming home in the dark street outside. Once I crept out of bed to look out of the window. Mr Thomas was clinging to the lamp-post and another man was playing an accordion. The accordion player was singing, 'She was a good girl until I took her to a dance, she was a good girl but then she had her first romance' – and, tilting towards the moon, Mr Thomas in his bowler hat was shouting above the accordion and the singing, 'Christ is come but I am damned.'

Keith and I used to play hide-and-seek in the nearby church-yard, our laughter resounding all loveliness amongst the sombre stone angels. We played cricket in the stretched summer lanes, we fished for minnows in the stream and became Cowboys and Indians amongst the bushes and trees of the Park. (I was always an Indian because my brother Leo had told me that Cowboys were Imperialists.) It was all greeny and water and swan until one afternoon the following spring.

We were mitching from school in the lane behind our houses and we caught house-flies with our hands. We would throw the living flies into the web between the stones of the wall and watch the insect struggling before the spider came out from his den to eat it up. Usually we pulled the wings off the fly first so that it couldn't escape.

'Catching flies,' I said, 'is a social duty,' when Keith became doubtful of our inquisitory practices. Then the big man approached us. We saw him coming down the lane but we didn't think he would stop to speak to us. He wore a gay coloured shirt.

'Hullo,' he said.

'Hullo, Mister,' said Keith.

'What are you doing?' the big man said.

'Nothing,' I said.

'Would you like some ice-cream?' he asked.

'Don't mind,' Keith said.

'No, we're going,' I said.

He looked down at us puzzled. His shirt was very bright-coloured. Suddenly he smiled artificially. 'You're a lovely boy,' the man said softly with an invalid's voice. He placed his hand on my friend's shoulder. He had hair on his hand. There was something very physical and secretive about him. Mother had said sometimes to me, 'If you're a bad boy I'll give you to the gipsies.' But he wasn't a gipsy. I could tell that. His sticky pathetic face leered at us and he lisped something we couldn't understand. All the time his hand lay remarkably intimate on my friend's shoulder.

'Go away,' I said, 'or I'll tell my father.'

The man laughed. 'Where do you live?' he asked.

'*There*,' I said.

He took his hand from Keith's shoulder, giggled and turned away. Quietly we watched him walk down the lane. The big man turned round and waved at us, and we didn't speak to each other at all. When he had gone I said, 'You'll have the Black Curse now.' Keith looked at me concerned. 'What do you mean?' he asked. 'Well, the man touched you, didn't he?' Keith went white.

18

''S all right,' I reassured him, 'you won't get the Black Curse unless we see him again.'

For weeks after that we wouldn't look at people and as we marched through the crowds we would stare at our feet. 'Don't dare look up, Keith,' I said, 'you might see the man and then you'll get the Black Curse.' Soon, however, we forgot all about the incident and it was not until the Wales *v*. England Rugby International match that we thought of it again. 'There'll be 50,000 people there,' said Keith gloomily. 'The man's bound to be one of them.'

These big rugby matches were great fun. The kind Welsh crowd would pass us down over their heads, hand by hand, laugh by laugh, right to the front. And then there would be a band playing and the fat man banging the fat drum. Tiddle-um, tiddle-um, tiddly um tum tum. Hoo-ray, Hoo-ray. And they sang the Welsh songs that floated sadly, but joyfully, into the air over Cardiff Arms Park, as little dark-headed men invaded the field in an attempt to climb the goal-posts and hang there the all-important leek. There would be the ritual of the crowd shouting 'Boo' and 'Shame' when the policemen ejected the intense spectators from the holy pitch. The policemen knew they were unpopular. They tried to shoo the invading spectators away with dignity, but the spectators ran round them towards the goal-posts, jigging and dancing, putting their thumbs to their noses. What a laugh it was. Yet nobody succeeded in attaching the leek to the crossbar. As one of the men next to us said, 'The buggers have greased the poles.' England came out in their white shirts and the crowd clapped politely, but the real applause was reserved for the men in red shirts as they strutted out from the players' tunnel, cocky and clever. The roar subsided as the band played 'Land of My Fathers'. Fifty thousand people (including somewhere in the crowd the Black Curse man) stood with their hats off at attention. When the National Anthems were over there was another roar. Somebody said, 'Jawch, England 'ave an 'efty team, much bigger than ours, mun.' The whistle blew, and soon after England scored. 'There seem to be two of theirs to one of ours,' the man with the

19

wart said. Another remarked, 'In the old days Wales really had a team, not a bunch of students.' 'It's the referee,' added his companion. 'Look at that, offside if there ever was one.' At last Wales equalized. 'What a movement, what a movement,' said the man who had been talking of the old days. 'Just like in 1923 when . . .' Three spectators near us wore red shirts and banged silver saucepans, urging the players to victory with screams of Llanelly encouragement and scathing criticisms. And we shouted too, oh how we shouted . . . When the noise was loudest we swore and nobody could hear us.

I lost Keith as the crowd pushed their way out into Westgate Street; but later going home I met him near the churchyard. Keith was morose and melancholy. 'I seen him,' he said. We walked silently through the lane. As I left him to have tea I shouted, 'You'd better watch out, the Black Curse.' He slammed the back door and ran into the house.

The next week I tortured him. I would go to the public baths and swim for hours in the chlorine water until the skin on my fingers was wrinkled and old. 'You'd better not come in,' I would say, 'you might drown.' And the Black Curse would make him watch me miserably from the balcony, whilst I splashed and raved, swam under water, stood on my hands, dived from the spring-board . . . Nor would I let him climb trees, for I pointed out to him that he might fall down and break his neck.

'How long does this Black Curse go on for?' Keith asked.

'Forever,' I replied joyfully.

How was I to know that the very next week Mrs Thomas would have a stroke? Keith's mother, only forty-four years of age, lay gasping, propped up in her bed with one side of her face and one side of her body paralysed. Her eyes were pulled over so that she was forever looking towards her right, where normally Mr Thomas slept. She couldn't speak, they said, though she could hear everything. The doctor reported that she had a large thrombosis in her brain. The following morning, at three o'clock, she died. That day the blinds were drawn in Keith's house. Neighbours stood outside their front gates, whispering. Incredulously, maybe for as long as two minutes, each person thought of his own

death, and in their hearts it was five-to-three in the morning. 'She was a good lady, Mrs Thomas,' they said. Others said, 'The poor boy.' And there was a sudden indignant anger against Mr Thomas, a match flame spurting in an unlit room, blown out almost as soon by a draught. Mr Thomas thought of all that might have been. He had been a brilliant architect at one time, of a good family, and fortunate in that he had a good education. He could have worked for himself instead of for *Tanner & Son*. Now, he was always afraid of losing his job because of the drink. Poor Blod, she lay there so quiet, so still, with her eyes turned looking to see if he had come to bed. 'Blodwen fach,' he said hopelessly, 'it was good at the beginning, wasn't it? Remember, before Keith was born? I didn't mean harm, Blodwen.' She still looked to the right in silence. 'Who had come to live in her?' he thought. 'She was a pretty,' he said aloud to the doctor, as if trying to defend her ugliness in death. 'Come away now,' answered Dr Meadows.

I went with my mother to give flowers to Mr Thomas, and he ushered us into their front room (their best room). Mr Thomas was dressed in black and he received my mother's condolences quietly. I didn't understand the slow punctuated conversation that followed. But I remember Keith's father remark: 'I swear to God, I shan't take another glass till I die. On Blodwen's body I swear it.' And he meant it, too. I observed a finger of sunlight pointing through a crack in the window blind, its fingernail scratching a round blob of sun on the tawdry deaf carpet. Outside an *Eldorado* man rang his bicycle bell. 'Ice-cream,' it tinkled. 'Ice-cream.' The dust danced, the dust climbed up and down the shaft of sunlight, the dust settled on Mr Thomas's black suit. The piano lid was closed, a coffin of music. And then I heard perhaps what I was waiting for: I heard Keith Thomas whimpering up-stairs. Keith's father said with dignity, 'Thank you for the flowers.'

That night, when Mr Thomas came through the road drunk and screaming despite his holy resolution, the whole street locked their doors and pulled down the blinds. The children could hear him from their bedrooms. 'Blodwen, my pretty, it wasn't me at all. Speak, Blodwen fach, speak. I know, I know, I know,' he yelled. Only Stokes joined him in the street. Stokes, who used to

go round the town with placards on his back, placards which read: CHRIST DIED FOR YOUR SINS on one side and REPENT BEFORE IT IS TOO LATE on the other. 'Kneel and pray,' begged the benign fanatic, 'kneel and pray.' 'I'm damned,' shouted Mr Thomas, 'I'm damned, it's too late.' But in the end they both knelt in the street, under the full moon, one praying and the other crying out 'Blodwen fach' between his terrible oaths.

Weeks later, I was playing in the Park with some other boys, when my friend approached me. It was the first time I had seen him since the funeral and his face was very white.

'You killed my mother,' he said.

'I did not.'

'You did.'

'I didn't.'

'You did.'

And then with a great effort he added, 'The Black Curse.'

Then Keith cried and I wanted to kiss him. But I cried.

*   *   *

It was a winter's evening; Sidney was blowing on his hands. 'No more school till Monday,' said Sidney. It was silly to come home from school tea-time with the lamp-posts lit to keep away the ghosts. It was that cold: in the middle of the road, steam rose from a drain. We stood there, looking downwards, watching the steam rising. 'It's the devil smoking his pipe,' I said.

> A dam and Eve and Pinchme
>   Went down to the river to bathe.
> A dam and Eve got drownded
>   Who do you think was saved?

A policeman came round the corner and we ran and we ran and we ran.

'You don't believe in Christmas, do you?' Sidney said to me.

'What's it like to be Jewish?' asked Philip.

''S all right,' I said.

'What's the difference?' demanded Philip.

'They puts 'ats on when they pray, we takes them off,' Sidney said.

'It's more than that, their blood's different,' said Philip, 'makes their noses grow.'

'Megan's coming round our house this evening,' I interrupted, making a face. Sidney and I didn't like girls because they wore knickers and Megan was especially silly. Lots of things were silly. Girls were silly, Miss Morgan our schoolmistress was silly, washing behind the ears was silly, going to bed early was silly. Now Philip was silly, because he didn't know what it was like to be Jewish. It wasn't anything really, except on Saturdays. We walked down the street wishing for snow and letting our breath fly from our mouths like ectoplasm. Soon it would be Christmas holidays, and presents and parties. The shops were crowded with voices. We pressed our noses against the window-panes, breathed, and wrote our names with our fingers on the misted glass. 'Leo loves Megan,' I wrote. It was all cotton wool in the windows, and the smell of tangerine peel, and a man with a long white beard.

'There's daft, i'n'it?' said Philip. 'Look, Father Xmas!'

'Where do flies go in the winter-time?' asked Sidney suddenly, and we all laughed sharing a secret.

When I arrived home, my brother Leo was squeezing a blackhead from his forehead; then he combed his hair.

'Megan Davies,' I shouted at him. 'Megan Davies.'

'Do your homework,' he said.

'Who loves Megan Davies?' I cried.

He hit me harder than he meant for I fell against the wall and a bruise came up like an egg on my head.

'Put some butter on it,' my brother said, 'and stop crying.'

'Bloody, bloody, bloody,' I screamed at him.

'Now then, enough of that,' he thundered. But the front door bell rang and he thought it was Megan, so I was given a penny to shut up.

It was only Uncle Isidore . . . I don't think I've told you about him. I'd like to tell you. Of course, he's dead now, but I remember him quite well. He's become a sort of symbol really. You know,

my parents still live in Wales, but we children have grown up and left home – as much, that is, as anybody can ever leave home. Anyway, when old Dafydd Morgan comes round the house at Cardiff these days, he and my parents get to talk about the kids.

'And what about Wilfred, your eldest son?' Old Morgan asks.

'All right,' says my father, 'not just an ordinary doctor but a psychiatrist.'

'Fancy,' says Morgan, 'Wilfred not just an ordinary doctor! Now my son Ianto 'e 'ad the gift do you know, just like his mother before she caught pneumonia, before she was . . . exterminated, God rest her soul.'

'And Leo, my second son,' interrupts my father.

'Ah yes, Leo, Leo, there's a boy for you,' smiled Morgan. 'A boy in a million. Very spiritual. And a credit to you; goes to chapel, I mean synagogue, regular, I understand.'

'A solicitor, Mr Morgan, very clever.'

'Yes, very clever. Fancy, a solicitor! A very spiritual solicitor, I should think. Pays, I always think, to go to chapel – I mean synagogue. The connections do you know? Apart, of course, as a remedy for the spirit. But what about your third son, the youngest?'

'Our third son, Dafydd Morgan,' says my mother, 'is no good. Won't do any work.'

'Just like Uncle Isidore,' exclaim my father and mother, in unison, lifting up their hands hopelessly.

'Fancy,' says Morgan. 'Now my son Ianto . . .'

Uncle Isidore wasn't exactly an Uncle. Nobody knew his exact relationship to the family; but my parents called him 'Uncle', and my cousins called him 'Uncle', and my uncles called him 'Uncle'. He used to visit our home regularly, once a week, to collect his half a crown and eat a bit of supper. He went around all my relations' houses to receive a silver coin and grumble. It wasn't even as if he were a religious man. He just lived that way and the rest of the time he would read at Cardiff Central Library, or return to his dingy bed-sitting-room and play his violin. Not that he was a competent musician. On the contrary, he would scrape the easy bits and whistle the difficult phrases. That was his

24

philosophy and his life. He always looked as if he needed a good wash, a shave, and a haircut. Uncle Isidore would pick me up and rub his face against my cheek. 'Like a baby's bottom,' he used to say to me. He smelt of dirt and tobacco. Eventually he died of kidney trouble. That's all I know about him. It doesn't seem very much. Uncle Isidore was just an oldish, untidy man, a sort of amateur beggar, who wouldn't work but read in the Reference Library and forever played his violin. It used to disturb people that he didn't have a reason for living. Dafydd Morgan would lecture him beginning with the inevitable sentence, 'The purpose of life is . . .' and end up his discourse hopelessly, saying, 'The Jews, bach, are generally an industrious people.' Now if Uncle Isidore had played his violin, say, like Yehudi Menuhin, my parents would no longer say, 'Our third son is like Uncle Isidore, what are we to do?' – but, rather, they'd exclaim, 'if only, oh if only our third son was like Uncle Isidore.' For I know that Uncle Isidore was an artist, a real artist – except that he just didn't have the necessary accident of talent. Yehudi Menuhin plays the violin and millions listen. Menuhin, thus, has a purpose in life. But when Uncle Isidore played, even the cat would rush for the door. Nobody listened. So, we say, he had no purpose in life. He was contemptible, a rogue, an outlaw. I never cried when Uncle Isidore died. Nobody did. There was a small funeral and my father and my uncles gave some conscience money for his burial. That's all.

When the front door bell rang, Leo gave me a penny to shut up. He thought that it was Megan Davies, but it was only Uncle Isidore.

'Workers of the world unite,' grinned my uncle at my brother.

'You should talk,' Leo said.

'Leo hit me,' I said.

'What?' cried Uncle. 'That is coercion. We can't allow coercion.'

'But he gave me a penny,' I said.

'Then you're a rich lad,' he exclaimed, and looked so dismal that I offered him the coin.

'That's all right, lad,' he said to me. 'I'll live without it.'

'Go on,' I insisted. 'Mama says you need it. Take it.'

'Ah,' said Uncle, 'your Mama is so right. She's a gentlewoman she is, and do you know, lad, she used to be the prettiest girl in South Wales – Jewess or Goy.'

'She still is,' I said, big-eyed.

'No, no,' said Uncle. 'Now she's the most beautiful.' Yes, Uncle Isidore had the soul of a gentleman.

The front door bell rang again.

'Megan Davies, Megan Davies,' I screamed.

Leo rushed to the door and I heard their voices together, and then the door slammed. I was left in the house alone with Uncle Isidore. He kicked the fire and the flames spat out of the coal, curling round his black boot. Mother would return soon and cook the dinner. Philip was silly asking me what it was like to be Jewish. Uncle Isidore stared into the fire with tremendous sadness. I wasn't sure whether he was awake or asleep. It was silent in the room but for the loud ticking of the mantelpiece clock. Suddenly he turned his head towards the window.

'You could stand there,' he said vehemently, 'all your life and look out.' And then he stared into the fire again. I walked over to the window, almost on tiptoe, afraid to disturb him. I gazed out. Down the road I could see snow falling under the lamp-post, and above, between the clouds, a few stars in the cold sky.

'Uncle?' I asked.

'Well?'

'Uncle, what's it like to be Jewish all your life?' I asked.

''S all right,' he said, and for a moment we smiled at each other.

*　　*　　*

My mother seemed very angry. She kept on talking and talking.

'Not in front of the *kinder*,' my father pleaded.

'Where're you going?' she barked at Leo.

'Out,' he said.

'Out where?'

'I'm eighteen,' he replied obstinately.

'You're not too old to put across my knee,' father said.

'I'm nearly eleven,' I said.

'I'm going to a political meeting, if you must know,' Leo lied.

'That girl, that *shickse*, I'll throw a bucket of water over her, that'll cool her ardour, my lad.'

'Which girl, Mother?' asked Leo innocently.

'Megan Davies, Megan Davies,' I cried joyfully.

'You be quiet,' my mother said.

'My God,' said Leo. 'What sort of house is this? There's no privacy at all.'

'I'll give you privacy.'

'Hell, Dad – can't I even – '

'Who do you think you're speaking to?'

It ended up with my father chasing Leo round the table swearing at him. As Leo went around the table for the third time, he grabbed the bread-knife. I stood behind my mother in the corner. Leo's face was white, my father's purple almost.

'The neighbours, what will the neighbours say?' shouted my mother.

Leo took the opportunity to dash for the hall, and in a flash the front door had banged behind him. We remained there very quiet and still, but for my father, who was breathing heavily.

'You wait till he comes in,' said my father darkly. 'I've had enough of his nonsense.'

There was a curious noise from the front door. Leo had pushed the bread-knife through the letter-box . . . Later, when my eldest brother Wilfred came in, he asked what had happened. My father leaned over the fire, silently, and mother went on with her knitting. My brother Wilfred was a medical student at the Cardiff Royal Infirmary.

'What's the matter?' he repeated.

'Leo chased Dad with a bread-knife and tried to kill him,' I volunteered. 'I think you ought to operate.'

'Go to bed,' said my mother.

'There's blood on the floor,' I continued. 'They tried to murder each other. Dad swore.'

'Go to bed,' repeated my mother. 'It's after your bedtime.'

'Will Wilfred tell me a story?'

'Yes. Up you go.'

'Good night Mama, good night Dada, good night table, good night walls, good night . . .'

'Up you go.'

And up I went, piggy-back, up the stairs, one by one on Wilfred's back; and I went to bed with the story of David and Goliath, of Jews and Philistines, and my brother's gentle, responsible voice, echoing in my head.

*   *   *

Saturday mornings, I used to climb into my mother's bed and lie between my parents and ask questions:

'Who made the world?'

'God.'

'Who made God?'

When Mam would go and prepare breakfast I would lie on the warm part where she had been. My father snored with his mouth ajar. His face was turned towards me and I could see the individual pores in the skin over his nose, clearly. His skin was like a used dartboard. He opened one eye fishily and saw me upside down. 'What are you looking at?' he said sleepily. 'Your nose,' I said. He closed his eyes again. The wallpaper in the bedroom was pinkish, so warm and kindly. He opened his left eye once more. 'What's wrong with my nose?' he asked. 'Nothing,' I said, but he turned over and I gazed at the back of his head. 'You're going bald a bit on the crown,' I remarked. Father grunted but he soon moved again, this time on to his back. 'You have quite a prominent Adam's apple,' I said. 'Be quiet,' he said. 'You have hair growing in your ears,' I continued. He pulled the bedclothes over his head. 'What are you doing that for?' I shouted.

Saturday was a grand day for there was no school . . . not until Monday. Saturday mornings Leo would often read me poetry from a little blue book.

'The one about the Merman, our kid.'

'No. And don't call me our kid.'

'The one about the Merman, and call once yet before you go, Marg-aret, Marg-aret.'

My brother sat up in his bed, so I lay down.

'This is by Gerard Manley Hopkins,' he said.

'Is he a revolutionary?' I asked.

'Well . . . in a way.'

'You always read revolutionaries,' I said.

Outside, it was raining. Saturday morning rain and the slish, slish, slish of wet tyres over the shining patent leather street with its caged pieces of sky in puddles. They say Manchester is rainy. Have you ever been to Cardiff? It's the rainiest city in the world. Wilfred told me a story about that: when Noah looked out from his Ark so many years ago, he patted the nearest giraffe and said: 'Soon it will be dry everywhere, except of course in Cardiff.' In 1934, one Saturday morning, it was rain over my home town and my brother Leo was reading me poetry from a little blue book. 'Glory be to God for dappled things,' he read. Mama was downstairs cooking breakfast; in the front bedroom Dad lay back snoring, his arm dangling over the side of the bed near an empty teacup. Keith's mother was dead in the wet graveyard and Uncle Isidore was still alive reading Karl Marx in the Public Library. Oh the rain in 1934 that fell over all the map. In the valleys, thirty miles from Cardiff, the rain fell absently across the town square and the queue at the bus stop suddenly started singing into the rain – the rain that stretched itself across the blind windows, the rain that pattered on the black umbrellas, the rain that dived into the slagheaps – the chapel of voices *together*, ever rising higher into the thin rain. Others lounged at corners, in doorways, smelling of wet mackintoshes, listless, dull with unemployment – depression in the valleys and the orator thumping his fist – they only went on singing *together*, louder and higher into the rain – then the bus arrived. The red-coloured bus arrived and they stopped singing, became conscious of the rain, the dampness seeping right through to their souls, the Rhondda Valley naked, bony, the green dress pulled off it, the pulleys stopped and a girl trembling near the coal-mine with a gentle fluttering movement

29

under her heart. One of the queue had a fit of coughing – spat from his mouth a yellow viscid fluid, mixed with coal and blood. All the people in the queue watched his convulsion of coughing, and like prisoners they filed through the pin-striped rain into the red-coloured bus, terribly mute, wet, *lonely*. 1934.

'Glory be to God for dappled things,' my brother read.

Alun and Gwennie had climbed the hills in the early morning to pick mushrooms. Then the bad rain fell, and they found a cave to shelter in.

'Why shouldn't we go to London, Gwennie fach?' asked Alun. 'Work is more regular. Safe work. Safe to get married and 'ave kids.'

'We've been through it before, Alun.'

'You'd like it there,' he said vaguely. 'Theatre and things.' But they wouldn't go. He knew it. A man has to keep his roots or he's lost. Alun's father had been a miner. The family always had been miners. And that was his life too, to come up blinking into the sunlight, or the rain, with the coal dust lathered on his face and black lines under his fingernails. And the soapy water in the zinc bath before the smoky fire-grate, and the yellow canary singing in its cage. It was a simple life and a hard one, but it was his. The men with white scarves around their necks and caps tilted on their heads, working when they were allowed to work, singing when it was time to sing. The choirs, the rugby matches, the chapel, the pub, the billiard hall, and being born and being loved, and the coughing. The English were alien. England was alien and yet the boys were going up North or to London, losing their own tongue, their own language, their own customs. Going to an alien country and feeling clumsy and different and disliked.

'Bugger the rain,' said Alun.

And Gwennie was thinking how one-third of a miner's life had to be spent away from the fresh air and sunlight. She didn't want Alun to get silicosis like her father and her grandfather. She didn't want to wake up in the morning hearing Alun coughing and gasping for breath. Only a week ago, she had heard one of the soap-box orators saying that four miners were launched into eternity every day, and nearly two hundred thousand were impaired every

year. A hazardous calling, the orator had said. A hazardous calling, thought Gwennie.

They were at the foot of the hills when they heard the explosion. Gwennie and Alun joined the silent knots of people who waited in the rain at the top of the pit. A fire was burning fiercely at the coal face, and the rescue party went down the pit with the aid of oxygen cylinders and canaries in cages, and one by one, pitifully, painfully, the trapped men were brought to the surface. The faces of many were badly disfigured. The rain fell. Gwennie said, 'Yes, Alun, we'll go to London, there'll be theatres and things.' 1934.

'Glory be to God for dappled things,' my brother Leo read from his little blue book.

'Breakfast, breakfast – get up or I'll throw a bucket of water over you,' shouted mother laughing. *Amo, amas, amat, amamus, amatis, amant*. When I was born my brother Wilfred bought me a *Comic Cuts* to read. I couldn't read then. Wilfred touched me to see if I was real. I was.

When breakfast was over I had to go to the synagogue, rain or shine, for it was Saturday morning. I used to sit next to Bernard and Simon. We would wear our skull caps and whisper to each other beneath the chant of the Hebrew prayer. A man with a spade-shaped beard would stutter and mutter at us now and then and again. 'Shush, shush,' his eyes said. Such and these times, we would stare at the prayer book and giggle. It seemed natural that the prayer book wasn't in English, but written and told in some strange language one read from right to left, some mystical language one couldn't understand. Obviously, one couldn't speak to God in everyday English. We stood up when the congregation stood up and sat down when they sat down. The men were segregated from the women lest they should be deviated from their spiritual commerce with God. The women prayed upstairs nearer to heaven; the men downstairs nearer to hell. The sermon would begin and I would stare at the red globe that burned the never-failing oil. The Rev. Aaronowich, a man with an enormous face, gave the sermon. Usually his tone was melancholy. Every New Year, Rosh Hashana, he would begin his speech, raising his hands, eyes round, mournfully direct, 'Another year has passed

... another nail ... in the coffin.' The congregation knew this preface to his sermon by heart. They could have joined in, if they so wished, in some sorrowful chant; instead (except for the elders who nodded their heads slowly as if watching vertical tennis) each would nudge and pinch his neighbour.

However, this Saturday morning in 1934, the Rev. Aaronowich was almost gay. I stopped staring at the red globe and ignored the scrubbings and scratching of Simon and Bernard. He spoke in English, with a Russian and Welsh accent, throwing in a bit of Yiddish when his vocabulary failed him. I think I could understand what he was saying. I believe he proclaimed that it was an honour to be alive, good to breathe fresh air, miraculous to be able to see the blue sky and the green grass; that health was our most important benediction and that one should never say 'no' to the earth. (Also, that the congregation should as Jews avoid ostentatiousness.) Never to despair, for when one felt dirty inside, or soiled, or dissatisfied, one only had to gaze at the grandeur of the windswept skies or at the pure wonder of landscapes – one only had to remember the beauty of human relationships, the gentleness and humour of the family, the awe and tenderness when a young man looks upon his betrothed – all things of the earth, of the whole of Life, its comedy, its tragedy, its lovely endeavour and its profound consummation – and I understood this for only that morning my brother Leo had read me from a little blue book words that sounded like 'Glory be to God for dappled things' – though, then, I didn't know what 'dappled' meant. And the Rev. Aaronowich spoke such beautiful things in such a broken accent that his voice became sweet and sonorous and his huge mask-like face rich, ruffled, handsome.

Afterwards, there was nothing to do but to stare at the red globe again, as the congregation offered thanks to God. In that red globe the oil of Jewish history burned, steadily, devotedly. Or was it blood? Blood of the ghettos of Eastern Europe. My brother Wilfred said a world flickered in that globe: the red wounds of Abel, the ginger hair on the back of the hands of Esau, the crimson-threaded coat of Joseph, the scarlet strings of David's harp, the blood-stained sword of Judas Maccabeus – David,

Samson, Solomon, Job, Karl Marx, Sigmund Freud, my brother said lived in that globe. Gosh.

The service seemed interminable, the swaying men, the blue and white *tallisim* around their shoulders, the little black *yamakels*, the musty-smelling prayer books, the wailing cry of the Rev. Aaronowich, the fusty smell of sabbaths centuries old. Thousands of years of faith leaned with the men as they leaned – these exiled Jews whose roots were in the dangerous ghetto and in dismayed beauty. Their naked faces showed history plainly, it mixed in their faces like ancient paint to make a curious synthesis of over-refinement and paradoxical coarseness. One received a hint, even as they prayed, a hint of that unbearable core of sensual suffering. As they murmured their long incantations, I saw in their large dark eyes that infinite, that mute animal sadness, as in the liquid eyes of fugitives everywhere. I was eleven years old then: I could not have named all of this but I knew it . . . I knew it all.

How different seemed the synagogue when empty. With people in it I felt safe – as if God were far away. I was wrong, of course, but that was how I felt. Once I entered the synagogue on a week-day, when no one was about. It was almost dark inside: the light glimmered through the stained windows, the red globe burnt outside the Ark in which were kept the scrolls of the Torah. The darkness had weight but the weight had stillness. It was so silent that I tiptoed. I was an intruder in the House of God. I was afraid. I wanted to run out, escape. Supposing God rose out from one of the corners, from the stillness, from the silence, from the dark? I thought I heard a motion from the other side of the synagogue. My heart turned over beating fast. Were there not footsteps coming towards me? I held my breath that I might listen better. Surely I could hear someone breathing nearby. He was behind me, I knew it, I was afraid. I ran out from the silence, from the dark, into the glittering sunshine and the loud street, not even daring to glance over my shoulder. I didn't want to see the face of God. It would have been a face of space and silence.

When the service was over, we walked the three of us into the late morning rain of a Saturday in 1934, and sabbath or no sabbath we boarded a tram. We held our pennies tight and tried to

look away when the conductor shouted, 'Any more fares, please.' It was to no purpose: we bought the yellow penny tickets and looked at their numbers. 'I've got a seven on my ticket,' I said. That was lucky. And the tram lurched down St Mary's Street. 'There he is, there he is,' shouted Simon. We poked our heads through the window and the wind and rain blessed our faces. Sure enough there he stood, as usual, opposite the Castle, selling papers.

'Paper Sir? . . . Thank you Sir.'
'Paper Lady? . . . Thank you Lady.'
'Paper Sir? . . . Thank you Sir.'
'Paper Lady? . . . Thank you Lady.'
'Paper Sir? . . . Paper Sir? . . . PAPER SIR? . . . Bastard!'
'Bastard, bastard,' we yelled.

He smiled back at us. 'You little bastards,' he grinned.

In Queen Street, an ex-miner played an accordion, a tombstone in one of his lungs. The music soared plaintively, insistently, across the rainy street: give, give, give, give, give. The traffic lights changed to green – the orange reflection rubbed off the wet surface of the road and a blue-green smudge usurped its blurred place. And the traffic passed on, passed on. The rain, thin and delicate, lost from the damp sky, sullenly fell forever. A car back-fired. Still, as the tram blindly hurled its way towards Newport Road, in the distance like a frail echo, I imagined the accordion music, its sad dark melodies of give and give and give and give.

'Bastard.' I liked that word. I used it on my brother Wilfred. 'You big bastard,' I said affectionately. Astonished, he made me promise not to speak it again. So I looked it up in a dictionary.

We sat down to eat: Leo reading the *News Chronicle*, and Wilfred and my mother chatting. The meal was good. Cold Meat and Pickled Onions and Chips. A meal with shape to it, see. Very tidy mun. 1934. Saturday. Cardiff. Rain. Glory be to God for dappled things.

*　　*　　*

I gave Keith one of my two frogs – the one that was healthy – not

34

the one that wouldn't jump around when you tickled its behind with a twig from a branch of the apple tree. So Keith and I became friends again. I kept my sick frog in an inverted glass jar next to the zinc bath in which swam the sticklebacks I had caught from the stream of Waterloo Gardens. I walked from my house to the wood-shed at the bottom of the garden to give my frog some of my father's cough medicine. I poured out the brown evil-tasting fluid into a saucer and pulled away the glass jar, but the frog didn't move at all: it just went on breathing in out, in out, the poor sick thing. I think it must have been an old frog. The wood-shed became my laboratory where I discovered the cure for cancer, colds, leprosy and Oswald Mosley. And the summer holidays came with a heat wave and the Brighton Trunk mystery and my father muttering, 'Funny, funny, look at my cough medicine! Who's been swigging it?'

'You,' said my mother.

'Not me,' Dad said.

'You take it in your sleep,' mother said.

'It's gone down like billy-o.'

'The weather,' mother said. 'Evaporation.'

'Somebody's been at it,' father insisted.

'That cough medicine, you take so much of it,' my mother warned. 'It'll give you a bad stomach.'

Keith never spoke of his mother now, and we were careful not to walk on the lines on the pavement lest we married coloured ladies when we grew up; we were careful not to pick dandelions lest we wet our beds at night; and at sleep time, after we had delayed quitting the living-room as long as possible, after we had said good night to all present (good night Mother, good night Dada, good night Wilfred, good night Leo, good night walls, good night ceiling, good night fire-grate – up to bed now this minute – go on, up to bed), we returned to the shadows of the red buried heart to dream of centuries we scored for Glamorgan.

And Monday morning came punctually, washing day, the frog still sick in the wood-shed, and our planned trip to Barry Island. Me and Keith to Barry Island. ALONE. Yes, Monday morning came walking into my bedroom banging the heat gong of sun-

shine. How was I to know what would happen before the day ended? Before breakfast, I went out to look at my frog, and there it lay, dying obviously, in its glass jar tomb. Everything had to die, I knew that. I ran into the living-room, wondering.

Wilfred had finished breakfast and sat in the armchair with his feet on the mantelpiece, reading the *News Chronicle*.

'Do you see many dead things?' I asked eventually, after I'd eaten my large breakfast.

'Pardon?'

'I mean at the hospital.'

'I'll get your sandwiches ready,' said mother, 'then you can call for Keith.'

Leo came in. 'Any post, any post?' He propped up the *Daily Worker* against the tea-pot and attacked his fried egg. 'Terrible,' he muttered from time to time. 'Terrible, terrible.'

'What is?' mother asked.

'Terrible, terrible.'

'The fried egg is all right, isn't it?'

'Yes, thank you, Mother. Terrible, terrible,' he muttered.

'Shut up,' said Wilfred. 'I'm trying to read.'

'Terrible,' Leo repeated.

The sun streamed into the room, over the breakfast table, over the half empty milk bottle, over the vase of pink carnations, over Leo's square hand that held his newspaper. Mother entered the room from the kitchen with fresh-cut sandwiches.

'At the hospital, Wilfred, do you see many dead things?'

He looked at me kindly.

'Would you like to be a doctor when you grow up?' he asked.

'I'd rather be an engine-driver.'

'It's very good to be a doctor,' said Wilfred.

'Terrible,' said Leo, not listening.

'Could I be an animal doctor, Wilf?'

'A veterinary surgeon? Well . . . perhaps. We'll see.'

He turned to Leo. 'A man came into Casualty last week complaining he was dead.'

'Go on,' said Leo, looking up from his paper.

'He was convinced he was dead.'

'Who?'

'The patient.'

'What did you give him, a bottle of aspirins?'

'I've got a headache,' said my mother.

'Well, this man, who complained he was dead . . .'

'It's time we had a National Health Service,' Leo said.

'Well, this man at the hospital . . .'

'Flag day's a disgrace,' said Leo.

'Well, the patient . . .'

'Poor man,' said my mother. 'In this hot weather too.'

'What did you do?' asked Leo.

'Dr Meadows asked him if he thought dead men could bleed.'

'I can answer, I can answer,' I interrupted.

'Shut up,' said Leo.

'The patient said that dead men of course don't bleed.'

'So?' asked Leo.

'So Dr Meadows took a pin and grazed his forearm drawing a little blood.'

'Yes,' said mother.

'The man looked down sorrowfully at the little trickle of blood on his forearm, and, after a while, looked up and said, without smiling, that that just goes to show dead men do bleed.'

'Was he dead?' I asked.

'Your sandwiches are ready. Here's the money for the ticket and don't get into trouble,' mother said.

Leo read the paper again and muttered 'Terrible, terrible,' now and then. Just before I left to call for Keith I looked at Leo's paper to see what was so shocking. On the front page there was something about a man named Harry Pollitt being tried for sedition. I did not know what sedition was. But perhaps Leo's comments were stimulated by the Test Match results. Yet these seemed good to me: Leo wasn't an Australian, though I knew he admired the invincible Don Bradman. I read out the cricket results for myself: England, 627 for 9, declared – Hendren and Leyland both with centuries.

'Wonderful, wonderful,' I muttered to myself. Leo was silly. Off I went, towel and bathing costume under my arm. Sand-

wiches in my satchel, money in my pocket, to call for Keith Thomas. We walked together through the morning, thinking of ice-cream, all the way to Cardiff Central Station. At Barry, we built sand up to our ankles until we had no feet at all. How were we to know what would happen before the day was over? We drank pop, and the gas in our tummies helped us not to sink in the frothing seas. Keith could belch louder than me. We ate tomato sandwiches and the sand was gritty in our teeth. All day it was lovely, eating, playing and quarrelling.

'Your father drinks,' I said.

'So what?' said Keith.

'Your liver goes wrong if you drink.'

'So what?' said Keith.

'My brother Wilfred is going to be a doctor.'

'So what?' said Keith.

'I'm going to be an animal doctor.'

'So what?' said Keith.

'So what what?' I said.

'So what what what?' said Keith.

Near us a couple played a gramophone, and five young men, tanned and proud, were playing with a beachball. They touched their toes, flexed their muscles, jumped high into the air, always conscious of their bodies, and the gramophone record went round and round filling the heat-laden air of Sandy beach, July 1934. Keith and I lay back after our swim on the scorching sands; looked up at an immobile aeroplane in the very blue sky; listened to the tinny voices singing on the battered gramophone: 'Lazy-bones', 'Stormy Weather', 'Wheezy Anna', 'Smoke Gets in Your Eyes', 'Miss Otis Regrets'.

Keith said, 'Simon can spit further than anyone in school.'

It was July 1934 and a heat-wave when the mercury jumped to eighty-three degrees in the shade, when fires started on the English heaths; and in the forest, terrible jaws of flame consumed the turf and the shrieking trees with their jagged yellow fangs. Even as Keith and I sunbathed at Barry Island, all day long elsewhere there was the great crashing of dead branches, and columns of black smoke sat in the windless blue-hot skies. Yes, that July

began with the torture of burnt trees in halcyon English woods; Captain Roehm shot dead in Germany, Dr Dollfuss shot dead in Austria, and a man called Hitler screaming: 'I beat down the revolution before it had time to spring up. I gave the order to burn out the tumours. He who lifts his hand for a blow against the State must know that death is his punishment.' In the Reichstag, they sang the Horst Wessel song with tears staining their eyes. In England, the amazing July of drought. In San Francisco, a general strike that paralysed that city and there were bullets in the streets and men, ordinary men, with curious grey flesh dead in the stricken gutters. The noise fell over the world: 'Stormy Weather', 'Lazybones', 'Miss Otis Regrets', and Mussolini strutting through the Piazza Esedra, Oswald Mosley posing on a lonely platform in London behind an immense red, white and blue Union Jack. 'We the English' – shouted Mosley – 'we the English are being throttled and strangled by the greasy fingers of alien financiers.' And he was talking about Dad and Mam, Wilfred and Leo, me and Uncle Isidore.

The record went round and round. The sea swaggered up the beach, crowned with white, erasing footprints, storming sandcastles. A woman with big breasts shouted for her niece to come out of the sea. She wore a yellow floral cotton dress that was dark brown under her armpits. Above her frock, the skin over her chest was brick red and peeling from the sun. Her knickers (pale green) went down to her knees.

'Her knickers are showing,' Keith said.

'She's got big breasts,' I whispered.

'Like big lemons,' volunteered Keith.

'Like big oranges,' I said.

'Like big electric bulbs,' Keith said.

We laughed at that. The absurd image of her breasts suddenly illuminated after some switch had been secretly turned on tickled us into an uncontrollable giggling.

'Like big grapefruit,' I said.

'Like big balloons,' Keith said.

'Stick a pin in,' I said.

Again we were moved to an almost hysteria. We were having a

wonderful time. Far away in Birmingham, even as we split our seismic sides, Mr Neville Chamberlain cleared his throat and barked at the annual open-air demonstration: 'Did anybody want to change the Constitution, to supersede the Mother of Parliaments, to abolish the House of Lords, to coerce the Monarchy, or to hand over their rights and liberties to dictatorship? That was what would have to be expected if Sir Stafford Cripps and his friends were to replace the present Government.'

The record went round and round.

> 'So she shot her lover down, Madam,
>   Miss Otis regrets she's unable
>   To lunch today.'

The aeroplane tuned the skies, and my frog was dying.

'Like big footballs,' I said.

'Like the world,' said Keith.

And the thought silenced us. Fancy: breasts big as the Earth. The sea crinkled its laced petticoat up the beach and the bathers popped up and down in the tide like yo-yos. But it was on our return journey that it happened.

Sand in our hair, in our mouths, in our navels, sand between our toes, we bundled into the train, into a carriage that was empty but for a man who sat in the corner behind a newspaper. Fresh, glittering still on our young retinas, were the muscular men playing beachball, the motherly woman with green knickers, the striped deckchairs, the dazzle on the sea. I took off one of my daps and poured sand out of it. The man in the corner wore shorts and Keith whispered me something about his legs, but what he said is our secret, and no one else shall ever, ever know. The train pulled out of the station, hissing and puffing in the hot weather. The fields and telegraph poles flew backward, rum tumpty tum. The man in the corner put down his newspaper and looked out of the window. We gazed at the photographs in the carriage, of other seaside places.

'I like Barry best,' said Keith.

'I like Ogmore best,' I said.

'I like Porthcawl best,' said Keith.

'I like Cold Knap best,' I said.

'I like Laverknock best,' said Keith.

'I like Penarth best,' I said.

'I like Southerndown best,' Keith said.

'I like Barry best,' I said.

'*I* like Barry best,' Keith said.

'Fight you for it,' I said.

But we didn't. Keith put his head out of the window and I said, 'Dogs do that,' so he pulled his head back in again.

Rum tumpty tum went the train. Smoke from the engine sat down on the green grass like a grey ghost.

'I'm going to eat a big dinner when I get back,' I said.

'I'm going to eat dinner and breakfast,' said Keith.

'I'm going to eat dinner, breakfast and lunch,' I said.

'I'm going to . . .'

Then the man in the corner wearing short trousers unaccountably screamed. I looked round startled. The man's face and body began to twitch. I stared, horrified. Rum tumpty tum went the train. The man's face went plum colour, and his body gave terrible jerky movements. It was very silent in the carriage but for the rum tumpty tum. The train was travelling so fast we couldn't jump out. We held each other's hand. The man's lids were wide open but I could only see the whites of his eyes. I began to shake uncontrollably. Rum tumpty tum, rum tumpty tum. A slow little worm of blood oozed out from the corner of the man's mouth. Then we entered a tunnel and somebody began to scream and scream in the dark. RUM TUMPTY TUM TUM. RUM TUMPTY TUM TUM.

'Keith!' I shouted, 'Keith!'

But it was Keith who was screaming. We came out from the tunnel. Keith's face was very near mine. Large, as I'd never seen it before, and he screamed and screamed.

'It's all right, Keith, it's all right.'

The man seemed to have fallen asleep. The newspaper had fallen to the floor but the man's shorts were wet. A trickle of water ran down his leg. Rum tumpty tum. The telegraph poles whizzed past and Keith was quiet now but for an occasional sob.

Perhaps the man had picked dandelions or something, but I knew he had the Devil in him or the Evil Eye, though Wilfred said there were no such things.

'We're nearly home, Keith,' I said.

Transfixed with fear, together, hands on each other's shoulders, we stared at the sleeping man.

When he opened his eyes, the man looked at us puzzled, vaguely, fugitively. He took a dirty white handkerchief from his pocket and wiped the blood from his chin and then stared at his handkerchief. Rum tumpty tum. Streamers of grey smoke passed the window. He picked up his paper and began reading as if nothing had happened. Our journey seemed to go on forever. Just before we arrived at Cardiff Keith began to cry. It's not that Keith is a crybaby but his mother is dead. The man gazed at Keith helplessly. He fumbled in his pocket and brought out his handkerchief. Houses were outside now, not fields. He was about to offer the handkerchief to my friend but seeing the bloodstains on it he hurriedly stuffed it back into his pocket. As we descended from the train he said 'I'm sorry' to Keith and walked off as fast as he could. There were so many people on the station and the engine was belching out mountains of smoke.

'A grown-up man wetting his trousers,' I said. Keith didn't answer.

'Perhaps we should have pulled the communication cord,' I said.

'We didn't have five pounds,' Keith whispered. Then Keith ran off.

It was the end of a long summer's day. 'He spoilt it, the man spoilt it,' I said to myself. Young people passed by, happy and talkative, with tennis racquets over their shoulders. You could see the sunset reflected on the window-panes, an orange coloured glitter. My hands still smelt of the salty sea.

It was the end of a long summer's day. 'He spoilt it, the man spoilt it,' I said to myself. In the distance, I could see Philip Morris painting. The skies reflected the orange coloured glitter on the window-panes. Beyond Mr Morris, a small boy, hand in

hand with an even smaller girl, came round the corner pushing a pram. If it was Dirty-face, where was his fierce dog? I hesitated, and I heard voices floating down from the front room of a house near by.

A woman seemed to be very angry: 'Shut up! Shut up! You think the world revolves about you. You think we all have to be on our toes because you're Jimmy Ford.'

'Aw, come on, love.'

'Don't you "come on" me.'

'You've no reason to be jealous.'

'My God, you're so full of yourself.'

This was interesting. Just listening was interesting but I could see now it was Dirty-face who pushed the pram. He walked slowly because of his little sister. I stood there not knowing whether to go forward or to retreat.

Inside the room the quarrelling voices became shrill. They were shouting all right. I didn't like it much when my father and mother shouted at each other. But this was different. This was really interesting. Alas, I had my own problems. Especially one. And he was coming closer.

For some reason Dirty-face had stopped. He seemed to be adjusting his sister's dress. Suddenly I heard the front door slam and a young woman, evidently angry, came down the steps. Hurriedly I bent down to tie up the laces of my daps, then I heard a telephone bell ring inside the house and a man's tired voice speaking.

'Yes, she's just gone out . . . No, no, Mary . . . She'll be back soon . . . I'd rather you didn't call me here again . . . No, please . . . Don't you understand, I . . .'

Even I understood that whoever had called Mr Ford had put down the receiver. Mr Ford used to come round our house sometimes to play chess with Leo. So I could imagine him now, a tall, stooping young man, vacantly puzzled, holding the black telephone that purred away without understanding.

Dirty-face had begun to move on. I walked towards Mr Morris quickly, for I knew that by talking to an adult I was safe from the belligerent Dirty-face.

'What are you painting, Mr Morris?'

He looked down at me kindly.

'Hello, kid,' he said. 'How's Wilfred?'

'He's all right.'

'Been to Roath Park lake?' said Mr Morris, nodding at the towel under my arm.

'No,' I said, 'Barry Island.'

'The light's nearly gone,' said Mr Morris, mixing his paints. 'Wouldn't be surprised if we had thunder later tonight.'

'I wish I could paint,' I said.

The sky had already begun to darken like a bruise and some people had just switched on the electric lights in their houses. Dirty-face was quite near now and I could see his sister had jam all around her mouth. If I had been in his position I would have put her in the pram, then one could have walked more quickly.

'Do you know my friend Keith?' I asked Mr Morris, keeping my eyes on Dirty-face.

'No.'

'He's my friend.'

'Is that so?' and he went on painting.

Dirty-face gave me a look and spat. He passed by, hand in hand with his baby sister. From inside the pram, a sad-eyed, brown-eyed, mongrel dog peered out. I would have made the dog walk, I thought.

'His mother's dead,' I said.

'Whom?'

'Keith's mother.'

Mr Morris didn't seem to hear me, intent as he was on his painting.

'Do you like frogs?' I asked.

Dirty-face was well past now. It was safe. From afar, I could hear the clanking noise of trains. I remembered the blood-stained handkerchief of the man who sat in the corner of the carriage.

'What's the matter, kid?' inquired Mr Morris.

'My frog is sick,' I said.

'The light is really bad,' said Mr Morris.

Dirty-face was up the other end of the street. He turned round occasionally, shaking his fist at me, and spitting.

'Sorry about your frog,' Mr Morris said.

'Well, so long, Mr Morris,' I said.

'Give my regards to Wilfred,' he said.

When I returned home Mama asked, 'Did you have a nice day?' 'Yes,' I replied. 'My, you're brown,' she said. I didn't speak much through supper. Mama said that I had returned home just in time because there was sure to be a thunderstorm and that would be a good thing for the farmers, for too much sun could be a bad thing – take Mrs Cohen who had sunstroke – and she was worried about Wilfred studying too hard and never managing to get into the sunshine so that he looked white as a ghost, poor boy, and he was never strong even as a baby, and everybody thought he would die except one clever woman doctor who prognosticated he had chicken-pox, not small-pox, and it was bad enough with Leo talking so much about politics, and it was a disgrace that he stood on a soap-box in Llandaff Fields for the family had always been Liberals, and Jews should always be Liberals, for as grand-father, *olavosholam*, used to say, all extremes were bad, and a curse on Hitler and Oswald Mosley, and that I should wash my hair and get all the sand out of it.

'You're not listening,' she said.

'I am,' I said.

After supper, I went out to look at my frog in the wood-shed at the bottom of the garden. The sun descended broken, dressed in cracked rose-coloured mirrors. Everything was hot and still, breathless, limp, caught in a sticky net. And there was no wind in the deathly apple tree. The scent from the honeysuckle was over-bearingly delinquent. I turned up the glass jar and, as I knew it would be, the frog was dead. Keith's mother is dead, I thought, and they buried her.

'It's going to thunder, come in, son,' Mam called. I dug up some earth though it was difficult for the soil was dry. The cater-pillars had made holes in the nasturtium leaves. In the earth, I scooped out a dark hole for my frog, my frog which was ugly to touch, slimy, dead, and guilty. The apple tree under which I made

a grave for the frog remained heavy, motionless, unreal. Whole hundredweights of clouds had piled up in the distant skies. The garden was electric, opulent but doomed, in the swooning air.

'Come in, son, it's going to thunder,' my mother called.

The grave had been dug. I poured earth over it, without ceremony. Near the wood-shed the spotted foxgloves seemed as if made of wax. Blooms of purple, rose purple, maroon, thick cream, pure white, apricot and surprised yellow, gasped in the deoxygenated atmosphere and a blackbird flew out from the apple tree making a great noise – flew out of the solid apple tree like a heavy black missile from a catapult. I had touched the frog corpse and I felt soiled.

'Come in, son, come in I say.'

And I went in and I lay down on the sofa thinking of my frog and of the man who wet his trousers in the train and wondered if there was any relationship between the two. The radio crackled like burning sticks and mother knocked it off because she was afraid that if thunder came the valves would be ruined. Perhaps in the earth, near the roots of the apple tree, the dead frog's belly would swell. Get bigger and bigger, bigger and bigger, rum tumpty tum, rum tumpty tum, bigger and bigger, bigger and . . .

'What's the matter, son?' my mother inquired.

'Nothing.'

'Don't you feel well, dear?'

'I'm all right.'

'Tummy-ache?'

'I'm all right.'

'You probably swallowed too much sea water. Sea water and ice-cream.'

'I feel all right.'

'Maybe sunstroke. You should wear a hat.'

'I don't like hats.'

'Mrs Cohen had sunstroke. I met her at the butcher's and – '

'Mam, do you always bury dead things?'

'Why?' she asked.

'Oh, I just wondered.'

'What a funny boy you are, you don't want to think about dead things.'

'Why not? Keith's mother is dead, isn't she? Keith thinks about her.'

'Perhaps you ought to go to bed and lie down.'

'Grandpa is dead, isn't he? You think about grandpa, don't you? You was there when grandpa was buried.'

'I don't want to hear such talk,' my mother said.

'But you *was* there when grandpa was buried.'

'Go up to bed and I'll bring you up some hot milk. You'll feel better in bed. There, dear – '

'Don't touch me, don't touch me.'

'Why, son, you're ill. I shouldn't have let you go to Barry without your cap. Do you feel dizzy?'

'I don't like dead things.'

'Now take off your coat.'

'Don't touch me.'

'Why not?'

'You'll get a sore on your finger.'

My mother became angry. 'Go to bed, go to bed this minute.'

'Father would understand,' I said. 'You're a woman, you wouldn't understand.'

Mother looked at me puzzled, then remarked gently, 'Go on up to bed now.' I climbed the stairs just as Leo came in. I heard their voices from the landing. My mother seemed quite upset. From my bedroom I looked through the window into the garden. I imagined I could see five young men playing with a beachball, dressed in bathing costumes on the green lawn, whilst the apple tree shed frogs instead of apples. Like big footballs, a voice said. Like the world, another answered. A blue hole in the grey sky looked down over the wood-shed, aghast. Then, downstairs, the wireless was switched on. I could hear the music from far away:

> 'Lazybones, lying in the sun,
>   Waiting for the day's work to be done,
>   Never get your day's work done.'

I heard my mother's voice shouting, 'Switch it off, it's going to thunder.' There was a swish-swash like wet tyres on a wet road. There was the sound of a million silken garments simultaneously being torn to shreds, there was a mutter, a groan, a crack, before the huge earthquake in the skies. I undressed quickly, jumped into bed. Something would happen: I would be punished perhaps ... by God. Thunder. Eels of lightning twisted through the heaving skies, into the bedroom.

Quickly, quickly, I said my prayers. 'The Lord, the Lord is One ... and look after Mama, and Dad and Leo and Wilfred and me. Keith too. Amen.' Again the lightning in the bedroom. The thunder came nearer and nearer. Once I couldn't count two between lightning and thunder. I put my head under the bedclothes.

Later when mother came up to see me she asked, 'Are you asleep, dear?'

'Yes,' I said.

*　　*　　*

Last week-end I had to go to Northern Ireland. I stood on the ship at the dock in Preston, waiting for the tide. Down below me sprawled the dirty brown water, hoofed, jigging and jostling in the wind. Above, as far as the delicate eye could see, the low grey sky. The engine of the boat chugged away and oil oozed out of its side making a rainbow-coloured scum on the swollen surface of the river. Seagulls glided, squealing in the wind. Aft of the ship, a dead fish floated on the waves, poisoned by the warm water from a nearby factory. The seagulls gathered over it inquisitively but wouldn't touch it. Uncle Bertie said, 'I better get back, you must come and stay with us again,' and the ship's funnel blew its sorrowful warning. 'Well, good-bye, Uncle,' I said. Uncle Bertie shook his massive grey head and his grey eyes watered a little. 'You look like Clive,' he said hopelessly. Again the funnel hooted and the seagulls screamed. I watched him walk across the dockside, tall and lonely. He turned round and waved to me and then he was gone.

Clive had been killed in France during the last war, the only son of Uncle Bertie and Aunt Cecile. They wouldn't believe that Clive was dead. They never locked the front door lest he should return one day. Uncle had said, should he return Clive wouldn't want to find the front door barred and locked.

It was good to see Uncle and Aunt after all those years. Uncle still towered in the air, six feet four inches tall in his socks. Aunt was plump, but one could still see that she used to be the rage and beauty of the Swansea valley, and she still indulged in those fatuous remarks that had no point. Remarks like: Marriage is an institution chiefly for men and women . . . so silly really. Uncle, of course, had calmed down: he was no longer the wild young man who had created the legend of two-fisted, crazy, wild Bertie. Yet he spoke as in the old days of people as if they were cars. 'That Miss Merrick,' he would say, 'is a nice job.' No one accused Uncle of having brains, but cars he loved and knew them intimately and cleverly. Once he loved cars, fighting and women – in that order. Now he was only preoccupied with his adoration for cars and his malice against the Germans who had silenced his beloved son. Sometimes when he spoke he planted oaths in his sentences like punctuation marks. Yet he was taken for a gentleman. My Uncle Bertie taken for a gentleman! You should have known him in the old days, back in 1934. . . . The funnel emitted steam, hooted desperately, and the boat slowly slipped away from the quay. Shivering a little, I stood looking over the railings of the deck, at the dead fish, the grey clouds and the seagulls. The boat left a trail of furrows behind it like a plough. Good-bye Preston, good-bye Uncle Bertie, Aunt Cecile. Uncle Bertie, I remember, in the old days . . . back in 1934 . . . in the summer of the Heat-Wave 1934 . . . I remember . . .

It was very hot and they sat under the apple tree playing cards: mother, Aunt Cecile, Leo and Leo's friend Jimmy Ford. Uncle Isidore lay asleep in the deck-chair, dirty and dishevelled as usual, and I rested on the lawn, reading. Mother liked to have Uncle Isidore in the summer garden for all the insects in the vicinity were attracted to him, ignoring the other customers who only smelt of mere soap and pedestrian water. I looked up watching

the excited insects fly about Uncle Isidore who lay back asleep, unperturbed, as he exuded mysterious smells – odours that proliferated exotically in Isidore's ragged clothes, ragged hair, ragtime beard.

The card-players talked about the theatre. Uncle Bertie strode through the drawing-room, into the garden, a huge figure of a man, with strong black hair, blazing grey eyes.

'Actresses,' Aunt Cecile was saying, 'are women who call everybody "darling" to obviate silly errors. Ah look,' she added, seeing Bertie, 'here's Bertie, isn't he splendid?' But Uncle Bertie was angry: he spoke in his special booming voice, 'Nobody, nobody insults our family and gets away with it.'

'What's the matter, what's the matter?' asked Uncle Isidore waking up startled.

'Nobody insults our family and lives,' boomed Uncle B. The card-players played on, ignoring him, knowing that it was best to be silent when Uncle Bertie had one of his moods. Uncle Isidore regretfully walked into the drawing-room. 'That madman,' he said as if to himself, 'he only thinks of cars, cars and fighting.' For a moment Uncle Bertie looked as if he would pick up Isidore by the scruff of the neck. Instead he shouted, 'What did you say, Isidore?' 'I was speaking to myself,' answered Uncle, quickly vanishing into the drawing-room. Uncle B. looked round puzzled. The card-players continued their game as if Bertie wasn't present.

'Nobody insults our family and gets away with it,' repeated Uncle.

Everybody pretended to be deaf. I felt sorry for him.

'It's hot,' said he. 'Hard on the tyres,' he added apologetically, taking off his shoes. He stood there, six-foot-four in his socks.

'Hello, Uncle,' I said.

'You know, lad,' he said to me in a loud voice so that the card-players could hear, 'I can't stand the family being insulted.'

I fell into the trap. 'What happened, Uncle?' I asked. He smiled, the first time he had smiled since he had entered the garden. Then he looked round fugitively. 'Where's your brother Wilfred?' he demanded.

'Out,' I said.

Uncle mopped his brow. 'Your brother Isaac,' he said simply to Cecile.

'Oh no,' said Aunt Cecile, throwing down her cards. 'You didn't hurt him?'

'Hurt him! Me! I, hurt your brother Isaac! Are you mad?'

'What happened?'

'Oh, he tried to hit me. He's a crazy fellah that brother of yours, but, Cecile, I assure you, I just kept him at arm's length until he calmed down. I didn't hurt him at all; but I don't like anybody insulting the family,' Uncle Bertie boomed.

'What did he say?' asked Leo.

'Say? He called me a big empty-headed swindler.'

'But what did he say about the family?' inquired Mr Ford.

'Well,' shouted Uncle, 'I'm a member of the family, aren't I?'

'So is Isaac,' cried Cecile.

'That's not the point,' argued Uncle. 'Anyway, I assure you, on my oath, I didn't hurt him.'

The card-players continued their game on the garden table, and the sun shone down through the apple tree, making a trellis of shadows over the card-players. Blackbirds whistled. Butterflies, boozed and drugged with August, crookedly fluttered through the air.

'Nobody should give birth to tadpoles except a frog,' said Aunt C.

'Ha ha ha, ha ha ha,' roared Bertie, before noticing that no one else was laughing. He tried subtly to change his laugh into a fit of coughing.

Uncle Isidore had found Dad's violin in the drawing-room, and he scraped on it happily. The music, right and wrong notes, swaggered into the garden, over the hollyhocks, over the foxgloves, over the wood-shed. It was pretty, sitting under the apple tree, the sun filtering through the branches on to the dappled card-players. 'Glory be to God for dappled things,' I said to myself.

'How's Leo?' said Uncle Bertie.

'Fine,' said Leo. 'Twist, twist, stick.'

'How's brother Wilfred?' said Uncle.

Nobody answered.

'I said how's Wilfred?' shouted Uncle angrily. 'How's his medical studies?'

'There seem to be more insects flying around now Uncle Isidore has gone inside,' said Leo, giving the air a sweep with his arm.

Uncle Bertie stood there nonplussed, not sure whether to go or to stay.

'It's time we had a doctor in the family,' he muttered.

'He's going to be a psychiatrist,' said mother.

'Twist, stick.'

'People who go to see psychiatrists should have their heads examined,' said Aunt Cecile.

'Twist, bust.'

When Wilfred returned from work, Uncle Bertie edged towards the drawing-room.

'Your Isaac,' said Wilfred excitedly, to Aunt Cecile. 'His jaw's broken in three places. I saw him. He's at the hospital. He said that – '

'I assure you I only kept him at arm's length,' shouted Uncle Bertie from the drawing-room. 'Anyway, he insulted the family.'

To make up to Aunt Cecile, Uncle Bertie decided to employ an artist to paint her portrait – to catch her beauty on a canvas for posterity – or as he put it to young Philip Morris, 'step on the accelerator and give us the works'. Mr Morris came to look Aunt Cecile over. Watching the artist gazing at Aunt Cecile, Uncle saw her again as if for the first time. He placed his rough hand on her fragile shoulder and shouted at Mr Morris, 'she's a beautiful job, my wife, isn't she?' 'She is indeed,' smiled Philip Morris, and Aunt Cecile said, 'go on with you.' 'Now I want this portrait beautiful,' explained Uncle. 'A good painting, I want. Precise, like a photograph, only in colour, do you understand?' Aunt Cecile smiled contentedly. 'Don't forget,' added Uncle. 'Nobody, Mr Morris, nobody insults our family and gets away with it.' Everybody felt sorry for Philip; but when the portrait was finished and Aunt Cecile couldn't recognize herself on the canvas, Uncle was, nevertheless, meek as a lamb.

'You look wonderful,' he said gently.

'I'm surprised you like it,' said Cecile.

'Ah well,' pronounced Uncle, 'I have a feeling for Art.' Everybody was puzzled by Uncle Bertie; he seemed gentle, a changed man since the portrait had been painted. Mild and kind, and kind of silent. Only when Wilfred came home one day and told us about The Challenge did we understand Uncle's meekness. Apparently, what had happened just before Mr Morris completed the portrait was that Uncle Bertie had been playing snooker in Ewen's Bar. 'Pot the blue,' said Mr Ken Williams, who was watching. Uncle Bertie turned round, glared at him, chalked his cue, then proceeded to try and pot the pink ball. He missed. Five minutes later, Mr Williams said, 'Not that ball ... this one.' Uncle Bertie raised himself to his full height and said quietly like a gentleman, 'Mr Williams, sir, you don't mind me telling you to shut your bloody trap, do you?'

The game progressed under the arc lamps on the green table; the white against the red against the white. Spectators gathered round, quietly smoking, or whispering together, and Uncle was losing. Uncle mis-cued and Mr Williams emitted a loud guffaw.

'Per-lease,' said Uncle patiently.

'Pot the black,' said Mr Williams, a minute later. Uncle Bertie put down his cue, walked over to Mr Williams, looked him up and down and said, 'I didn't quite hear what you were saying.'

'I said pot the black.'

'Why, Mr Williams?' asked Uncle softly.

Mr Williams looked round uneasily. One of the spectators dropped his cigarette-end on the floor and stepped on it. Uncle Bertie's opponent leant on the billiard-table.

'I'm just trying to be helpful,' said Mr Williams.

'I don't want you to be helpful, Mr Williams,' said Uncle.

'Well, you're just making silly errors.'

Uncle Bertie didn't seem to hit Mr Williams very hard. He just bunched up his fist, swung his arm and Mr Williams's knees buckled. He fell to the ground at thirty-two feet per second, per second. It took twelve men to throw Uncle out of Ewen's Bar. At least it started with twelve, but ended up with eight. The door

wasn't very wide: Uncle converted it into Horatius' bridge.

But why Uncle had been so subdued of late was because Mr Ken Williams had challenged him to fight Mr Jake Williams at the Club over eight rounds.

'Wants me to fight his big brother, the baby,' said Uncle Bertie.

Uncle naturally accepted; but he was worried for he'd never fought in the ring, had never worn boxing gloves.

'He's making us the laughing stock of the town,' mother said.

'He's mad,' said my father, 'just mad.'

Uncle Bertie found sympathy enough though, from me and cousin Clive. It was the end of our summer holidays; it was our last fling. We used to rise early in the morning, that late August, and pace Uncle on our bicycles. Yes, Uncle was in training.

'I'm not taking any chances,' said Uncle. 'I've never seen Mr Jake Williams.' Uncle worried so. Up St Fagans, down Fairwater, we'd race ahead of him and people stared and scratched their heads. Returned to the garage he'd dance around a sack filled with straw and paper, punching it, hammering it, until his fists ached. Once he slipped and fell into a pool of oil. His face black, he walked into the house and mother said we didn't want any coal today, thank you. After that, he took to skipping as Clive and I twisted the rope round faster and faster, until he was puffed. He sat down on the stone step, gasping as we stared at him philosophically. 'Leave me alone,' he bellowed at us, though we hadn't said anything. 'When you're my age you'll feel as if you needed a new engine too.' Uncle was old, do you see, thirty-eight at least. Sometimes, he'd just forget to train or, alternatively, claim that he was getting stale. Then he'd feed us on ice-cream whilst he talked on and on about Rileys, Rovers, Humbers, Austins, Fiats, Lea Francis's, Bentleys and other cars which he had owned or would own.

When the men at the Club met Mr Jake Williams, Uncle became the favourite. Even Dad put a pound on Uncle.

'Why, he's a midget – practically,' said father. 'I saw him myself, he's no match for our Bertie. I put a quid on him at 3 to 1.'

'You ought to be ashamed,' said mother, 'encouraging this farce.'

'Well, he's my own brother – there's such a thing as loyalty.'

A row began which I couldn't understand, though I knew it was about gambling and money and horses, and Dad kept on repeating, '*Shweig*, not in front of the *kinder*, not in front of the *kinder*.'

When Uncle Bertie saw Jake Williams he gave up training completely. 'Kids,' he said to Clive and me, 'it'll be a massacre.' And it was. Everybody who was anybody crowded into the Club. 'Children not allowed,' said Mr Lewis. 'He's my Dad,' said Clive. 'He's my uncle,' I said. As Mr Lewis thought it over we slipped in. A square had been ringed off in the centre of the hall and two spotlights shone down from the balcony. The whole male side of our family turned up in their best suits, with red carnations in their buttonholes. Bertie had bought them the carnations. Uncle Isidore edged his way in without paying. 'Why did you bring your violin, Isidore?' asked Mr Thomas. 'I'll play in the intervals,' he answered.

Uncle Bertie became annoyed when Cecile wouldn't go. As Aunt explained to mother, 'I'm not going to encourage him.'

'He's mad,' said father, 'mad, mad.'

'You're mad,' mother replied, 'from the same family.'

'What's he want to fight everybody for?' said Dad. 'He's perverted.'

'A pervert is somebody one meets outside the channel of normal intercourse,' Aunt Cecile quickly interceded.

There was a great roar in the Club as the contestants entered the ring. 'Come on, Bertie the Bull,' shouted the man next to us. Clive said, 'Dad isn't a bull.' 'We trained him,' I said proudly. Bertie said to one of his seconds, 'I wanted Cecile to sew a *Magan David* to my shorts, but she said fighting was irreligious.' Uncle, tall and huge in football shorts, jumped up and down in his corner, gave a knees bend and almost fell through the ropes. Half the crowd cheered. When he indulged in some shadow boxing, by accident, he knocked one of his seconds out, and *all* the crowd cheered. Jake Williams was only of average stature, so the odds lengthened to 6–1. There was a hold-up as they revived Uncle B.'s second, and Clive said, 'That's my Dad.' Curly Townsend, the

well-known football referee, introduced them to the audience: 'Ladies and Gentlemen. This contest of eight rounds between Bertie . . .' The rest of his sentence was drowned in the mighty applause, '. . . and Jake Williams, lightweight champion of . . .' There was silence, but for Mr Ken Williams's repugnant laughter. '. . . better known as Killer Williams . . .' Stunned silence. The odds dropped, the odds turned round. Uncle didn't seem to mind, he just danced up and down in his corner. The bell rang and the boxers came out of their corners slowly. As the shouting died, Uncle Isidore could be heard playing 'God Save the King' on his violin. Everybody stood up to attention, including Jake Williams. Just before Isidore finished Uncle Bertie took a swipe at Killer Williams who was standing stiffly with his arms by his sides. Curly Townsend, the referee, fished in his pocket and blew a whistle, beckoning Uncle to his corner, and the crowd roared. 'It's not started yet, Bertie,' said Curly. 'The bell went, didn't it?' remarked Uncle. 'Didn't you hear the National Anthem?' cried Curly. The bell went again, and as the roar subsided Uncle Isidore could be heard playing 'Land of My Fathers'. Again everybody stood at attention and Uncle Bertie took a swipe at Jake Williams, who this time ducked and quickly stood at attention again. When the bell went for the third time Uncle Isidore played 'Trees' so everybody ignored him. Curly Townsend repeatedly blew his whistle but they ignored him too.

It was as Uncle said it would be, a massacre. After all, Killer Williams was a professional. Uncle's right eye closed up and his nose commenced to bleed. By the second round he'd been knocked down four times, and each time he became more angry. 'Take off my gloves,' he cried. 'Take off these bloody things – how can I hit him properly with gloves on?'

'Come on, Dad,' shouted Clive.

The bell rang for the third round but Uncle wouldn't fight on unless they took off his gloves.

'It's silly,' he shouted, tearing off his right glove, 'fighting with these things on. Be reasonable, Mr Williams, be reasonable, Curly, what do we want gloves on for – we're not children.' The crowd roared. Curly Townsend blew his whistle and went over to

Killer Williams shouting, 'Mr Jake Williams is the winner by a technical knock-out.' Uncle stood there disconsolate, one glove on, one glove off, one eye open, one eye closed, and his nose bleeding. The crowd cheered and booed. As Jake Williams stood there with his arm raised, bowing to the spectators, Uncle Bertie dashed over and landed a swift upper-cut with his hammer of a bare fist on his opponent's jaw. Killer Williams sank to the ground, glassy-eyed, and the half of the crowd that was cheering, booed, and those that were booing, cheered. Uproar. Curly kept on blowing his whistle, and Uncle Isidore played 'God Save the King' and everybody stood silently to attention, except Mr Jake Williams who lay horizontal . . .

That was a long time ago . . . back in 1934. But yesterday Uncle Bertie, now older and grey, spoke of this great fight at his home in Preston.

'Do you remember, Uncle Bertie,' I said, 'back in 1934 when you fought Jake Williams?'

'Do I remember, do I remember,' said Uncle. 'I murdered him.'

'Drink your soup up,' said Aunt Cecile.

'He was a dirty fighter that Jake Williams,' said Uncle.

'Clive was alive then,' said Aunt Cecile.

We ate on in silence. All of us, I think, were dreaming of different things.

'His fighting days are over,' said Aunt Cecile.

Outside there was a screech of brakes and a dull crash. Uncle leapt up from the table. 'Damn it!' shouted Uncle. 'If that lorry driver's knocked my new Triumph at all . . .' He walked briskly to the front door.

'You stay where you are,' Aunt Cecile said to me.

Outside, I could hear Uncle and the lorry driver arguing. Aunt smiled, 'If music be the food of love . . . eat on.'

Uncle returned, moody, grumpy. 'He insulted me, Cecile,' he burst out. 'He buckled the bumper of the car. He insulted the family and I wanted to hit him.' Uncle stood up, tall, wilting, shaking with rage. 'I'm over fifty . . . I haven't the strength to hit a man any more. Haven't got the strength.'

'Sit down,' said Aunt Cecile. 'Finish your meal.'

'It's a dreadful thing to be old,' said Uncle, looking out of the window.

That was yesterday. But I remember him as a young man: strong black hair and grey eyes. I stood on the deck of the ship in the Irish Sea, between the grey waters and the grey skies, in the year 1951, feeling the spray moisten my cheeks as I thought of another time, another year: 1934.

*   *   *

Sammy, apparently, was a sort of third cousin, and he came to London from the United States on a travelling scholarship. Everybody said that he must be very, very clever. We decided that we should make a party for him when he came to Cardiff. Wilfred had taught me the words of 'Yankee Doodle Dandy' but Leo said that 'The Red Flag' was good enough for him and would be good enough for Sammy. Wilfred had told me all about America and Leo had too, so I didn't know what to think. It was a wonderful new land of poverty, of skyscrapers without doors, of new culture, vitality and drugs. It was a land which belonged to the Red Indians, but there weren't any Red Indians any more. It was a land with a way of life and gloriously built cemeteries. It was a continent of 'oh yeah' and 'sez you'. It was a state of unemployment, it was a street which was paved with gold. It was a house of graft where democracy thrived. It was gaudy, it was big.

'Are Americans taller than Englishmen?' I asked.

'Columbus was a Jew,' mother asserted.

Father never spoke a word.

'Do you think Sammy would have met Charlie Chaplin?' I asked.

'Naturally,' said mother. 'Do you think that Sammy is a nobody?'

We sat that Saturday tea-time drawing up a list of suitable people to come to the party for Sammy. Mrs Goldblatt was invited because she had a brother in New York. Father didn't like Mrs Goldblatt. 'She's a *yachne*,' he said, 'an awful gossip.'

'So?' said mother, 'what's news but gossip? Is it a crime?' Father said, 'If you invited everybody who had relatives in New York it wouldn't be a party, it would be a fête.' 'You're anti-American,' said mother.

'Can I ask Keith?' I pleaded.

It was then the real argument began. Mother thought of Keith's father, and how lonely he was, and then how she had considered Mrs Thomas a real friend, and it was a shame and a disgrace that Mr Thomas never got a proper chance to meet good people, and if he had decent friends he mightn't drink so much, besides Mr Thomas was an educated man and Sammy would enjoy meeting a man who had read Aristotle and Socrates and Plato.

'What's so wonderful about that?' asked my father. 'I could read Aristotle, Socrates and Plato – does that put money in your pocket?'

'*You* could read Aristotle, Socrates and Plato!' my mother laughed at him.

'So,' said my father, 'couldn't I? All you have to do is to take the books out of the public library. When you've read books too rare for the library, then you can call yourself an educated man. What's this Aristotle? Anybody can read Aristotle.'

'You're reading a thriller by John Kennedy – that's a credit to you, I suppose,' argued mother.

'Why not?' answered father. 'I can count on one hand the people who have heard of Mr John Kennedy – but this Dr Aristotle – everybody has heard of him. Even I've heard of him!'

'Let's ask Mr Thomas,' mother implored. Tears came to her eyes. 'Think of it. A poor widower living in a big house with a boy only as big as our youngest son.'

'He's got a maid there too,' said father. 'She looks after him.'

'He's driven to drink,' continued mother. 'A man without a woman in his life is driven to drink, I tell you. If the Government was run by women there'd be no wars,' added mother irrelevantly.

'He drank before his wife died,' said Dad.

'His wife always was an invalid,' said mother.

59

'Why, not long ago you said his antics killed her.'

'Think of the poor lonely man,' said mother.

'Why not invite Uncle Isidore too?' father remarked sarcastically.

'Why not?' said mother.

'Anyway,' said father, 'we'll have to get more bottles in.'

'I think Mr Thomas is going away next week,' I said.

'Go round and ask Keith if his father's going away next week,' mother commanded.

'He's at the pictures,' I said.

'He'll be back by now,' mother said. 'Go on.'

I walked over to Keith's house, fed up. It was fun making lists of people to come to our house. And I was going to miss the arguments. Still it was a *mitzvah* to ask Mr Thomas. I knocked at Keith's house in Marlborough Road but received no answer, so pulled the string in the letter-box and let myself in. Standing in the hall I noticed once more the peculiar smell of Mr Thomas's house. The stairs in front of me up to the landing, and the living-room straight down the corridor.

I remembered the day I came to tea when Mrs Thomas was alive. 'What's the matter?' Keith's mother had asked, 'is there something burning?' 'I thought we were going to have bananas and cream,' I had said. I remembered the day before the funeral when I came round with my mother to visit Mr Thomas. Outside the *Eldorado* man tinkled his bicycle bell, 'Any ice-cream, any ice-cream?' and inside the shaft of sunlight, the dust descending upon Mr Thomas in his mourning suit, and the piano lid closed. There had been other times, long before, when the lights were lit behind the curtains, and from outside, in the street, you could hear Mrs Thomas's fine delicate voice singing, 'Drink to me only with thine eyes'. Drink to me. I stood in the hall knowledgeable with what alcohol can do to a man. It lifted him up only to make him sink lower. Mr Thomas gentle, drunk. Mr Thomas quarrelling, drunk. Mr Thomas slamming his fist down on the kitchen table shouting, 'A man has to be master in his own home.' Mr Thomas crying, 'she was a pretty, my Blod,' and wobbly and drunk, drunk with feathers in his head, with the noise of alcohol

in his head, and Keith staring at him afraid, unsure, pale as snow.

The stairs in front of me, and the living-room straight down the corridor. A house is alive because voices never leave it: a woman's voice reading the Bible, a gentle whisper in the night; the arguments over money; a boy's simple prayer; light and shade; sudden joy that a man, a woman, a boy can never forget; dark sorrow that marked a man, a woman, a boy, irretrievably, irrevocably. The house knew. Rain on the roof, snow on the roof, sunlight in a cascade about it. Bricks and mortar mixed with voices. And far away, the kitchen clock ticking, ticking. The house knew: Mr Thomas came there, a young man, certain of himself, his future. And the morning the doctor came round, serious-voiced. 'I'll call him Keith,' said Mrs Thomas, 'after my father.' And Mr Thomas coming down the stairs proud as a peacock. And the night Mrs Thomas cried with joy. 'You're safe,' she said to her husband. 'Of course I am, Blod fach, don't you worry – and I'll be back soon forever.' He looked so fine there, did Mr Thomas, in his officer's uniform, and the neighbours came that night and there was singing and a bit of drink.'When the war's over we'll have a boy, you see, Blod.' And she looked up shyly, tenderly at her husband. Bricks and mortar. Voices never leave a house.

I stood in the hall and it was a dark house. 'Anybody in?' I shouted. There was no answer. At least, I thought, Phyllis the maid should have been there. Perhaps I should wait. It was true what mother said: the matinée would be over now and Keith should return any minute. I thought I'd let myself into the living-room and sit there until somebody came, then I heard a creaking noise from the lounge. I walked near the door and listened hard. Who was in the room? Only Phyllis, Mr Thomas and Keith lived in the house now that Mrs Thomas was dead. And as far as I knew no visitors came, except perhaps an occasional friend of the maid's. I stood there not knowing what to do, whether to stay or go – knock on the lounge door or not. Now, clearly, I could hear a panting noise and the sound of a bed creaking again with a curious regularity. The panting noise grew louder, became a weirdly recurring moan. Suddenly, there was an animal cry,

almost of pain and the creaking noise finished. I heard a woman's voice mumbling and then it was quiet.

I walked out of the house and banged on the knocker hard and let myself in again. Nothing happened. Presently Mr Thomas came out from the lounge and looked at me sternly. 'Keith isn't here,' he said. Just then my friend came in. Phyllis walked into the hall, her plump face flushed and her eyes bright, glittering. Keith stared at his father and the maid inquiringly. Then Phyllis ran upstairs, and the three of us, Mr Thomas and we two boys, stood there in the hall, watching her climb up.

'Did you see a good film, Keith?' asked Mr Thomas. The boy didn't answer. From the landing, Phyllis shouted down, 'I'll be back in a minute and make you some tea.' Then she disappeared out of sight. I tried to tell Mr Thomas about Sammy and America and the invitation to our party but he wasn't listening. There was the sound of Phyllis moving about in the bathroom upstairs. Keith's father looked stupid in his green tie, white shirt, and black trousers. He put his hand on Keith's shoulder.

'Are you all right, Keith boy?'

And then he did something he had not done for years: he bent down and kissed his son's cheek. Mr Thomas's chin was prickly and he smelt of stale alcohol and tobacco.

Keith looked at him. His father was smiling.

'Are you all right, son, all right, Keith boy?'

'I want my mother,' the boy said. 'I want my mother.' Mr Thomas's face crumpled, the smile tragically fell from his look, and his mouth moved helplessly, hopelessly. I said, 'Good-bye, Mr Thomas, good-bye, Keith,' and I went for the front door. As I was shutting it, I saw them, father and son, standing there in the hall, and the maid, Phyllis, coming down the stairs.

When I returned home, they weren't arguing or cataloguing any more lists. I didn't know what to say about Mr Thomas. I still wasn't sure whether he was going away next week or not. Mother looked at me and said, 'Poor Mr Thomas will be disappointed.'

'Can't we have a party anyway?' asked Dad.

'Sammy has just wired to say he can't come to Cardiff next week as he's going to Paris,' mother told me.

'That's the sort of thing that happens if you get a travelling scholarship,' explained father.

'I wonder if the boy knows anybody there in Paris,' mother said.

'There's Jews everywhere,' said father.

'It must be awful for Keith,' I said suddenly.

My father and mother looked at each other.

'I mean not to have a mother or brothers.'

My mother walked over towards me, and put her hand on my arm.

'It's a pity for Mr Thomas,' she said.

Father put some more coal on the fire and my brothers came in hungry, whistling, talking, making all the house alive.

'Come on, Mother,' they said, 'let's have some supper.'

'I'm not a machine,' she answered.

'Supper, supper,' they clamoured.

Before bedtime I strolled out into the garden. In the kitchen, as she washed up the dishes, my mother was singing:

> 'Oh Danny boy, the pipes, the pipes are calling
> From glen to glen and down the mountain side.'

The other side of the lane I could see Keith's house, dark against the skyline. Standing there, I visualized Mr Thomas looking out, his white face framed in a black window as he listened to the small sad noises of the neighbourhood – a door bang, wind taking the trees, my mother's throaty voice:

> 'The summer's gone and the last rose is falling,
> 'Tis you, 'tis you must go and I must bide.'

* * *

Near the door at the back of the bare Hall I could see Mr Thomas standing disconsolately, trilby hat in his hand. His parched wrinkled face was tilted towards the naked electric bulb as if he expected some austere angel to descend from the cracked ceiling and embrace him. But then all the audience appeared strangely moved as they intently listened to the chairman who spoke from

the raised platform. You could have heard a pin drop. When somebody coughed it seemed a horrible intrusion, a vulgar familiarity. For my part I felt a righteous pride that, up there on the platform, sat my brother Leo, obviously a person of some importance. Mrs Ford, Jimmy Ford's mother, held her handkerchief tightly in her skeleton hand. There was a murmur of assent when the chairman sat down. He drew his chair nearer to the wooden table and poured out, from the stone jug, a glass of cold water, wiping his perspiring forehead with the back of his hand. But it was not warm in the October Hall. One of the other men, not my brother Leo, rose to speak, fingering his bright red tie.

'We are gathered here,' he said, 'on one platform, myself a communist, Ted Pattison an anarchist, and a socialist' – here he indicated my brother Leo – 'to pay tribute to a valiant comrade, Jimmy Ford, who now lies dead in Spain. Jimmy, as we all knew him, understood well the historic significance of . . .'

On the floor lay a trampled pamphlet – orange, white and black – which showed a good-looking young man in a torn tunic. The face was just familiar to me despite the bandage around his head and his ageless smile. Beneath the indistinct photograph was written simply, *Memorial Meeting for Jimmy Ford*. The speaker told the audience of Jimmy's courage, of Jimmy's sense of realism, his selflessness; but I could only remember Mr Ford's tired mechanical voice, his tall stooping figure, his eyes vacantly puzzled and how, when he came round to play chess with Leo, he had the habit of twisting a lock of sandy hair about his index finger. Or how mother would always make him sardines on toast for which he seemed to have a special addiction . . .

We sat there in the bare October Hall in the days of blackshirts, Potato Jones, Unemployment and Tommy Farr. Mrs Mary Ford walked in, just as the speaker was thumping the table, making the water shake in the glass as he shouted, THERE CAN BE NO VICTORY WITHOUT SACRIFICE, and she joined her mother-in-law quickly. The speaker seeing her, forgot momentarily his rhetoric, hesitated, and his voice seemed spent. All the audience eyed her pinched, translucent face, her frail shoulders

draped in black. Mr Thomas who had come to sit behind me said, 'He was just a kid.' And then, 'It's a hell of a world.'

Because I felt embarrassed I hummed to myself:

> 'Roll along, Cardiff City, roll along,
>   To the top of the League where you belong;
>   With a bit of luck
>   You'll win the F.A. Cup.
>   Roll along, Cardiff City, roll along.'

At Brunete, the International Brigade had marched through the dark; nobody dared speak at all, but the night air hummed with the murmur of marching thousands. Lorries, lights damped out, extinguished, rumbled over the cart-grooved roads. Madrid seemed a long way now: the drinks, the earnest conversations, the ambulance, and the sandbags, and a Spanish poet reciting, 'Singing I defend myself and I defend my people when the barbarians of crime imprint on my people their hooves of powder and desolation.' Now there was darkness and anonymity. Before dawn trickled its grey oil into the Spanish skies the various units had taken up their positions. In the dawn light Jimmy Ford looked at his silhouetted comrades for comfort. The man on his right was from Manchester – that's all he knew about him. Yesterday each had mingled through the lines looking for someone from his home town. And when they found a compatriot from a town away, or a street away, they would talk avidly, their location of birth giving them some kinship. Names of streets, pubs, dance halls were swopped as if they were names of exotic treasures. To be born in Cardiff and to meet a man from Newport was not to be solitary. But now everybody stood unspeakably alone. Waiting there, Jimmy tried to recall home, Cardiff and Mary – and what this war in Spain meant. Nothing would stay in his mind. He fingered the creased and greased peseta notes in his pocket, and there, beyond the tobacco fields, a white roofless farmhouse caught his attention. It was obviously deserted. Singing I defend myself, but nobody sang. He hardly heard the noise, though he saw the yellow and red tongues of flame spitting

from the artillery guns. Soon after, the enemy began a counter-bombardment and he could smell the acrid smoke and odour of cordite. The shells were unaccountably landing on the San Theresa cemetery, this side of the tobacco fields. Tombs, stone angels, memorials, crosses, were hurled into the air. Nobody said anything. It took a long time for the dust to settle. Together they marched forward despite the incessant whining hail of shrapnel that ricocheted off the stony surface of the road. Involuntarily, Jimmy with his free hand pulled out the peseta notes from his pocket. It was the only thing he could give away, but though he spoke no words came and the youth from Manchester marched on oblivious of Jimmy's fate. The Fifteenth Brigade, ragtime idealists, advanced; but Jimmy Ford lay horizontal, akimbo, on the dusty road near the tobacco fields, the vision of a white deserted farmhouse leaking out of his surprised eyes. An hour later the small wind blew some peseta notes across the blind quiet grasses skirting the empty road.

And the meeting fell silent in that dry, cold Hall as Leo concluded his speech; Mary Ford couldn't stop sobbing and her mother-in-law sat bolt upright, staring in front of her, slowly nodding her head back and fore, back and fore, incapable of consoling her son's wife. Uncomfortably the audience sat there, angry and resolved, as Leo sat down. They sat there in straight wooden chairs touched with divine pity, divine anger because of a boy unjustly dead on some road in Spain. Yet, if they had spoken, they would have used worn-out phrases, words that were but currency of second-hand emotion.

The chairman sipped some water from his glass. 'Perhaps Mrs Ford would like to say a few words,' he said. Slowly, painfully, Jim Ford's mother rose to her feet. There could be no victory without sacrifice, somebody had said. They waited for her to say something, prayed with all their hearts that she should find the right words. She stood there, dumb. And the audience became more angry, more resolved, watching her stand there inarticulate. Mary Ford stopped sobbing, looked up at her mother-in-law's face moulded as hard as stone. Finally Mrs Ford said quietly: 'I brought Jimmy into the world. You have all been most kind.

Thank you.' Then she sat down again and the chairman, clearly moved, recited:

> 'They shall not grow old, as we that are left grow old:
> Age shall not weary them, nor the years condemn.
> At the going down of the sun, and in the morning,
> We shall remember them.'

Suddenly there was a disturbance. Mr Thomas walked out, knocking a chair down. People looked round to see what happened. Mr Thomas walked through the door marked EXIT. The meeting fumbled to a close and a box was passed from hand to hand, into which folk stuffed sixpences, shillings, florins. A washed-out looking woman stood at the end of my row shaking a box half-filled with coins. They didn't expect me to put anything in because I was just a boy. Anyway, I had no silver to give. The chairman was saying: 'Comrades, give generously. Give all you can. Jimmy Ford gave generously. . . . He gave his life.'

Eventually everybody in the Hall stood up to sing *The Internationale*.

> 'Arise ye starvelings from your slumbers,
> Arise ye criminals of want.'

Sadly, the male and female voices resounded in the mean Hall. I noticed Mary Ford was singing too. The portly chairman loudest of all. Now and then you could hear his voice racing a syllable in front of the rest.

> 'Then, Comrades, come rally,
> And the last Fight let us face.
> The Internationale
> Unites the Human Race.'

Afterwards, gradually, they moved towards the door marked EXIT. It seemed all so sad, brave and tired: the voices singing and the door marked Exit, Exit; the woman shaking her box of coins; another lady selling the *Left Review* at the back of the Hall. Leo began talking earnestly to Ted Pattison on the platform,

and nearby, the communist, Alan Fellows, spoke to a group of sympathizers gathered around Mary Ford and her mother-in-law. I sat patiently waiting for Leo. Now everybody had left except those assembled on the platform. Distinctly I heard Jimmy Ford's mother saying, 'It's all very well, Mr Fellows, but you're not dead in Spain.' Mary pulled at her arm but her mother-in-law's voice rasped louder, 'You can say that easily, Mr Fellows, but you're not dead and your mother is not mourning for you.' The portly chairman interceded: 'That's not fair, Mrs Ford. Alan is doing a fine job, he's ...' I couldn't hear the rest of his remarks and old Mrs Ford never replied.

Leo and Ted Pattison didn't seem to hear the argument, they just continued talking avidly. Ted Pattison was nodding his head and waving his arms. At last Leo shook hands with everybody, and stepped off the platform, and together we walked through the door marked Exit.

Outside we strolled under the X-rayed trees of October. Leo didn't speak at all and I almost had to run to keep up with him. All the time I was thinking: Mr Thomas was crying. Mr Thomas was crying but he wasn't drunk. I wondered if Keith had ever seen his Dad weeping. Mr Thomas was crying. Mr Thomas was crying like a baby, but he wasn't drunk. Drunk people often cry. Wilfred said so. But Mr Thomas was as sober as his black suit. Fancy Mr Thomas crying. Leo didn't cry. He looked sad but he didn't cry. Leo made the speech but he didn't cry. Mr Thomas listened to his speech. Mr Thomas cried. I saw it. Tears were streaming down his face and he walked through the door marked Exit. If I was bigger perhaps I could go to Spain. It was worth fighting for. Maybe if I got killed they'd have a memorial meeting for me. It was very sad all these young men dying. One week Leo would show me a short story by Ralph Fox in *Left Review*. The next week there would be his obituary. There'd been an article by Christopher Caudwell, then a week later his obituary also. One week a poem by John Cornford, the next another obituary, and so on and so on. Nobody seemed to care except a few like Leo and some of his friends. Even Keith wasn't angry about it until he read Cornford's *Huesca*. Why didn't the Government do some-

thing? The Germans and Italians murdered them and some old fogey would talk talk talk in Parliament.

Leo and I take a short cut home through Waterloo Gardens. We walk over the gravel pathway, paved with the brown, the rust-gold, the anaemic green of the fallen leaves. They crackle beneath our feet and Leo recites:

> 'A handsome young airman lay dying,
> And as on the aerodrome he lay,
> To the mechanics who round him came sighing
> These last dying words he did say:
> Take the cylinders out of my kidneys,
> The connecting-rod out of my brain,
> Take the camshaft from out of my backbone
> And assemble the engine again.'

'Poor Jimmy Ford,' I said. Leo looked away. 'Non-intervention,' he laughed bitterly, 'non-intervention.' 'Mrs Ford was so upset.' I said. Near the summer-house, yellow chrysanthemums scattered the sentenced air like abbreviations of colour. 'If you feel so strongly about Spain,' I said, 'why don't you go there?' Leo gazed down at me from his twenty-one-year-old eyes, as if he had been struck a blow. Scrawled across the wooden summer-house, in white chalk, was SIDNEY LOVES SHIRLEY. Underneath it in bigger letters someone had written: WHOEVER THINKS THAT IS CUCKOO. 'Why don't you fight for Spain?' I repeated, though I had no wish to ask the question again.

The other side of the summer-house we see Mr Thomas. He sits on a park bench withdrawn into himself. From a little brown bag he pulls out slices of bread which he breaks into crumbs before throwing the food on to the gravel pathway. As we pass him the sparrows, that excitedly scurry about his feet, fly off, whirr into the air timidly. He looks up with disenchanted sadness, raises his proper trilby hat. 'Good evening,' he says. 'Good evening,' Leo replies. We walk on in silence across the autumn park, knowing the sparrows already have returned to peck at the crumbs on the pathway, and that Mr Thomas has somehow come to the point of his destiny, there, where the evening gathers, as

the darkness comes out from the trees, and the waterfall of the nearby brook crashes down into the imperturbable and absurd night.

* * *

In the hall, the stone bust of Clytemnestra stood on its stone 'Greek' pedestal. It had been newly whitewashed and I remembered how, when I was five or so, when visitors were about to leave the house, I pressed her one stony nipple that peeped over a fold of her stone dress. My father was in the middle of a farewell conversation and Dafydd Morgan had a fit of coughing. I turned round, still with my finger pressing the nipple of Clytemnestra, and mother, who was watching me, quickly averted her gaze. I posed in that position for quite a while as Clytemnestra stared down at the floor blankly. The visitors seemed a trifle embarrassed, talking a little too quickly, and Dafydd Morgan's loose cough exploded in the stuffy stiff air of the hall. The moment seemed to last forever – my index finger on the stony nipple, the accelerated conversation – before the door banged and mother ushered me into the living-room gently, without explanation. Though now I was fourteen, I felt a secret compulsion, as I stood there in the afternoon hall, to touch Clytemnestra again. I could hear the voices behind the door of the drawing-room so that now my mother's indignant comments distracted me from my silly intention.

'Mrs Goldblatt was there. A *baitsema*, I tell you. Such a woman! And she was wearing her straight black hair, shoulder-length, with a schoolgirl's fringe. With a schoolgirl's fringe cut across her forehead! And at *her* age! She had on long jade earrings, a shell necklace and a low-cut sweater with a long black taffeta skirt. Imagine! And she smoked through a cigarette-holder as long as a fountain-pen. And fingernails! Long! Plum colour like her thick lipstick. Powder – excuse me, Leo, I'm not exaggerating – an inch thick. Making sheep's eyes at all the young men, and flashing her diamond rings in their faces to dazzle 'em.'

I heard Leo saying, 'She certainly impressed you,' and mother replying, 'Why, I hardly looked at her, I couldn't be bothered.'

Before I went into the room I looked in the mirror with satisfaction. I had gummed down my hair with Wilfred's hair-cream and had a parting worth an advertisement. Not that it was really anything to do with Lydia Pike. After all, how could I be in love with her when we hadn't even exchanged pleasantries; but I thought of her a great deal. 'Hullo, Lydia,' I said to Clytemnestra, touching her cold nipple before I walked into the living-room with a casual indifference. They looked up from their chairs when I came in, then resumed their conversation as if nobody had entered. I leaned against the sideboard, raising my left eyebrow, for I had seen how effective this pose was in the mirror.

'What's the matter, are you ill?' asked Leo.

I gave him a look which I had also practised but it didn't seem to work out, so nonchalantly I hummed:

> 'I'm the man, the very fat man
> that waters the workers' beer.
> What do I care if it makes them ill
> if it makes them terribly queer.
> I've a yacht, a car and an aeroplane
> and I waters the workers' beer.'

'Shut up,' said Leo.

'I'm the man, the very fat man,' I sang.

'What do you want to pour so much of that poison on your hair for?' asked Dad.

'I'm not keen on curly hair,' I explained.

'You'd better give up eating crusts,' Mama said. 'Besides I'm tired of finding the loaves with all their outsides cut off.'

'You'll get bald when you're older,' Wilfred said. 'Leave *my* hair-cream alone.'

'You need a haircut,' Leo said.

'What did I give birth to,' asked Mam, 'a tailor's dummy?'

'It's unnatural to be so clean at fourteen,' remarked Leo.

'Leave me alone.'

'You dirty the pillows with such a greasy head,' scolded Mam.

'Oh stop going on about it.'

'Now don't be impudent,' said Dad.

'Leave off,' I said.

'Don't speak to your father that way,' said Leo.

'It's your father too,' I said.

'Enough,' said Dad, 'or I'll put your head under the tap.'

'Anyway, what are you smothering your head with hair-cream for? *My* hair-cream,' asked Wilfred.

'Yes, why?' asked Leo.

I looked at their inquiring faces: Leo with his dark smouldering brown eyes, Wilfred wiping his spectacles with the end of his tie, Dad with his greying hair, and Mother with her corrugated brow.

'Haven't you a tongue in your head?' demanded father.

I wanted to rise from my chair and break something.

'What have we given birth to, a mute?' mother asked.

I looked down at my feet, hurt.

'Leave the poor boy alone,' said father.

'Go on now, wash your hair,' Leo said.

'Leave him be,' said Mam. 'You're always teasing the boy.'

'Who, me?' asked Leo. 'I like your cheek.'

'Do you realize you're speaking to your mother?' shouted father.

'I realize it,' Leo said.

'You're not too old to prevent me giving you a hiding,' threatened Dad.

'Oh stop arguing with your boys,' said mother.

'They're your boys too,' said father.

Through the November streets we roamed: Bob, Basil, Ken, Alun (who had just moved into the district) and myself, the youngest. We hung round Lydia Pike's house just to receive a glimpse of her. Alun hadn't seen her yet. We waited expectantly.

'She goes to The Parade,' volunteered Bob.

'The Parade's the girls' high school,' I informed Alun.

'I'm not interested in women,' said Alun.

'Nor am I,' said Bob with alacrity.

'Nor am I,' said Basil.

'Nor am I,' said Ken.

They looked at me anxiously.

'Nor am I,' I said.

We stood there at the corner, half-way up Cyncoed Hill, the other side of the disused quarry. The new row of grey shaled houses overlooked the chimney-pots of Cardiff as they slanted down to the Bristol Channel. Soon they would erase the view by building houses on the south side of the street, and so destroy the feeling one had of almost being in the country; for further down the road, to the east, the tarmac came abruptly to an end and a stony skeleton of a path continued onwards through a gate, into a field, following a lovers' walk past a famous spot where a middle-aged woman, a few years before, had been casually murdered.

Lydia Pike's house, with its garage and front lawn, stood unfriendly behind us. And its blind windows gazed out, over the smoky beer-coloured weather of autumn, at the distant sea on which some child artist had drawn with a lead pencil the silhouette of a static cardboard ship.

'Let's go then,' said Alun.

'No point waiting here,' said Basil.

'Absolutely no point,' I said.

'Stupid, isn't it?' said Ken.

'Besides,' said Bob, 'what would we do if she came?'

'Ask her for a date,' said Basil.

'Bet you you wouldn't,' screamed Bob.

'Bet you a shilling,' I said.

'I'm not interested in women,' said Alun.

'If I was interested I'd make a date,' Basil pronounced.

'Bet you wouldn't,' I said.

'Let's go,' said Alun. 'None of us are interested.'

'Where'll we go?' Ken asked.

'Nowhere to go,' Bob said sadly.

'May as well stay here,' I said.

'You're a bunch of ladies' men,' jeered Alun. 'Women,' he added knowingly. 'Women ... *Ach y fu.*'

'Well, where'll we go?' asked Basil.

'Anywhere, but let's go. It's cold standing about,' said Alun.

The noises of the evening gathered together on a web of silence: the sound of a faraway train, a lone dog barking, shouts

of a 'rag and bone' man coming down Cyncoed Hill, a queer chirping cry of some unseen bird. And beneath all these, the whine of silence that oozed from the gouged-out eye of the disused quarry.

Lydia Pike came round the corner on her own. We politely moved out of the way, clearing the pavement. She minced past us in her black sweater, nose tilted in the air, her blown golden hair falling like water over the back of her shoulders. She ran up the steps, gave us a dazzling look, and in a moment she had disappeared inside the house and not one of us had spoken a word.

'Let's go,' said Basil.

'Yes,' said Bob.

'Silly waiting here,' I said.

Suddenly, some anonymous futuristic man, a long way away in the power house, touched some gigantic switch and the lampposts jerked to life; and, though it was not dark, the electricity demarcated the country from the town more absolutely than any fumbling sunshine of a windy summer afternoon . . . We began to walk away silently.

'Where'll we go, Alun?' asked Bob.

'Boy,' said Alun. 'She's certainly got a pair of tits on her!'

We looked at him surprised, aghast, mouths open; then with a certain reverence.

A week later, when I was wearing my new mack, I spoke to her for the first time. Bob Williams and I were walking across the bridge that spanned the stream in the park, when we saw her ahead of us. It was after tea, on Sunday, in the last rays of the lean sun. It had been a beautiful day, sunny, crisp and clear, so that now a linear streak of crimson gashed the western skies which were, for the most part, suffused with canary coloured clouds that tumbled down behind the sharply defined rooftops. Everywhere, people began to feel uneasy, disturbed, restless, for they realized that Monday was almost upon them, with its dull routine work. Week-ends were so short! In the morning, they rose late, read the Sunday newspapers, still wearing their dressing-gowns, smelling the Sunday joint, the cooking odours from the

kitchen, hearing the church bells gulping out their signal to the more faithful who, outside, with their set mask-like faces, hurried to church in their best costumes or suits. Some, more energetic, braved the morning air to clean their shining automobiles before they were recalled into the living-rooms to carve the sizzling joint. Afternoon was upon them so soon, the sun throwing down its ancient text on a yellow faded page, while fathers of families watched the death of leaves and wood, the autumn bonfires, crackling, the blue gauze of smoke near the rear wall of gardens. Serious-looking daughters wrote letters painfully. Mothers washed the dishes under the gleaming taps and, upstairs, a clock was ticking always in an empty room. Tea-time would be over, and the uneasiness, the restlessness begin, for Monday would be swiftly upon them. Sunday evening was the worst: it was ineffably miserable because the clock would turn again and it was turning now. The awful feeling of the end of things and the sensation of returning home to a cold room with an empty fire-grate, the sense of things that had happened before like a premonition of a quiet disaster.

'I hate Sunday evenings,' said one boy to another. A cloud, oddly black in the painted sunset, and the three of them looked up. It was Bob who had asked her to accompany us to the pictures. 'Tomorrow evening . . . with both of you?' she queried, and seeing us awkward there, had laughed at us, had laughed in her throat, and I was so close I could see the film of moisture over her tongue and small white teeth. She seemed so assured and cool. I bet she knew all. I bet she knew things adults whispered about.

'How old are you?'

'Fifteen,' I lied, for I knew that was her age.

'I'm sixteen,' Bob pretended, also adding a year on.

We looked over the bridge at our faces in the stream, at the inverted trees and the drowned, ever-altering skies. Her face seemed like an apparition in the waters.

'Do you know the story of Narcissus?' I said. 'My brother told it me.' I expect she thought me pretty silly: I know Bob did, for afterward she asked me: 'What did you tell that stupid tale

for about that boy getting drowned kissing himself? You wait when I tell the gang.'

It was dark when we had left her. Walking down Cyncoed Hill, the lights of Cardiff below us seemed so sad, like certain sorts of music, do you know? We met the others, under the lamp-post, outside the closed shops.

'Tomorrow evening, me and Bob,' I told them. 'We've to meet her in the foyer of the Queen's Cinema.'

'Not a bad film – *Night Train to Madrid* – I wanted to see it, anyways,' said Bob apologetically.

'Where did you get your new mack? Been a fire?' asked Basil, examining it under the lamplight, pretending he couldn't care less about our date.

'What'll you do, each hold a hand in the dark?' mocked Alun.

'I'm glad I'm not you,' said Ken. 'You'll have to pay for her.'

'One tit each,' shrieked Alun.

There was no moon up and by the Park it was dark and cold. Their malice towards Bob and myself was at first almost imperceptible. Gradually their remarks grew harder as the hours passed by. It was first innocent malice, then maliciousness, then a white hatred that had to be dissipated in some disguised action. Suddenly Bob and I had become outlawed as if we had betrayed them and we disgustingly tried to humour them, absolve ourselves of a sin we had not committed.

'Look out!' said Basil solicitously. 'Careful! Your new coat! Fresh-painted railings.'

Why did they laugh?

Ken put his hand on the railings, before wiping it on my new mack, and I didn't realize properly what he was doing, for it was very dark and we were gathered together in that part of the street which was equidistant from two lamp-posts.

'Don't be crazy,' I shouted. 'It's brand new.'

The others followed his example, joyfully running to the iron railings of the Park, then back to me, wiping their hands on my back. Oh, the swines! I tried to protect myself, but they locked my arms, dragging me to the Park railings, rubbing my mack against the new paint. Bob looked on uneasily neutral. Oh, the

bastard, the disloyal bastard! They were laughing shrilly and Alun was shouting something in Welsh. It was like a war cry. I couldn't see what colours the railings were in the dark. I broke away from them in tears. 'I'll get even with them, each one of them,' I thought. 'Keith will help me.' I ran home. I could hear their laughter down the street and in the dark I cried freely.

I was afraid to go home but I had to. Mother would give me hell: the new mack smeared with God knows what coloured paint. She was always saying I never took sufficient care of my clothes and now the mack – the very first time I had worn it. What could I tell her? Friends, they called themselves! That was the worst: they were supposed to be friends. I entered the house quietly and peeled off my mack in the hall. Mother was always going on about money being short in the house nowadays – things were not what they were – and how glad they were that Wilfred was a doctor, for Dad couldn't afford to support him any longer. Gosh, a mackintosh must cost pounds and pounds! I examined the mack under the light in the hall. Oh, it couldn't be! I looked and I looked. I couldn't believe my eyes. Of course it was very dark outside but ... What miracle had happened? There was no paint there – not a smear. So the railings weren't wet at all! They had fooled me and I had made a hopeless fool of myself. Oh, the rotten swine, oh, the rotten, rotten bastards ...

Bob called for me the next evening to go to the pictures and I thought he looked at me most sheepishly. Well, he was a fool too. I had decided to say, 'About the mack – I knew, you know – all the time – I fooled you all.' But I thought better of it.

'Put your new mack on,' said mother, 'that old one is a disgrace.' And I looked to see if Bob would be smiling, but he seemed preoccupied. He never spoke at all until we were sitting upstairs in the tram. 'Supposing she doesn't turn up,' he said. His forehead had little red marks on it where he had obviously been trying to squeeze a pimple. He looked worried and subdued. 'She will,' I said. 'No damn silly stories about Greek characters now,' said Bob. The tram seemed to thunder down Newport Road awfully quickly. The nearer we got to our destination, the more I began to regret our date, but Bob had begun to whistle unconcernedly.

'Don't think it'll be much of a film,' I said.

'She's a smashing looker,' said Bob.

'Yes,' I said.

It was our first date. It was one thing fooling around in the Park, but going formally to the pictures with Lydia Pike, of all people, well . . .

'Smashing figure,' said Bob, as the tram passed the Cardiff Royal Infirmary where Wilfred, my eldest brother, was doing his first job as a house physician. People in town were milling about in all directions, rushing to catch trams and buses and trains after the day's work.

'Wouldn't care though if she didn't turn up,' I said.

Bob looked at me questioningly.

'Nor would I,' he said.

'You got red marks on your forehead,' I said.

We were both miserable getting off the tram. The pavement was flooded with people outside the Dutch Café. Behind us, the conductor shouted, 'All aboard what's goin' aboard,' and a bell rang, and the yellow tram No. 2A ground its way onwards to Victoria Park.

'I suppose we better go,' I said.

'A date's a date,' answered Bob. 'Anyway . . . the others will ask us.'

'Yes,' I said. 'A date's a date.'

We arrived punctually, right on the hour. We looked around the foyer but Lydia Pike wasn't there. The commissionaire was shouting out the prices of the seats and we looked at each other hopefully.

'Perhaps she won't turn up,' said Bob.

'I refuse to wait for a woman,' I said.

'Let's wait one minute and then go in,' Bob suggested. We counted sixty quickly; we looked at the clock and noted that she was already two minutes late. Every girl that passed by looked a little like Lydia Pike.

'Let's go in,' I insisted. 'Don't want to miss the second feature.'

'Hell, she might see us inside,' Bob pointed out. 'Let's go to another cinema.'

'The Empire,' I said. 'Better programme than here.' We looked round like two foxes.

'Quick,' Bob said, 'let's go before she comes.'

We walked out swiftly into Queen Street, then ran as fast as we could down the road to the Empire. Only after we had bought our tickets and were going into the dark did we feel free and want to chuckle.

When I returned home that night, mother shouted from the kitchen: 'Is that you? I've got your supper ready.' Standing in the hall, in my brand-new, unstained mackintosh, I put my finger again on the nipple of Clytemnestra, the murderess. The stone face seemed to sag a little and assume the features of honey-haired Lydia Pike, and I think I was smiling, with my finger incriminating me, when I heard Leo's voice from the stairs saying, 'What the hell's the matter with you?' He leaned over the banister, looking at me from his dark, smouldering eyes, smilingly startled.

* * *

Lol was three years older than I. Seventeen years from his shadow he stood, tall and well built, with a lolling massive head full of air, instead of brains, and with no neck at all worth talking about. If Modigliani had painted him, he would have just looked about normal. As Keith had said – if Lol was blessed with a neck he would have been a giant almost. Lol's father who'd recently come out of jail had become rich suddenly, so now Lol, dressed in big-shouldered suits and gaudy extravagant ties, lounged round street corners talking to newspaper boys.

I was lying down on the grass near the quarry, chewing a blade of grass when I heard his voice.

'Hello,' he called. Lol sat down beside me, pulled a stem of grass from the earth and started chewing at it like me.

'Whassermarra with your brother Leo?' asked Lol. 'Saw 'im in town with a white thing round his leg.'

'Broke it,' I said. 'Mam's pleased because that's stopped him going to Spain.'

'What's wrong with Spain?' demanded Lol.

'Don't you know, Lol? – there's a war going on.'

He looked at me incredulously. We sat there awhile looking over the rooftops at the distant Bristol Channel shimmering in the sun that shone out of a bald blue sky. Below us the dark primitive quarry with its rusted stone jutting in and out savagely. Stone abandoned, cold, cruel, ancient . . .

'Why ar't you at school?' he asked me finally in his Canton accent.

'Don't feel like it,' I replied.

'Wish I was you,' he said miserably.

'Why?'

'Dunno. Wish I was anybody but me.'

Lol pulled his creased trousers up from his suède shoes, revealing gay yellow socks.

'What do you do all day?' I asked him.

'Goes to the pitchers venyer every afternoon,' he said. 'Likes gangsters best.' He made a fist of his right hand, then slowly extended his index finger like a gun. 'Bang, bang, bang!' he said.

'What else do you do?'

He frowned, trying to think. 'In the mornin', these weathers, I likes goin' for a walk early. Picks mushrooms.'

'On your own, Lol?'

'Oh yes, in the mornin', very early. Sometimes I takes a bus to Rhwbina – I gets up especially early – and I takes a threepenny bus ride. They gives you a blue ticket for threepence. I collects 'em. Tickets. I got lots. And I goes walking in the 'ills. It's dirty, misty I mean, early mornin' and you know, sort of true. Know what I mean? Fresh air, when you breathes. Very good for you, fresh air, Dad says.'

Lol began to breathe violently in and out, in and out, expanding his chest, making a noise like an engine with brakes on, until his face was red.

'Good for you,' he explained. 'Fresh air.'

'You pick mushrooms, Lol?'

'Yes. It's easy. You find 'em, then you pick 'em.'

'And you're on your own?'

'Natcherly. It's nice, mun. Fresh air. Mist. Bloody birds sing-ing.' I laughed and he smiled at me benevolently.

'What you going to do when you grow up?' I asked him.

'I'm 'aving elecuit lessons.'

'What lessons?'

'You knows, for speaking proper,' he said.

'You mean elocution lessons,' I said.

'Yes, 'em,' he nodded vaguely.

'What for?' I asked.

He took a blade of grass out of his mouth once more and looked at me with bright eyes.

'Goin' to be a film star,' he said proudly and he threw back his head, closing his eyes, pointing his finger at me. 'Bang, bang, bang!' he bellowed.

'What do you want to be a film star for?' I asked him.

'Go away,' he said. 'You're 'aving me. Leave me be.'

'No, serious, Lol. Why do you want to be a film star?'

'Garn,' he answered.

'I'm interested. Honest.'

Lol looked at me suspiciously. His brow puckered, and his big head lolled forward on his chest.

'They gets their pitchers in the papers.'

'And . . .?' I asked.

'Shut your gob,' he ordered. 'You're 'aving me.'

'No, I'm not, really, Lol.'

'You knows Lydia Pike,' he shouted. He stood up and looked around at the house across the street. Fiercely, he said, 'If you touches 'er, I'll do you in, proper.' He pointed a finger at me. 'Bang, bang, bang!' he screamed. 'Bang, bang, bang!'

'Don't be silly, Lol. Sit down.'

'Shurrup!' he yelled. 'You're 'aving me.' And he walked away leaving me there, on the sparse grass, near the old disused quarry, under a sun that was too dazzling to look at.

The next evening after tea I walked out of the house, and there he was again, evidently waiting for me. There was a steamroller down the road and you could smell the new tar. Shadows of houses were slung across the street because the sun was low in the sky.

'Steamroller,' said Lol, nodding his head.

'Yes,' I said.

'I been waiting over an hour for you,' he remarked.

'Why?'

He didn't answer and we walked towards the Park. I wondered what was inside the new briefcase he carried.

'What do you want, Lol?' I asked.

He combed his greasy hair and straightened his sky-blue and dandelion-yellow tie.

'I just wants to walk with you.'

In the Park, we watched the tennis-players for a while, and afterwards stared at the waterfall, watching the foam bubble like shaving soap.

'Let's go into the summer-'ouse, bachan.'

'What for?'

'I want to tell you something.'

'Can't you tell me here?'

'Too many people about.'

'They're not listening, Lol.'

'I want to *show* you something.'

'What?'

'Come to the summer-'ouse.'

We passed the magnolia tree. Its wax blossoms had already begun to fall. The shadows stretched themselves across the grass. They were long. Because of Lol I felt uneasy. You couldn't be sure of Lol. Only last year I remembered, the day Dirty-face and his dog suddenly came round the corner, the other side of the street. I was with Lol then. The dog growled, recognizing us. Dirty-face was shouting, 'Come back, boy, come back, boy!' and there was a shriek of brakes before the motor-car gathered speed again to disappear down Albany Road. The dog lay in the gutter and Dirty-face looked down upon it, stupefied. We ran across the road, Lol and I. 'The car didn't stop,' I said. The dog was stretched out in a pool of its own urine and something was funny about its back. Its hairy belly heaved in and out as it breathed. And the brown eyes gazed at Dirty-face sadly, with a sort of 'You are responsible' look. The smell of burning rubber from the auto-

mobile's brakes still hung finely in the air. 'Could you go and get a vet?' Dirty-face asked me, nearly crying. Just then the dog barked. It barked and whined rather as it would in the night when a stranger approached.

'There, boy,' said Dirty-face. 'It's all right, boy.' Dirty-face had bent down to stroke the dog's head. Suddenly, the dog cocked up its ears, listening to something.

'What can it hear?' I asked.

'Go and get the vet!' shouted Dirty-face.

But by then the eyes of the dog stared on brownly at nothing and its belly was still.

'He's dead,' whispered Dirty-face.

'It's not,' said Lol.

'Poor chap,' I said.

'It's not dead,' shouted Lol. 'It's not, it's not.' Dirty-face burst into tears. 'It's not dead,' screamed Lol. All the muscles of his face seemed to tremble at the same time and he brought down his fist again and again on the dog's belly and face.

'Stop it, Lol,' I shouted.

But he still flayed the dog, screaming now something incomprehensible. A man intervened finally and they took Lol to a doctor who gave him an injection.

I had been frightened by Lol then. And, yesterday, when he had stood over me as I lay on the grass near the quarry, he had been odd, strange. You couldn't be sure of Lol.

Wilfred said once that Lol was harmless. Backward, of course, but harmless, and I was not to pull his leg, like the other kids did. I was to be kind to him, Wilf had said. Yet last year as he was striking the corpse of the dog, he was dangerous surely? And yesterday, he had been a bit crazy; the way he shouted about Lydia Pike. Harmless ... hell. What did he want to go to the summer-house for? What did he want to show me?

'Show me here, Lol,' I said.

He gripped my arm tight.

'Come,' he said urgently. 'I gotter speak to you private.'

Near the summer-house I looked back, and the blossom lay under the magnolia tree like bits of useless paper. I was glad that

there were a couple of lovers in the summer-house. The man looked at us meaningfully. 'Get to hell out of here,' his eyes said and the girl looked down at the floor.

'Let's go, Lol,' I said.

'We stays 'ere,' said Lol.

The man coughed, waiting for us to leave. There was a musty, dusty, stuffy odour in the summer-house.

'We stays by 'ere,' repeated Lol loudly.

The seamed walls, lettered with signatures and initials of lovers of past years, looked down upon us askance.

'Let's go and get some sun, Arthur,' said the girl and, though I prayed they would not, the couple walked out. The man turned round before he left, scowling at us.

We were alone. The voices and the sound of the tennis-players seemed far away.

'Whassermarra with you?' said Lol. 'What you shake for?'

'It's cold in here,' I said. 'The sun never gets in.'

'I'm 'ot,' said Lol, and he took his coat off. 'Did you see how that girl's dress was all creased and mauled?' He smiled.

'What do you want to tell me, Lol?' I asked.

Lol blushed.

'I want – '

His sentence was interrupted because the man who had been with the girl reappeared in the doorway. He walked over to the corner of the summer-house, where he had been when we first came in, and picked up a pair of gloves which the girl must have left behind.

'You kids got nothing better to do than sit in a summer-house?' protested the man.

'Shurrup!' said Lol.

The man started towards us, but Lol stood up; so he changed his mind. He said something obscene and Lol pointed his finger at him shouting, 'bang, bang, bang!' The man looked at him amazed and walked out.

'Some people got some cheek,' I said.

'I should 'ave bashed 'im,' said Lol. 'Like in the pitchers.'

84

'Well, Lol?' I asked casually.

Lol pulled out a writing-pad from his dispatch-case. 'I wants . . .' he said. 'Listen,' he went on, 'I want . . . I want you . . . to write a letter for me.'

'Sure, Lol,' I said, relieved. 'Who to?'

'If you 'ave me, I'll get you,' he warned.

'Who to?' I repeated. 'I mean whom to?'

'What?' asked Lol.

'Who to?'

He looked at me, sizing me up.

'To Lydia Pike,' he explained.

I didn't dare laugh, though I did almost in surprise.

'What about?' I asked, and then, 'is that what you wanted to tell me?'

'You knows. About me. About me 'aving talking lessons and my becoming a film star. About me being strong an' being able to bash anybody what asks for it. I'm no good at writing,' he added, 'though my Uncle Fred is a clerk. Your cousin, Clive, told me you're goin' to be a writer and I can't spell proper. That's my trouble – spelling.'

'I haven't got a pen,' I said.

He pulled out a fountain-pen from his inside pocket.

'Begin,' he commanded.

Lol stood over me, forcing me to write.

'*Dear Miss Lydia*,' I wrote, '*Excuse my presumption in writing to you . . .*'

'What's that word?'

'Presumption?'

'What's 'at mean?'

'It means impudence, cheek, boldness.'

'What's cheeky about it? Lots of folk write to folk. Uncle Fred 'ad a letter last week. Leave out the cheek word.'

'*Dear Miss Lydia*,' I began again, '*Excuse me writing to you but I want to tell you about myself and . . .*'

'What do you want to write "excuse me" for?' said Lol. 'I haven't belched or farted.'

'*Dear Miss Lydia, I'm writing to you because I want to tell you*

about myself. I'm taking elocution lessons and I'm going to be a film star . . .'

'With pitchers in the papers.'

'*. . . with my picture in the journals.*'

'Good,' said Lol.

'What else can I write?'

'*You* write it. I'd do it if I 'ad your education – if I could spell proper.'

'Do you want me to say you like her?'

'Don't be soppy,' said Lol. 'Tell 'er I think she's neat.'

'*. . . I should like to make your acquaintance and I think you're most attractive.*'

'That's nice. I like big words. That's what I want. Now say about me being able to bash anybody. Ask 'er if she'd like anybody particular bashed.'

'I think I'd leave that out, at the moment, Lol.'

'Well . . .'

'I'll put your address on it and sign your name.'

'I can sign my own name.'

'Fine, Lol.'

'And what'll you put for a PS?'

'A PS?'

'Natcherly.'

'You don't have to write a PS.'

'Now don't do that to me. Don't 'ave me. Do what's right by me. You wouldn't want to 'ave me bash you.'

'But Lol. You don't have to add a PS, honest.'

Lol looked at me uncertainly, searching my face to see if I was taking him in.

'OK,' he said. And then he signed the letter, folded it up and put it in an envelope which he had extracted from his briefcase.

'You're my pal,' he said tenderly, when I wrote Lydia Pike's name and address on the envelope.

We went out into the sun again. The end of the sun. The magnolia tree in the dusk. Lots of insects about. The tennis-players going home and the sound of the waterfall. Near the shops stood the red pillar-box.

86

'Got some money for a stamp?' I said.

'A stamp? What for?'

'You have to put a stamp on it, Lol, otherwise they have to pay the other end. Pay double.'

'I'm not goin' to post it,' said Lol.

'Not going to?'

'No. I was only jokin'. Christ, catch me writing stuff like this to a girl!'

I looked at him surprised. 'Do what you will, Lol,' I said, and started off home.

'Think I'd write letters to girls,' he called after me. I could hear him laughing. Gosh, to think Lol had kidded *me*! Yet at the corner of the road, I looked back and he was still standing by the pillar-box, with the letter in his hand.

'What you looking at?' shouted Lol. 'Beat it.'

*   *   *

A cold wind blew through the streets of Europe. Wilfred and Leo were discussing the events in Germany. It was November 1938.

In every part of the Reich, synagogues were set on fire or dynamited. Jewish homes were smashed and ransacked. Individual Jews were arrested, hounded or baited by bands of Nazis who toured the streets of Berlin smashing up all Jewish shops. Large crowds joined in the wholesale looting; nor would the police interfere. Fire brigades remained silent except to protect neighbouring Aryan houses from the infection of flames. Youths broke into the remaining synagogues to use them as urinals. This in Berlin, Munich, Vienna, Nuremberg, Stettin, Frankfurt-on-Main.

'It can't happen here,' said Wilfred.

This in Cologne, Lubeck, Leipzig, Breslau, Stuttgart.

'It's unlikely to happen here,' said Leo.

This in Hanover, Hamburg, Constance, Reichenberg.

'Supposing it did?' asked Wilfred.

This in Germany.

'No. It wouldn't happen here,' said Leo.

In Frankfurt and Munich all male Jews arrested between the ages of eighteen and sixty were sent to concentration camps at Oranienburg near Berlin, Dachau near Munich.

'Mosley has no support,' said Wilfred.

'If Grynszpan hadn't gone to the German Embassy it would have taken place anyway,' said Leo.

'Who is Grynszpan?' I asked.

'They killed Grynszpan's parents,' Wilfred continued. 'Wouldn't you have done the same in his place?'

'I don't know,' said Leo.

'Who is Grynszpan?' I repeated.

'Read the paper,' commanded Leo.

I picked up the paper and read: 'Decrees have taken away the last possibility of economic existence from the German Jews . . . They cannot obtain the barest necessities of life . . . Not food, not shelter . . . Few visas can be given to those Jews who are besieging the foreign consulates . . . Flight across the frontiers . . . Refugees turned back by neighbouring countries . . . Work of Jewish relief organizations brought to a complete standstill by the arrest of the responsible officials and thousands already dependent on them left penniless . . . Jews afraid to return home . . . Jews hiding in the woods . . . in the fields . . . Fate of those arrested unknown . . . Infirm Jews and the Jewish aged turned out of the hospitals and old people's homes. . .'

'There's nothing in the paper about Grynszpan,' I said.

My brothers looked at each other.

'Who is Grynszpan?' I asked imploringly.

'Not a person,' said Leo, 'but a condition of history.'

'I'll try and explain to you,' said Wilfred.

'*L'addition*,' called the youth. Outside, November crept like a cold dark implacable tide through the streets of Paris. Though it was but the middle of the afternoon the lights of the restaurant had been switched on – it hung there in a frozen cascade of stiff electricity over the table Grynszpan occupied. '*L'addition, s'il vous plaît*,' repeated Grynszpan.

Georges, the waiter, walked over to the table fascinated, wondering whether, after he had presented the large bill, this customer, whose dress suggested the worst of poverty, would be able to pay. Grynszpan couldn't understand enough French, so, finally, the waiter wrote down the figures on the paper cloth that covered the table. The youth counted out the money, examining each note, assessing its value, and the eyes of Georges and Grynszpan, when this ceremony was over, met momentarily like an accident. There was something in the dark emotionless eyes of this pale youth that erased the habitual smile from the waiter's mouth. He helped the boy into his shabby frayed overcoat. '*Merci*,' said the youth.

The waiter noticed the lifeless cold set lips of the boy and then Grynszpan had gone out into the November street. Georges watched him through the plate-glass window, remembering how this customer had taken such an eternal time to devour his meal. It was as if the youth had tried to taste every crumb of meat, every single molecule of fat, carbohydrate, protein, like a man at the beginning of a long farewell, like a man partaking of food for the last time.

'*Garçon!*' shouted somebody and Georges, shrugging his shoulders, shuffled off to another table.

Eventually a taxi stopped for Grynszpan. '*Au consulat allemand*,' he commanded. The cab-driver looked at him doubtfully, but Grynszpan pulled some money out of his pocket and the driver, suddenly all smiles, gesticulating, talking loudly, beckoned him into the taxi.

It was simple to lie back there on the leather seat watching Paris pass by, pass by. This was how life was for the fortunate, good meals, the best wine, transport by taxi. The cab-driver glanced curiously at the face of the boy through the cracked mirror above the steering-wheel. It was a long mask-like face, drained of blood, a face too old for the voice that had issued out of it, for the head and body to which it was attached. And then a bicycle careered crazily in front of the taxi, and the cab-driver pressed angrily on his horn, which in turn prompted like some involuntary reflex the surrounding traffic to hoot and to toot in

unfailing sympathy. Here was the language of Paris traffic, the dead vocabulary of a city.

Grynszpan's right hand strayed into his overcoat pocket. The object there lay as a threat, cold and reassuring in his hand. He felt no fear now, only hate; no grief – that had gone with his tears – only hate for the murderers of his parents. And yet, now, murder seemed such an easy, such a little thing.

'*Vous êtes allemand?*' asked the driver.

'*Non.*' Grynszpan paused. '*Je suis polonais.*' Then added in a voice hard as a laugh, '*Je suis juif.*'

The taxi-driver said no more. He understood. Later that night he would tell his wife casually that he took a young Jew to the German Embassy. 'Polish, you know.'

Outside the German Embassy, a beggar braced himself, put on his face to meet the face that would alight from this taxi. He moulded his features into a resemblance of abject agony. He tried to make his face look like that of Jesus on the Cross – and then he would stretch out his clawlike hand for the pieces of silver. The beggar watched Grynszpan come out of the taxi with rage. He had been cheated. Yet, seeing the youth pay the cab-driver generously and the driver salute, he felt a certain pride. For here was one dressed like himself, one who evidently had hungered, had known humiliation, had known the body-louse. The shoddy figure of Grynszpan somehow renewed his faith. Today the youth had alighted from a taxi, well tomorrow perhaps, he himself . . . Well, one never knew: the world was a miracle. When Grynszpan emptied his pockets, giving away all his money, the beggar accepted it without a look of gratitude, without even surprise, but took it as if it were his rightful inheritance.

Once the youth had passed through the doors of the German Embassy he stood there shocked by the silent dignity of the place. And the thick, grey-coloured luxurious carpet beneath his feet intimidated him. The carpet more than anything, even more than the knot of officials who inquiringly looked at Grynszpan from the other side of the foyer. The carpet made him conscious of his own appearance, his own inadequacy. He noticed how, when he walked over to the desk, it was as if he walked on cotton wool.

The carpet was so thick that it disturbed his balance organs: he walked over like a drunkard, but with no noise. They stared at him dispassionately. 'State your business,' the taller man said. Grynszpan's left hand lay as dead on the shining desk. Somebody near the stairs had a fit of coughing and the officials looked across annoyed, seeming to suggest that to cough here was a singular discourtesy. The shorter man meantime examined the pale small hand that lay on the blotting-paper, noting like a detective the millimetre of dirt rimmed under each fingernail.

'I want to see the German Ambassador,' Grynszpan said, and he felt the blood flush his face. He cursed himself. There was no need to blush. And his voice had sounded so meek as if he only wanted to see the German Ambassador in order to ask permission to see his bride-to-be. The short official had the habit of frequently half-closing his eyes: the lids would flicker for a moment and the pupils disappear upwards out of sight.

'How old are you?' asked the taller man.

'Seventeen,' he replied.

'What do you want to see him about?'

A door opened somewhere and Grynszpan could hear a typewriter clicking. Then a harsh voice shouting something in German. Feet shuffled and the door closed.

'It's private,' the boy said.

Supposing they wouldn't admit him to the Ambassador. Should he make a dash for it: run up the stairs?

'Go away and write a letter,' said the short official. The lids flickered, the pupils went upwards showing the whites of the eyes and the little twisted blood-vessels.

'It's urgent,' stated Grynszpan, looking steadily at the shorter man's eyes. He heard his own voice coming back queerly. 'It's urgent, it's urgent, it's urgent.' Not like his voice at all. Perhaps it was because his mouth was so dry.

The taller official became afraid – the boy looked so pale – from another world almost: the clothes rotting on him as if they had been buried underground for a long time. Another man, too short for his weight, ambled over to the desk and whispered to the other two. Grynszpan gazed downwards and noticed that one of his

own shoe-laces was undone. How terrible the carpet was. If there was no carpet he could have made a run for the stairs, his voice could have been stronger. There was something about its luxuriousness, its thickness, that he could not understand. He hated it, as much anyway as he could hate a thing.

'What's that?' asked the taller official, startled. Again the third man whispered something: it was obscene the way he leant over to speak into the ear of the official. The whisper grew large, inflated itself, burst on the thick carpet where the two words 'Jew boy' fluttered dying, emotionless. Grynszpan noticed the hairs that sprouted out of the taller official's ear. Now six eyes looked at him, coldly. It was then Herr Ernst von Rath strode from the street, through the glass doors, into the foyer of the Embassy. He had just been accosted by a particularly impertinent beggar. He walked in angrily. Grynszpan realized it was someone important by the way the others looked up. The doorman had clicked his heels.

'Throw the Jew out,' shouted the tall official.

When the youth pulled a gun out of his overcoat pocket, everybody stopped thinking. They all appeared like figures in a photograph, caught in one pose eternally. They waited there listening for something. Von Rath stood precisely still staring at the gun stupidly. The short official's pupils shot under his upper lids as if he didn't want to see anything. And Grynszpan aimed at von Rath's face. As a child, Grynszpan, in street corner fights, had never been able to punch his opponent in the face: he had always directed his blows to the body. Grynszpan absurdly remembered this now as he pointed the revolver at von Rath's mouth that had fallen open in stupid surprise. It was strange; and then the gun went off and Herr von Rath, the Third Secretary of the German Embassy in Paris, sank to the deaf carpet, holding his stomach with both hands. And Grynszpan smiled.

They were all yelling at him now, kicking him and punching him. '*Jude*,' they were shouting. '*Jude, Jude.*' The short official was twisting his wrist trying to break his arm, but the boy hardly felt it. 'Mama, Dada,' he said under his breath, 'Jews of Germany ... I did what I could.'

He heard a crack and he knew they had broken his arm, but there was no pain, only the delight of seeing, near the hunched body of Herr von Rath, a bright spot of blood like ordure staining the light, grey, luxurious carpet of the German Embassy.

*   *   *

By the following spring, Lydia Pike had become my girlfriend. I had given her a packet of liquorice allsorts, played tennis with her – gone to her birthday party and helped to blow out the sixteen candles. We played Postman's Knock, Winking, and Hyde Park Corner – after that – as Keith complained – 'We were as good as married.' Now, in the longer Spring evenings, we'd go out walking together and she'd take my arm as soon as we were in the country where nobody could see us – and I'd talk of Politics, God, Death, Art, in fact all things that began with capital letters. Now and then very daringly we'd speak of Sex.. I couldn't say whether Lydia Pike was clever; but she listened intelligently.

'Don't you think she's a bit dumb?' asked Keith.

'Lydia dumb!' I roared indignantly. 'She's sensitive – she has greater sensibility than any other woman I'm acquainted with.' I looked at Keith quickly in case he asked me to enumerate the very few females I knew – but he looked away preoccupied. One of the things Lydia and I would discuss constantly was Ogmore-by-Sea, for mother had agreed to allow me to go camping there in Hardy's Field when the summer came; and Dad had no objection as long as I matriculated. They assumed that I would go with Keith, but what they didn't know was that Lydia and Nancy Roberts would be our neighbours, for they, too, were camping there in their green tent. It wasn't a question of telling my parents lies; it was merely a matter of omitting one or two important facts. As Keith put it resolutely, 'We pursue the code of British Foreign Policy.'

Not that mother would object essentially; though her attitude to girls was a little odd. Sometimes she'd speak of '*Shikses*' whose only occupation, it would seem, was to make 'sheeps' eyes'

at her three sons. Or: 'the modern girl doesn't wash – they put on the paint and the powder – what they need is Lifebuoy Soap.' My mother was old-fashioned, I suppose – thought girls who weren't chaperoned were potential scarlet women. . . Dad, on the other hand, remained silent about the opposite sex – and about sex in general. If I would have asked him any questions on that subject he would have blushed to his roots.

Leo, though, was, as ever, voluble. He advised me: 'If you take a girl to the flicks see you buy her something to eat before you take her home. Tell me, and I'll supply any extra money.' I never asked him for cash on that score, but I took his advice and Lydia and I would often feed at the chip shop on the way back from the Globe Cinema. Wilfred, too, would have been sympathetic but he'd taken a job at a mental hospital, for he was specializing in psychiatry, and he wasn't living at home any more.

I was thinking thus of my family's attitude towards women as I stood outside Keith's house waiting for him to finish his Sunday evening piano lesson. It was mild weather with an unidentified bird singing. The trees had produced a rash of green boils and a yellow fever of daffodils had fired the green grass near the brook in Waterloo Gardens. Spring-time, spring-time and a ghost moved across the heart with Persephone rising from her chains in the earth, climbing into the clear April air. Standing there listening to Keith playing the scales I saw the sun begin to fall with Pluto's wound in the West.

'Again, Keith,' I heard Miss Cobb say through the muffled window. I wished Keith would hurry up or we'd be late for our appointment with Lydia and Nancy.

Now Keith played the wrong notes of Rachmaninoff. Perhaps they'd turn him into a bloody concert pianist. Already he'd let his hair grow long. . . I imagined Keith finishing some piano concerto at the Empire. There was a silence, a hush, an interval of breathlessness, before the whole audience rose to their feet clapping. 'Bravo, Keith Thomas,' somebody shouted. Keith bowed, smiled. Miss Cobb excitedly whispered, 'He was my pupil once.' Shouldn't care to be a concert pianist myself though. There were so many things to be – another Grynszpan for ex-

ample – firing bullet after bullet into the astounded corpse of Adolf Hitler. Or better still, a cricket hero. Look: Glamorgan are playing Yorkshire. I'm batting with J. C. Clay and we need ten more runs to win. Clay: 9 not out. Abse: 92 not out. I capture the bowling. I look around, note the positions of the vertical men in white, note the large crowd gathered at Cardiff Arms Park, sitting in striped deck-chairs, lying on the scented grass, packing the pavilions. The clock, at the back of the Rugby stand, points to three minutes to seven. The long shadows stretch across the turf. Verity bowls – a beautiful leg glide. Now I'm 96 not out. Six more runs to win. The atmosphere is tense, the audience silent, for there's only one more wicket to fall and this is the last over of the match. Keith in the pavilion dropped a pin and the sound of it distracted me for a moment. I pat down the pitch, I demand the screens to be moved over to the left, because of the dazzling sun. Verity runs up to bowl. One pace, two, three, four, five, six, seven, eight, arm over. I lean down . . . smash through the slips all along the carpet. 'A Hammond shot,' I heard one of the fielders say admiringly. 'Lovely shot, son,' says J. C. Clay. The ball doesn't quite reach the boundary but we run very hard, cross four times – *despite my injured leg*. A century up. Everybody is clapping: the crowd, the Yorkshire players, and J. C. I wave my bat in the air acknowledging them and see the Glamorgan Captain, M. J. Turnbull, smiling in the pavilion. Two runs to win and now the last ball of the match. Verity again runs up to the wicket – in the distance I hear the City Hall clock striking seven – arm over. 'No ball,' shrieks the umpire. It's going to be a six; yes it is: the little leather ball goes sailing right out of Cardiff Arms Park, right over the posh Angel Hotel, drops now out of sight (that'll be in the *Echo* tonight, darro). We've won. Cheers, applause. In the corner of my eye I see in the crowd my whole family cheering. J. C. Clay and I are walking back to the pavilion (myself limping) between a lane of spectators. Glamorgan are now the Champion County. In the pavilion, Turnbull, Smart, Laver, Emrys Davies, Dai Davies, are throwing up their caps. There's Lydia Pike looking at me with shining eyes – who wants to be a concert pianist? Lydia's coming towards me. She squeezes my hand and –

'What's the matter?' asked Keith.

'Who me? Nothing. Why?'

'I thought you were in a trance.'

'Just thinking.'

'What about?'

'Oh, er ... trying to work out whether Ends justified the Means.'

'Yesterday you said Marx was all wrong,' said Keith.

'Where's Miss Cobb?' I asked.

'Talking to my father,' said Keith, combing his long hair.

We walked into the gravel sunlight towards Lydia Pike's house. When we were half-way up the hill, he pulled a packet of cigarettes from his pocket.

'Have a drag,' he said.

'Let's wait,' I said doubtfully.

He looked at me, his eyes blue as a poison bottle.

'Scared?' he asked.

'It'll be dark soon,' I persuaded him.

Keith ignored me and lit up expertly, cupping his hands to keep the match from going out in the light breeze.

'Remember what we were talking about yesterday?' he said, blowing out a cloud of grey-blue smoke.

'What?' I said. 'Dialectical Materialism and the Spanish War?'

'No ... afterwards ... what you were saying about the Oedipus Complex.'

'Yes.'

His cheeks sucked in, pulling at the cigarette, making the fag-end glow brick-red.

'Tell me,' he said. 'Can you still have an Oedipus Complex if you haven't got a mother?'

'Dunno,' I fenced, 'I haven't read all Freud yet ...'

Keith suddenly hid the cigarette behind his back and I looked up the hill to see Mr Blackburn, our English Master, come around the corner from Melrose Avenue.

'Crikey! Old Blacky,' grunted Keith.

96

Mr Blackburn took long steps, using his umbrella like a walking-stick.

'Good evening, boys,' he said, stopping.

'Good evening, sir.'

The smoke came out from behind Keith's back, just faintly.

'You should wear your caps,' complained Mr Blackburn. 'You're not ashamed of your own school, are you?'

'No, sir.'

'Have you done your week-end essays?' he asked.

'Yes, sir,' we said.

'Last week your essays were uncommonly alike,' said Mr Blackburn. 'You were asked to write on "Tea" and you insisted on depicting the horrors of exploitation. Both of you.'

'A coincidence,' said Keith, raising his eyebrows.

'Remarkable,' I stuttered.

'Some paragraphs were *identical*,' said Mr Blackburn.

'Telepathy,' muttered Keith.

'I beg your pardon?'

'How odd,' said Keith.

'Most odd,' agreed Mr Blackburn.

'We think alike, sir,' I volunteered.

Keith was getting worried. If the conversation continued the cigarette would burn his fingers.

'Is there something burning?' asked Old Blacky.

'It's my hair-oil,' mumbled Keith. 'It has an oriental smell'.

'I don't want you to think alike this week,' went on Mr Blackburn, not listening. 'It's English literature I'm interested in – not political diatribes, or anarchist propaganda. Good evening.'

'Good evening, sir.'

Keith carefully transferred his cigarette anteriorly as Mr Blackburn strode down the hill.

'Bloody Tory,' said Keith.

'He reads the *Daily Telegraph*,' I said.

Near the quarry, Lydia Pike was waiting for us, honey-haired, grey misted eyes, what a figure, Lydia Pike (I bet she doesn't wear a brassière). We looked down, the three of us, into the dark hole

of the disused quarry. The grey stone was rusted with mustard colour; at the bottom, rainwater had collected. I imagined a thousand men, stripped to the waist, toiling – striking picks into the stone sides of the quarry to the rhythm of Capitalist whips.

'Nancy can't come out tonight,' said Lydia.

'Oh, what a pity,' Keith said casually in his best accent.

'She's got a headache,' explained Lydia.

'Not bad, I hope,' Keith inquired, pronouncing every syllable carefully.

'No.'

'A pity,' said Keith.

He lit another cigarette. Then said, 'Either of you care to partake of the brown weed?' He spoke with breeding, slowly, changing his voice. 'Either of you . . . care . . . to . . . partake . . . of the brown . . . weed?'

'No, thanks,' said Lydia.

I took a cigarette and blushed when the match went out. It took three matches to light the damned thing. My face bloomed like a geranium.

'I like men to smoke,' said Lydia, 'it's so manly.'

We walked towards the fields; it was dusk now and the skies had changed to translucent green and purple. We strolled through a gate, puffing cigarettes madly, Lydia between us. On an allotment, a man wearing bicycle clips looked up at us amused. Towards Cyncoed you could see the wooded hills. Below us, the lights of the City and the Bristol Channel. The grass lay wet with dew and in the farther field there was a ground mist. Behind us, the allotment man, now chopping wood, disturbed the loneliness of the fields.

'I think I'll turn back here,' said Keith suddenly.

'Why?' asked Lydia. 'It's quite early yet.'

'No, I've to be home early,' Keith said, inspired. 'Dad's got sciatica – and he's not to worry about me . . .'

'Psychosomatic?' I said.

'Yes,' said Keith sadly, 'psychosomatic.'

'What is?' asked Lydia.

'His sciatica,' I explained.

'You know what psychosomatic means, surely?' said Keith.

'Of course she does,' I said.

Lydia smiled . . . I didn't like it that Keith thought Lydia stupid. Keith threw his cigarette-end on the grass and stepped on it professionally.

'Do you have to go, Keith?' I said.

'But definitely.'

'Shall we walk back with you?' asked Lydia.

'Heavens, no!' I protested. 'Keith's not afraid of the dark, are you?'

'No,' said Keith mournfully.

'I'm sorry you have to leave us,' I said.

'We could walk back with him,' suggested Lydia.

'No . . . oh no . . . please . . . please . . . don't spoil . . . your walk . . . because of me . . .'

'Not at all, Keith,' Lydia sympathized.

'Well . . . you'll probably get back quicker if you're on your own,' I said.

'Yes . . . probably.'

'What a shame your father has sciatica,' said Lydia.

'Well, good-bye, Keith,' I said finally.

'Good-bye,' he frowned, shaking hands with Lydia. 'Give my condolences to Nancy.' And then to me, 'If you can't be good, be careful.' . . . I laughed awkwardly. We watched Keith strolling down the path, past the allotment. The man who had been chopping wood came out on to the path, pushing his bicycle, and Keith opened the gate for him.

'Shouldn't we walk him back?' asked Lydia.

'No,' I said, 'he likes walking home alone.'

Keith turned round and waved. Then he shouted, 'Shall I leave some fags with you?'

'Don't bother,' I called back.

He waved again, sadly, and disappeared into the road, leaving Lydia and me high up in a spring-chilled field, close to a moon that hardly shone because it was not yet dark.

We continued through the fairy-tale fields up to our ankles in grey mist and I gave my school scarf to Lydia to keep away the

cold. She looked lovely in my green and gold scarf. I hummed the school song to myself:

> 'Green and Gold, Green and Gold,
> Strong be our hearts and bold.
> To remain unsullied our Great Name
> Adding to Ancient Glory, Modern Fame.
> Green and Gold, Green and . . .'

I nearly stepped on some cow-dung, humming. At the top we gazed down at Cardiff, at the lights dotting the shadows below, window lights, lamp-posts, flashes of electricity from the trams. Away towards the direction of Newport a train rushed through the dark, a chain of lights, like a glimmering thought, across the blank mind of the countryside. Somewhere down there amongst the lights, Mother would be in the kitchen preparing the evening meal. Leo would be in his room writing a speech for some Labour Party meeting, rehearsing it perhaps before the mirror. Dad would be in the armchair under lamplight reading the *South Wales Echo*, the spectacles slipping down his nose, and his mouth silently forming the words as he read.

'I think Keith is very nice,' Lydia said.

'Yes, he's a good chap,' I condescended.

'And attractive too.'

I looked at her – was she joking? 'Do you think so?' I asked doubtfully. I tried to see Keith through the eyes of Lydia. A scruffy, scraggy youth with red-brown hair falling over a high forehead without fuss – the freckled wide flat face, the snub nose, and eyes blue as a poison bottle . . .

'Oh, I don't mean physically,' said Lydia.

'No?'

'But he attracts me mentally.'

'That so?'

I was taken aback. Imagine *anybody* being attracted to Keith *mentally*. Perhaps Lydia was a little backward after all! But Lydia slipped her hand into mine.

'Of course *you* attract me mentally *and* physically,' she reassured me.

'I don't know why,' I said, 'there's nothing to me.' I looked at her beautiful face. 'Nothing at all really.'

'Oh, but there is,' protested Lydia.

'Besides, I'm no good for women,' I pointed out. 'I'm so selfish, so egocentric, inconsiderate. And I'm moody, shockingly moody. I think of suicide quite a lot, you know. I'd be hopeless to live with. Can't do anything in the house. Only concerned about myself. Yes, I'm an evil influence on women.'

'You shouldn't speak of yourself that way,' said Lydia passionately. 'You're a good person.'

'Oh no,' I protested. 'I'm rotten really. I know myself. Rotten through and through.'

The fields traced our signatures in moonlight and shadows. Under the clear stars we looked at each other with wonder, anew.

'You're beautiful in this light,' I said.

Lydia looked down at her feet.

'I'm going to kiss you,' I said.

She feebly tried to stop me. After she said: 'You're not like other boys. You kiss differently. You don't make me feel sick when you kiss me.' I wondered how other boys kissed her and *which* boys.

'How do you mean?' I questioned her.

'You keep your lips closed when you kiss,' she whispered. What did she mean? Of course I kept my lips closed. Was there another way of kissing?

I tried to embrace her again but she pushed me away saying: 'A girl mustn't be cheap with her kisses.'

We turned back down the path and later I stepped on the cow-dung which earlier I had avoided.

After lunch, Whitsun bank holiday, mother astounded me.

'I've asked your girlfriend to tea,' she said smiling, as she arranged the yellow tulips in a vase. Father knocked his pipe against the heel of his shoe and Leo looked up from his newspaper.

'I met her with her mother this morning,' mother explained. 'She seems a nice girl, and she told me she was a good friend of

yours.' Dumbstruck, I gazed at Leo, who pretended to return to his newspaper. Lydia surely wouldn't accept such an invitation: she'd know how much it would embarrass me. Gosh, I hope Lydia didn't say anything about Ogmore.

'What are you encouraging him to go out with girls for?' said father. 'He's got his matriculation in a couple of months. Plenty of time for girls when he goes to University.'

'No need to blush,' said Leo. I could have killed him. Father started to ramble on. He didn't talk often but now it was as if he'd been wound up. 'He should study more. Where did he come in his Easter exams? Seventh. Imagine a son of mine seventh.'

'Seven is lucky,' said mother.

'Seventh,' father said dramatically, pronouncing the word 'seventh' like mother would have said 'Adolf Hitler'. 'Wilfred always came first. Leo always did well in school. It's only since he left that he's become lazy.'

Leo winked at me. Dad had a habit of criticizing his sons in their presence. However, since Wilfred had left home he had become a model of perfection . . . 'Latin,' continued Dad, 'that's what you must study.' Father put his pipe in his mouth, thinking.

'I got 62 out of 100 in Latin,' I protested.

'Sixty-two!' exploded father. 'You think that good enough – even Leo, that dumbkopf, could do better than that. Why, when Leo was at school his Latin master wrote to me personally. Said Leo was in a class of his own.' Dad looked at me with pride. Leo burst out coughing.

'If you don't get your matriculation, I'll break your neck,' said Dad. He was working himself into a temper. 'What are you coughing for?' he shouted at Leo. 'It's no coughing matter . . . I work hard so you may all be educated. Be given the chances I never had. From morning to night so that you may pursue a richer and better life.'

'What are you shouting for?' said mother. 'We're not in the next room.'

'And he tells me he got 62 in Latin. He must get 102, then he can be pleased with himself.'

'All right, all right,' said mother. 'He's a good boy.'

'A good boy.' Dad stood up. 'All he thinks about is football and cricket. Writes poems instead of doing his homework. He'll become like Uncle Isidore!'

'Well, *you* couldn't write poems,' said mother.

'Who wants to?' shouted Dad. 'Does poetry make you any money?'

Leo interrupted him. 'Sixty-two is a very good mark.'

'What did you ask her around here for?' I scolded mother. 'Do you want to deliberately embarrass me?'

'What's the matter, aren't we good enough for her?' Dad brought his fist down on the table. 'Do you think we're Tailors or Shoemakers? What's her father do anyway?'

'He's a civil servant,' said mother. 'Very high up.'

'I thought he was an architect,' I said.

'A civil servant,' sneered father, turning up his palms as if he was weighing the heaviness of the air, 'a *civil* servant.' That was his last word on the subject. He put down his pipe and opened up a packet of *Players*. He never said another word hardly all afternoon and only opened his mouth to cough out cigarette smoke.

'You'll damage your lungs,' warned mother.

Mother brought out the best crockery and prepared a tea fit for a queen. Evidently she had taken to Lydia. Certainly, mother asking a girlfriend of one of her sons to tea was a record. A phenomenal precedent.

When the front door bell rang I fell over a chair in an endeavour to reach the hall first. But it was too late: mother was out of the kitchen in a flash. I stood near the sideboard, my hands sweating. This would be an ordeal: worse than being at the dentist. I heard voices in the hall and mother saying, 'That's Clytemnestra.'

'Do you want to borrow my shaving tackle?' Leo mocked me.

'Shut up!' I hissed.

Nancy Roberts, of all people. There was some mistake. What was she doing here? God, this would give Keith a laugh.

'Come in, my dear,' said mother. 'This is Nancy.'

Of course, of course, Nancy Roberts's father *was* a civil servant. Nancy smiled uncomfortably. Father stood up like a gentle-

man, shook hands with her and gave a grunt. I saw that he was about to offer her a cigarette but midway through the gesture he realized what he was doing. There was an awkward silence until mother said, 'That's a pretty dress.'

'Thank you,' said Nancy.

'Did you make it yourself, dear?'

'No . . . my mother bought it for me. At Howell's.'

'A good shop Howell's,' mother affirmed.

'Very good shop,' said Dad, trying to make conversation.

'Yes, it is a good shop,' agreed Nancy.

We relapsed into silence again, and Leo suggested we should eat. We sat down at the table, mother choosing our chairs for us. There were tomato sandwiches, cucumber sandwiches and chocolate éclairs and, after – bananas and cream. Mother took a fork and started to mash the bananas – before passing them on to me.

'Don't bother,' I said.

'Why,' said mother, 'you like them mashed.'

'Yes,' I protested, 'but I can do them myself.'

'I have practically to feed him,' said mother, and for the fourth time that afternoon I blushed scarlet. 'He's such a baby . . . He's so particular about his food . . . won't eat anything but chips.'

'I believe you know Philip Morris,' Nancy Roberts said.

'Oh yes,' Leo assented.

'He painted a picture of my sister-in-law,' mother said.

'Aunt Cecile,' I explained.

'He's a good artist,' mother said.

'You know him, do you, Nancy?' asked Leo.

'Yes.'

There was yet another silence. Father looked round the table waiting for somebody to speak. And mother poured out tea, an amber stream, into the egg-blue tea-cups.

'He's a good friend of mine,' Leo continued.

'He's a friend of the family,' mother insisted. 'He comes with us to Porthcawl sometimes on Sunday afternoons . . . Don't smoke when you're eating,' mother said suddenly to Dad; then sweetly to Nancy Roberts, 'I bet your father doesn't smoke when he's eating?'

'No,' said Nancy.

Father said, 'I'm not hungry,' but he mumbled it so that you could hardly hear him.

After tea we sat round the fire that father had prepared, for it was a cold day though it was spring. Nancy Roberts picked up a book, *Red Star Over China*, which lay on the arm of the sofa and said to my father, startling him, 'Do you think there'll be a war?'

Father looked round the room for aid and Leo kindly helped him. 'We can only hope not. With Collective Security perhaps, but . . .' He changed his mind.

'I read Beverley Baxter in the *South Wales Echo*,' volunteered Nancy.

'He's always going on about the Red Sea of Bolshevism,' I muttered.

'Politics, politics,' my mother sadly commented, as she cleared the tea-table. The world of happenings crept unobtrusively into the room. The noise outside: the sound of marching feet tramping through Austria, Sudetenland, Czechoslovakia. A man with a lock of hair falling over a fanatical forehead. A man with rather bulbous eyes screaming to a cast of millions and the torches flaring and '*Sieg Heil*', '*Sieg Heil*'. An echo from America, the sound of a dance-tune, 'Jeepers Creepers, where did you get those peepers?' And a sick man with an umbrella stepping down from an aeroplane looking relieved at the magnesium flashes that accompanied the barrage of cameras . . .

Father poked the fire and Mam said that it was cold for this time of the year and they spoke of summer and perpetual holidays. Now the tablecloth had been cleared, mother returned the vase of yellow tulips on to the polished table. The grey light filtered through the window on to the flowers – and those yellow aristocrats fainted in the heat of the fire-warm room. Their green stems long and undulating, topped by yellow petals, stared down at the polished table seeing their own smudged reflections. They were like yellow swans peering down at a surface of shimmering water. Soon perhaps the tulips would dip their heads through the wooden table . . .

The conversation continued, polite and fairly, the hands of the

mantelpiece clock turned round until it was a respectable time for Nancy to go. Eventually she shook hands with everybody and mother commanded me to see her home. Nothing happened that afternoon – a girl came to tea, we had bananas and cream, a yellow petal fell from a yellow tulip – and the noise outside. *Sieg Heil, Sieg Heil,* seemed a long way away, unreal.

In the hall Nancy Roberts asked, 'Who's Clytemnestra?'

'A murderess,' I answered, and then we were through the door into the cold fresh air in the street where nothing ever happened.

'What the hell did you come to tea for?' I asked.

Nancy began to cry and I put my hands in my pockets.

'I'm sorry,' I said. 'I'm glad you came to tea. Honest, Nancy; it was lovely having you. Cross my heart, fall down dead if I tell a lie. Really, Nancy. Honest Injun.'

Nancy looked out from tear-broken eyes vehemently: 'I didn't want to come to tea. My mother forced me to.'

Lydia was already five minutes late. Keith and I loitered round the corner from the hospital wearing our Sunday clothes and swearing the afternoon away. Nancy Roberts had been warded already a week now. Even though my family had decided that I was to be a doctor I'd never been inside a hospital before. I knew what went on there though; often, when the family were engaged arguing I'd slip into the front room and look at the gruesome pictures in Wilfred's text books. Especially on pages 204 and 205. Also, I'd heard stories Wilfred had told Leo of hospital life and medical student training. The Post-Mortem Room for example. The Pathologist, I knew, wore a salmon-coloured apron and salmon-coloured gloves and he stood always poised over a dead body, with a little silver scalpel in his hand. The Pathologist had unpleasant pouncing eyes like a dentist. And the smell in the white-tiled room made me feel sick even to think of it. I tried to imagine the scene as Wilfred had related it: the students all standing round the body laid out on the porcelain table, and all the time they (the students) just smoked their pipes, talking casually about John Barrymore and Norma Shearer. How could they, with the poor man lying there naked, a glassy wax corpse?

'She's ten minutes late,' complained Keith. 'Women are the limit. I wish we'd seen Nancy and were coming back now.' But I hardly heard him for I stood there in the Sunday dry sunlight looking at a vision in the street: the Pathologist bringing down the sharp silver scalpel into the dazzled white flesh of the dead man. Why didn't the corpse cry out in pain? If only the students stopped talking and listened – if there was silence, full, complete, then perhaps we might hear the very tiny cry of the dead man which would undoubtedly transform us all forever.

'You're not very talkative,' said Keith.

'Don't feel like talking,' I answered, staring at a pool of sunlight in which a dead man lay back with a plum-skin face and a white body. He was so still, so silent. Wilfred had told Leo how the porcelain slab had grooves in it to drain the surplus blood away; the grooves now made a herringbone pattern of red, and when they opened up the corpse, his belly was full, containing a factory of colours. Philip Morris would have liked to paint that. Perhaps when the Pathologist sliced the brain in search of a haemorrhage or a tumour, one would hear snatches of conversations from the past, old nostalgic songs falling away from the little knife. Imagine in the silence of a Post-Mortem Room hearing very faintly, falling from the scalpel as it cut through the brain, a conversation from 1901 . . .

The sun went behind a cloud and the shadows scurried across the waiting street.

'Jiawch, Nancy's a lucky dab having her appendix out,' Keith said.

'Why?' I asked.

'Well, she won't have to take the exam – but she'll be healthy enough when the time comes to camp in Ogmore.'

'Dad'll murder me if I don't pass,' I pronounced.

'Wish my appendix would burst,' said Keith.

'Here's Lydia.' I looked down the street and saw honey-haired Lydia walking through my vision of death – through the old porcelain slab, through the crowds of students, to come close as a hand. Pretty and fresh, all grey eyes smiling with light, so that

the Pathologist disappeared in smoke and the dead man turned to dust, climbing up a sunbeam.

'Do you like my hat?' Lydia asked.

'No,' replied Keith curtly.

She had lipstick on too – and a new cotton dress, so that you could see her breasts blind and breathing beneath the green cloth – not to mention silk stockings *and* high heels.

'Crikey!' Keith exclaimed. 'Don't you look . . . old.'

'Sophisticated,' corrected Lydia, pulling a mirror from her bag.

'Gee,' taunted Keith, 'I don't go out with women, I don't smoke, I don't drink, I don't swear – but damn me if I didn't leave my bloody cigar-case with that old whore in the bleeding pub!'

'Don't be so crude,' scolded Lydia and I tried to change the subject.

'What's new?' I said.

'Llewellyn Rees is going to visit Nancy this afternoon,' said Lydia.

'You're late – quarter of an hour.' Keith was annoyed.

'Always the gentleman,' snapped back Lydia.

Llewellyn Rees was captain of the school cricket eleven. It was his last term at school – lots of chaps bought him ice-cream, or gave him sweets trying to suck up to him, hoping that they might be chosen for the cricket team. Rees was nearly eighteen at least.

'What's Rees visiting for?' I asked.

'He's a friend of Nancy.'

'Since when?' asked Keith.

'He took her dancing,' explained Lydia earnestly.

We were dumbfounded. Keith could only say, 'I didn't know Nancy danced.' We crossed the road, dodging the traffic, out of the sunlight, and walked over the square shadows of the dark shops towards the hospital.

'I don't like him though he's quite handsome,' said Lydia.

'He's pimply,' said Keith.

'Oh no,' objected Lydia. 'I think his skin is tender – and he gets a rash from shaving.'

We were defeated until Keith remarked, 'Looks are not everything.'

''Course not,' said Lydia.

'There's a soul,' I pondered mournfully.

Outside the hospital a woman sold flowers; the doors revolved exits and entrances. A man limped slowly into Casualty and the hospital machine began to move laboriously, but with a curious precision.

'We should buy Nancy flowers,' suggested Lydia.

'She wouldn't want flowers,' Keith protested.

'I've brought her some PK chewing-gum,' I said.

'The tulips would be nice,' said Lydia. 'I would have liked the tulips.'

'Gold-digger,' whispered Keith, but Lydia didn't hear him. Keith didn't seem to get on well with Lydia nowadays. And she was different when he was around. When it was just Lydia and me – it was different, she was sweeter, she was *smashing*.

'I'll pay half of it – if you both contribute,' said Lydia.

'You'll have to carry the tulips then,' I said.

'I wouldn't be seen dead carrying flowers,' Keith said.

We walked into the ground floor of the hospital, Lydia holding a bunch of mauve tulips which didn't smell even. It was a damn nuisance having to visit Nancy Roberts. It was Lydia who suggested it. 'Nancy would like to see Keith,' she had said. And Keith said awkwardly: ''Course she wouldn't. I'll write if you like.' That was two days ago. We waited for the lift. Somewhere, in this building maybe, a post-mortem was going on. Somewhere upstairs a world of nurses, in antiseptic blue and white, moved carefully from bed to bed. Perhaps a child was being born or maybe, right now, an intense drama was being enacted in the quiet operating theatre under cold, glinting, implacable lights.

Nancy Roberts smiled from ear to ear when she saw us and we sat round her bed awkwardly whilst she admired the tulips.

'You shouldn't have,' she said.

'Where's Llewellyn Rees?' asked Keith.

'Oh, I don't know. Why should I?' queried Nancy.

'But you said – ' Lydia stopped herself.

'I'm glad he didn't come,' said Nancy.

'Oh . . .' said Lydia.

'His eyebrows are awfully bushy,' said Nancy.

Keith and I grinned.

'He's a member of the WHA,' said Nancy.

'What *is* the WHA?' I asked.

'You tell him,' said Nancy.

'No, you,' echoed Lydia.

A nurse came by, smiled at us and began putting green screens around the patient next to Nancy. A number of visitors had seated themselves around different beds. The ward had become transformed. The world had come in with presents, flowers, voices. Sunday afternoon. The secret pain lay there, disused for an hour.

'The Wandering Hands Association,' whispered Nancy.

In this ward I couldn't smell the antiseptic anaesthetic odour which permeated the Casualty Department that I had noted like a memory when we had entered the hospital. I recognized Mrs Shapiro a few beds away. A nurse said to her, 'Are you comfortable?' 'Thank you, my husband's got five shops,' she replied.

'I like your hat,' said Nancy.

'What was it like?' said Keith suddenly. 'The operation . . .?' Nancy smiled. She had been waiting for the question. And she answered with a prepared speech long as a story.

We left the ward solemnly; glad to leave its formality, glad to quit the mansions of the sick and old. Down the whirring lift through the faint ether-odour of the Casualty Department into the street of many colours. Outside the hospital stood a white ambulance. The flower woman still stood there smiling, and a student passed us with a stethoscope conspicuously sticking out of his pocket. Keith nearly bumped into a man who stared at the doors of the hospital vacantly, afraid perhaps to go in.

We accompanied Lydia home, up the hill, talking and dreaming. Between fragments of conversation I saw myself, self looking

upon another self – and that other, a white-gowned, white-masked surgeon. I had recurrent daydreams of myself playing cricket for Glamorgan, scoring the winning goal for Cardiff City, or agitating a responsive crowd, like Leo did, demanding a Government of the People, for the People. Sometimes I imagined myself as another Grynszpan. But now, looking down at the haggard patient before self's other eyes, I saw that reclining figure assume the familiar features of Nancy Roberts. I said to the beautiful brunette nurse, 'This is inoperable, I will operate.' Only a gasp of amazement and admiration disturbed the silence of the operating room. The anaesthetic bag inflated and collapsed, inflated and collapsed as Nancy Roberts stood on the threshold of 'Life' and 'Death'.

'We must save the life of Nancy Roberts,' I said to the nurse who looked like Kay Francis.

'Impossible,' she answered. 'Even you couldn't do it.' The breathing continued, diminished; the spectators in the gallery clenched their fists until their knuckles turned white.

'I must try,' I said modestly. 'Now pass me more blood.'

They brought me a bottle of red fluid.

'No,' I said, 'the green blood.'

'Green?' they asked, surprised.

'Yes,' I commanded. 'Blood saturated with chlorophyll. It's the only way to save Nancy Roberts.'

'Where shall we get it?' they queried.

I took a syringe and needle, sticking it into one of my own veins, and the green corpuscles trickled out, remarkably. When I completed the operation the bladder of air expanded rapidly.

'There you are,' I said. 'Next patient.'

'Don't work any more today,' pleaded a blonde nurse. 'You've been operating twenty-four hours solid, without food, without water, without sleep.'

'I'll take a glass of water,' I remarked. 'The rest can wait. You must not put self first in a profession like ours.'

'Sir,' said the Kay Francis nurse, 'the next operation is on a man called Keith Thomas – cancer of the brain.'

'Wheel him in,' I sighed.

At the gate of the house we said good-bye to Lydia Pike, and Keith and I walked down Penylan Hill again.

'You've been very quiet,' said Keith.

'I've been thinking,' I said.

'What?' he asked.

'I think I'll become a doctor after all.'

'Thought you were going to be a poet and an assassin,' Keith reminded me.

'No,' I said. 'One must choose the difficult path. It's too easy to be a poet, or to knock off a few heads of Europe. Too easy. I'll take the difficult path. Anyway, I believe in Democracy.'

'What'll you be tomorrow?' smiled Keith.

'Dunno,' I said.

*   *   *

I had rung the bell three times, knocked on the door, but still no one answered. It could have been worse – it could have been raining. Indeed, the clouds gathered soiled and grey, threateningly. I stood in the porch, irritated, for the parcel I carried seemed to be growing more heavy, more awkward every minute. It was task enough carrying the damned thing to the Rev. Aaronowich's without having to take it all the way back home again. Secretly I gazed through the letter-box to see a section of the old-fashioned empty hall: the hall-stand, erect and dignified, wore its hooks and respectable-coloured overcoats, mackintoshes, hats, umbrellas, while further away I could see the staircase undulating upwards silently. No sign of life at all. For luck, once more, I rang the middle bell of the first floor flat and heard the dry chirp of its echo distantly in another part of the house. For the last time I brought the knocker down in a pattern of noise that would have disturbed the dead.

Going out of the wrought-iron front gate into the pavement of plane trees and red pillar-box, I felt compelled to look upward and saw, to my surprise, the large smudged face of the Rev. Aaronowich behind the upstairs window. We looked at each other, ghost staring at ghost, before his face moved out from its

sculptured vacancy into an expression of liquid recognition. He waved without strength, feebly, and moved away from the window presumably to descend the silent stairs and open the heavy front door. I walked up the front garden again, shifting the parcel from one arm to the other.

It seemed hours before I heard footsteps in the hall and saw Rev. Aaronowich's shadow through the stained glass of the front door. At first, thinking he had forgotten my presence, I had been tempted to ring the overworked bell again. Certainly, during these latter years, he had gained a reputation for lovable absent-mindedness which was not so lovable to those inconvenienced by these same lapses of memory.

The front door creaked as the Rev. Aaronowich opened it slowly, carefully. He looked over my shoulder, frightened, as if he expected hooded figures of conspiracy behind me – as if someone lay in wait for him and used me merely as some plausible decoy. Surprised, he said, 'You are alone.'

'Mother asked me to give you this,' I said, thrusting the parcel forward.

'Come up,' he commanded, and I followed him slowly, for every four steps he stopped, out of breath, to hang on to the polished wooden banister.

He led me into his book-lined study. I had never visited his house before. I noticed a *menorah* on the mahogany sideboard, standing between ordinary brass candlesticks. On his desk stood a big silver-coloured wine cup, which doubtless he used twice a year, *seder* nights, on Passover – for the Angel, for the unexpected guest, for Elijah. But these were the only paraphernalia of religious ritual – otherwise it could have been any scholar's study.

'I haven't seen you at *shul*, Michael, for a very long time,' he accused me when his breath returned.

I didn't think it worth while to protest that my name was not Michael. 'No, sir,' I said instead. 'I'm studying for my matriculation.'

'Does that make you less of a Jew?' the old man asked, hunching his shoulders. 'The Jews in Germany tried to forget they were Jews – and look what's happening to them. The tragedy

there,' he went on, 'is not that they are being persecuted, but that they don't know why they are being persecuted . . . Jews always have been hounded, hunted – but formerly they always knew why. The Jews in Germany think they are Germans, so they ask: Why? Why? Why?' He nodded his head sadly. 'You should go to *shul*, understand what Judaism is,' he said.

I had put the parcel down on the table and waited patiently to be dismissed, but he drew up a chair and said,' We must have a little talk.'

'I'm sorry, but I have an appointment,' I lied.

'First a little talk – and a cup of tea perhaps?'

I didn't wish to be rude and the old man seemed intent on keeping me there.

'Hitler,' he said, 'is a very evil man.' Then again, nodding his head knowingly, 'so was Haman – you know what happened to Haman.' He cocked his head on one side as if straining to hear something: the front door bell perhaps? Now he looked at me urgently. 'I should like you to stay, Michael, and have a cup of tea – my wife won't be long.' I started to tell him that my name wasn't Michael, but he didn't appear to be listening. Through the window I caught a glimpse of Mrs Aaronowich in the small oblong garden, struggling with the Monday washing. The sheets were hung in a row and the convex wind blew and puffed out their boasting white chests. They billowed out, proud and pompous, waiting to be decorated with medals of sunlight. But the sky was damp grey over the washing-line, over the patch of grass and the fading wallflowers.

'And why don't you come to *shul*?' asked the Rev. Aaronowich. 'You haven't been since your *bamitzvah*.' I couldn't tell him how both Keith and I agreed that public prayer was repugnant to us – whether in church or in synagogue, whether spoken in English or in Hebrew. A prayer should be personal and spontaneous, Keith and I agreed, not a tract repeated parrot-like – a tract worn out by clichés told to a public God with terrible familiarity.

'I see you've become an atheist,' he said. 'All boys of sixteen become atheists . . . it is part of their future religious orientation,'

he said, smiling and with certainty. But the smile suddenly loosened itself from the big mask of his face, which now tightened up, to emphasize every single line in the geography of his features. I saw that he stood near the desk in pain, for he held his brown-freckled soft hand over his heart and this frightened me. He must have guessed this, for heroically he searched for his smile again and choked out, 'Just indigestion ... don't be alarmed.'

He caught his breath and moved towards the sideboard very slowly, opening a top drawer to pull out a round, white, small box.

'Are you well, sir?'

He took out a little red pill and swallowed it down, leaning heavily on the sideboard, shutting his eyes.

'Are you all right?' I repeated.

He didn't answer and I sat there afraid. Supposing the old man pegged out? I imagined him crumpled up dead on the carpet, near the desk, myself rising from the chair and the clock on the mantelpiece suddenly ticking loudly. Or supposing he fell to the floor screaming in pain, appealing to me? What should I do? I shivered and wished like a coward that I could leave. As casually as possible I walked over to the window for reassurance.

Mrs Aaronowich was bending down over her washing-basket, fiddling with pegs, her grey hair blown like a short scarf in the wind. A ginger cat sat on the square patch of grass inanely watching her. We seemed to wait in the room indefinitely before the Rev. Aaronowich opened his eyes. He seemed surprised to see me. Then said: 'I feel better now, thank you ... You were telling me, I think, of the essential differences between Judaism and Christianity?'

'I don't think I was,' I protested mildly.

'Oh no,' he apologized, 'that was Samuel yesterday. You look like Samuel,' he added limply. He looked out at me from faded, rheumy, blue eyes. 'Do you know the differences, the essential differences, between Judaism and Christianity?' he smiled.

'I think so.'

'Well?'

'First' – I started awkwardly – 'First . . . we . . . Jews . . . don't believe in Christ: that is to say, not as God . . .' I looked at him to see if he were listening. He was. 'I mean we believe that God is One – that there is only One God.' The Rev. Aaronowich sat down in the armchair and said softly, 'Hear, O Israel, the Lord Our God is One.' He leant forward. '*Shema* is a Hebrew word meaning "Hear". It is the first word of the passage, Deuteronomy, chapter six, verses four to nine, which form the "*Shema*" – as God is One, He is not only Unique but a Unity, Indivisible – so for we Jews, Michael, there cannot be a Son of God, except in the sense that all men are "the sons of God".' He paused, stared at the door anxiously, because of a sudden sound of footsteps. His skin was drawn tightly over his large wide cheekbones and little worms of blood-vessels, purple, minute, threaded their way under the pores.

Mrs Aaronowich came into the room and he sat back evidently relieved, as if he were afraid that it might have been some malignant stranger who had just a minute before stood on the landing. She, for her part, looked at me petrified and hurriedly put on her glasses. Yet recognizing me she seemed disappointed.

'No, Sarah,' the Rev. Aaronowich said, 'it is not he.' She took off her spectacles, helplessly wiping the lenses with her apron. Mrs Aaronowich was a short, dumpy, home-made woman. Her blown grey hair fell over a high forehead. Replacing her spectacles in their case she stood near the door nervously twisting her thick gold wedding-ring round her finger.

'A cup of tea for me, Sarah, perhaps – and young Michael here.'

'Michael?' asked Mrs Aaronowich. She vanished again, presumably into the kitchen to put on the kettle and to disturb the special china that was reserved for visitors and pupils. No, it is not he, the old man had said.

The Rev. Aaronowich's accented voice crackled and he spoke again like a duty. 'And you are quite right, Michael, when you say that all men are the sons of God.' (Had he forgotten that he himself had said this?) He rambled on, sometimes stopping to

116

catch his breath. 'It results from this point that Judaism teaches there is a direct way between man and God – there being no Mediator. Yes, we are a religion without Mediator, without Sacrament, without Priest – whereas Christianity teaches that between Man and God is Jesus, the Church, the Priest.' His voice droned on curiously broken, half alien, half Welsh. Under the table when he wasn't looking I pretended to wind up a gramophone, but nobody was there to share my tasteless joke . . .

'Both Judaism and Christianity teach that when a man has sinned he must truly repent of the wrong he has done.' The old man suddenly spoke more loudly as if addressing a larger audience. 'According to Christian teaching, however, man's soul is from birth soiled by sin so that it is only through the great sacrifice of Christ on the Cross that complete forgiveness be possible. For them, Christ is not only the Mediator, but also the great Intercessor between man and God. According to Christian teaching, only through Jesus is God willing to cleanse man utterly of sin . . .'

The Rev. Aaronowich sat there in his black mournful suit talking avidly. How many years, decades, had he carefully prepared the Saturday sermon? I imagined him sitting at his desk, a spry young man composing his weekly piece. The months, years passed, he grew older, fatter, greyer, balder, but still he sat before his desk in the same attitude, relating everyday life to rabbinical teachings. Now he merely sat sunken in an armchair, retired, faithful to his own God and to his own inwardness, but without the necessary audience to explain, discuss, teach. He sat older by far, speaking sermon syllables to a youth who could not move away without giving deep offence.

'Human nature, the Christians would have us believe, is wicked and corrupt from the very beginning . . .' He looked at me.

'Original Sin,' I said, to show I was listening.

'Judaism on the other hand teaches that the soul of man is pure. As we say in our morning prayer . . . What do we say in our morning prayer?' He looked down at me sternly. I was the con-

gregation and I sat there dumb, embarrassed, ignorant. Mrs Aaronowich came in with a pewter tray, biscuits and tea-pot, saucers and cups, sugar-basin and milk.

'Quite right,' he said, though I hadn't spoken, 'we say in our morning prayer – ''My God, the soul which Thou hast given me is pure . . .'' ' The front door bell rang stridently. Suddenly they were caught there as in a photograph, the old man finishing a sentence, his right hand in mid-air, his wife about to put her tray on the square table – but both listening to the front door bell ringing, ringing.

Needlessly I said, 'Someone's at the front door' – and they went on breathing: the camera handle beginning to turn again. Dr Aaronowich brought down his right hand on to his black trousers and she turned round from the table, her lips parted.

'You haven't forgotten,' she said.

'Tell him to go away,' Dr Aaronowich said.

'I can't do that,' she whispered. 'Even a stranger is welcome in our house' – and then more loudly to me, 'You must be very busy, dear – no doubt you want to go.'

I rose from the table, glad. I felt restricted in this formal atmosphere – the heavy furniture, the little lace cloths, the books precisely arranged – all these combined to contrive a certain respectable claustrophobia. I rose, but Rabbi Aaronowich was plucking at my elbow, signalling me to sit down. 'Michael is my guest,' he said. 'Finish your tea and . . .' The bell rang again, furiously, freezing him into silence. Nothing seemed to matter in the room but the bell as it malevolently buzzed louder and nearer, filling the whole room with a sense of noise and shrill disaster.

Mrs Aaronowich looked at her husband pleadingly. 'He wrote to say he would come – and now he's here I can't tell him to go away – as if he were a . . .' Words failed her.

'Tell him I'm busy with a pupil,' the old man said roughly.

When the bell rang again Mrs Aaronowich, without saying another word, went downstairs to answer it. The rabbi gaped down at his feet, at his laced boots, and made a strange noise in his throat like a sob. He fumbled for a handkerchief and lifted it to his overbrimming eyes. 'Oh Absalom, my son, my son,' I

heard him mutter. And then I guessed which hooded figure it was that rang the front door bell so persistently. The stories from years ago sounded like a whisper in my head – of Jack Aaronowich, their only son, who had married a non-Jewish girl against the wishes of his orthodox parents. It had caused a scandal amongst the Cardiff Jewish community who, with their prejudices, heart deep, had pencilled darkly the character of Jack Aaronowich. 'Broke his mother's heart,' they had said. 'They sat *shiva* for him,' they had said. 'Taken ten years of Rabbi Aaronowich's life,' they had said. And Jack Aaronowich had become a sort of land, a legend. A land of vice and a legend of calculated seediness. 'You'll end up like that boy Aaronowich,' mothers had scolded their sons – so that in the young imagination Jack Aaronowich had become the apotheosis of evil, of a wasted and mean life. One imagined him lolling and loitering in some billiard hall in Soho, white faced, diseased, drugged, slobbering under the harsh arc-lights, beyond hope and help! Nothing had been heard of him for seven years ...

There were voices outside and the old man continued to look down at his feet; yet cautiously stuffed the handkerchief back into one of his pockets, taking out a red pill instead.

'Just wait there a minute,' I heard Mrs Aaronowich say. 'Just a second, Jack.'

Sarah Aaronowich entered the room once again, her bright eyes questioning, her pleasant face flushed, her grey hair curling over her forehead. She stood near the desk waiting for her husband to say something. Coldly the old man stared at the floor.

'What is it, Sarah?' he asked almost savagely.

Mrs Aaronowich stopped smiling. Timidly she said, 'It's our son.'

'Our son?' The Rev. Aaronowich looked up, stared right through her, his rheumy eyes steady. 'Our son Jack is dead, Sarah,' he said gently. His wife gazed at him perplexed and I heard someone coughing outside the closed door.

'It's Jack, *our* Jack,' said Mrs Aaronowich.

'Excuse me,' I said, 'I must be getting along. Thanks, thanks

for the tea.' I moved to the door and they ignored me. They just looked at each other, gazing deeply into each other's eyes, searching for something that was lost, long ago.

On the landing I passed Jack Aaronowich who winked at me, obviously embarrassed. His pretty wife held his hand. When I looked round from the top of the stairs I saw Jack Aaronowich raise his arm to knock very quietly, very deliberately on the ambiguous door.

* * *

The mechanical voice of the loudspeaker floated disembodied over Smith's bookstall, across the station clock, mingling with porters, passengers and sad farewells. The voice said Newport, Swindon, Reading, Paddington. It seemed the voice of Fate. More appropriately it should have called out Abyssinia, Austria, Czechoslovakia, Spain. Dead, dead, 1939. Then there was a shriek that I thought came from Europe, but it was only the plaintive call of the train, and the big engine blew two ghosts of steam out of its unstitched sides. Lots of people rushed out of the Refreshment Room.

'We'll be back on Monday,' said mother. 'Be a good boy.'

'Study hard,' said my father, smiling uncomfortably.

'He'll be all right with me,' said Uncle Bertie, towering massively, good-humouredly, over the crowd. Mother, father, Leo, bundled into the Paddington train.

'Bring me back some wedding cake,' said Uncle Bertie, 'and all good wishes to Sammy.'

'What did you say RSVP meant?' I asked Leo.

'Remember to Send the Vedding Present,' he replied.

'Garn,' I said.

They sat in the GWR third-class carriage with its pictures of Mevagissey, Torquay, Porthcawl and an elongated map of Southern England. Mother looked soulful leaning out of the window. Mother was always ready to shed a lonely tear – at deaths, weddings, good-byes, illnesses, *bamitzvahs*, births. Songs like 'My Yiddisha Momma' prompted her generous sentimental soul to rise to her eyes in a tearful grey mist.

120

'Don't waste your time at Uncle Bertie's,' shouted my father over mother's shoulder; mother only planted a damp kiss on my reluctant cheek. 'Heavens,' she said as the train gave a little jerk forward, 'did I turn the gas off in the oven?'

The train moved forward and hands leapt out of the windows waving, waving, smaller and smaller, out of sight.

The voice began again. 'The next train to come into platform two ...' But Uncle Bertie took my arm and strode towards the nearest exit. I said to Uncle, 'I once saw a man have an epileptic fit in a train.' All he remarked was: 'That cousin of yours, Sammy, getting married. What a mug!'

My American cousin Sammy was, as you've guessed, going to be married in London that week-end and my family had been invited up for the wedding. Wilfred was going to travel from Abergavenny where he was now working as a doctor. It would be a regular family reunion, and my mother had bought a new hat. Only I couldn't go to London because of the proximity of my examinations. Uncle Bertie and Aunt Cecile had offered to look after me for the week-end and after many doubts and reservations mother had agreed. There had, though, been a terrible argument first.

'I wouldn't let my son stay with that *meshuggana* Bertie,' mother had said.

'He's my brother,' Dad protested.

'Cain was Abel's brother,' replied Mam. 'Everybody says your Bertie is mad, everybody. He *is* mad!' proclaimed mother definitely.

'Things are very bad for him now in the business.'

'Bad, bad ... he's bad,' said mother. 'Do you know he even carries a gun on him now?'

'Since when?' asked Dad.

'Since last week,' said mother. 'He's got a holster under his coat.'

'You believe everything,' said father. 'And you talk too much in the butcher's shop.'

Whenever Dad wished to defeat my mother in argument he would accuse her of gossiping. Having pulled out his trump card

he would never say another word, but shut his jaw tight, deaf to any of my mother's protestations.

As Uncle Bertie and I walked back through crowded St Mary's Street I asked Uncle about the gun.

'Yes,' he said. 'You can never tell when you may meet a burglar.'

When he hesitated before a jeweller's shop, peering distractedly through the window-pane, I imagined him mask over face, trilby hat well down over his eyes, gun in hand and a brick in the other.

'That,' he said, pointing to a necklace, 'is *Art*.' He nodded his head agreeing with himself. 'Wish I could buy it for Cecile,' he added.

Ever since Philip Morris painted Aunt Cecile, Uncle Bertie had a thing about Art. Everything he liked, he described as Art, Great Art, whether it was a motor-car or merely Aunt Cecile's cooking. Now Uncle Bertie stared and stared through the shop window unwilling to come away. A policeman near by gazed at him curiously.

'The Bobby is watching you,' I said.

Uncle Bertie turned round nastily and said to the policeman, 'Anything wrong?'

'No, sir.'

We shuffled away with Uncle Bertie muttering, 'If you vant to buy a vatch, buy a vatch; if you don't vant to buy a vatch, get avay from my bloody vinder!'

'Remember to Send the Vedding Present,' I said, and we smiled at each other.

When we returned to Uncle's house in Albany Road (he lived near The White Wall in the only house in the street that had not been recently painted), Cecile rose from the chair, full of complaints. Why didn't Uncle do this, why didn't Uncle do that? There's no money coming into the house, she protested, bills, bills, everywhere.

'Wait until Dad sees Mr Simon,' said cousin Clive loyally.

'Why did you pay off all Uncle Isidore's debts when he died?' grumbled Aunt Cecile.

Uncle Bertie pretended not to hear but pulled the black mangy cat on to his lap, and stroked it, until it purred fiercely.

'Makes a noise like a motor-car,' said Uncle Bertie, looking at the cat proudly.

'And talking about cars, why don't you sell the Rover?' said Aunt Cecile.

'Things are not that bad,' said Uncle Bertie. 'There's going to be a boom soon.'

'You've said that for ten years,' nagged Auntie. 'You don't realize. It's about time we had some luck. I tell you if we dropped a piece of toast on the floor it would fall butter-side downwards.'

'You wait until I've had my little talk with Mr Simon,' said Uncle.

'Yes, you wait,' said Clive.

'You'll probably say the wrong thing and offend him,' said Aunt Cecile.

'Me, say the wrong thing?' objected Uncle.

'All we need is cancer,' said Auntie gloomily.

'Cancer, *schmancer*,' replied Uncle Bertie, 'what does it matter as long as you've got your health!'

'Or sell some of those china figures,' said Cecile, pointing to the sideboard. 'They're worth a few pounds.'

'That is Swansea china,' shouted Uncle exasperated. 'That is *Art*. My God,' he added, pushing the cat to the floor, 'don't you appreciate *Art?*' He brushed down his trousers vigorously, trying to remove the moulting hairs of the two-eyed cat.

'Come on, love,' he said, 'let's have a cup of tea.'

'Can't you wait until Mr Simon comes?' she said, but she went into the kitchen all the same.

When she was out of hearing, Clive winked at his father as if they shared a secret.

'I've got the bottles,' my cousin said.

Uncle rubbed his hands gleefully.

'Come into the garden,' Clive said to me.

'How many bottles?' asked Uncle.

'Six.'

And they motioned for me to join them as they walked through the open garden doors.

The garden lay resplendent in the promise of summer. August would be soon and the exams over. August would arrive with tennis-players and sipping iced lemonade on the veranda. There would be the salt smell of the sea on the hands and emptying sand from holiday pockets. There would be a sentimental tune like 'Deep purple' and the sound of someone diving into the swimming-pool with a blank explosion. Summer nights would saunter along the low-down streets and lighted windows would float high up in the black air.

'Do you think she'll hear?' asked Clive.

Near the wall, at the end of the garden, Clive had arranged six medicine bottles all in a row.

Uncle didn't reply to my cousin's question but just pulled the gun out of his holster, aiming at one of the bottles. There was the loud report of a gunshot and one of the bottles flew into a spray of pieces. From the lilac tree, three birds shot out as if fired from a catapult.

'Well shot,' applauded Clive.

But they waited to see if Aunt Cecile would come out of the kitchen protesting. Nothing happened except in the listening air the distant ring of a front door bell could be heard. Uncle Bertie fired again. This time Auntie pushed her head through the kitchen window. 'What are you doing?' she shouted.

'Just testing, just testing,' lied Uncle.

'That's the front door bell,' Aunt Cecile cried. 'It's probably Mr Simon.'

Uncle Bertie returned his gun into the holster and ambled back into the house.

'Your Dad's a character,' I said to Clive.

'See that dustbin?' said Clive. The dustbin was full of holes. 'He's a good shot, isn't he?'

Mr Simon was a bent, benign little man, with grey side-boards and grey hair which he brushed sideways in an endeavour to hide his baldness – but his parting was two inches wide, anyway. He

looked out from two brandy coloured eyes mildly. His thin scraggy neck was surmounted by a winged collar many sizes too big for him and to this collar his right hand would tremble from time to time. His fussy black trousers fell over old-fashioned spats and gleaming black shoes. He put on glasses when he was introduced to Clive and me, and having scrutinized us carefully he replaced his spectacles in his inside pocket.

'I hear you're in the Art Game,' said Uncle Bertie, all pleasantries over.

'I sell picture frames amongst other things,' Mr Simon remarked kindly.

'Well, to come to the point,' said Uncle, beaming.

'Have your tea first,' interrupted Auntie, smiling at Mr Simon.

'I don't mind if I do,' said Mr Simon, patting the cat deliberately, as if it were red-hot.

Uncle Bertie was impatient. 'The fact is, I can put my hand on thousands of frames.'

'Well then, I'm interested,' said Mr Simon, reaching for a scone. 'I hope this will be just the beginning of a profitable business relationship.'

Aunt Cecile poured out the tea carefully. 'How is business generally, Mr Simon?' she asked politely.

'There's going to be a boom, a boom any day now,' interrupted Uncle with such emphasis that Mr Simon withered in his seat and his tenuous eyes opened widely over his teacup, as they gazed at the company.

'Would you and Mr Simon like to go into the front room to discuss business?' asked Aunt Cecile.

'For the details, yes.' said Uncle, 'but first let us – as a famous statesman said – let us generalize in the parlour.' He began to laugh at this and Mr Simon accommodatingly joined him in a correct high-pitched chuckle.

'Thousands of frames you have access to,' Mr Simon said, sucking in his breath.

'Thousands,' said Uncle Bert, pulling out his hands as if he were telling a tall fishing story.

125

'I could buy thousands,' said Mr Simon.

'Yes,' smiled Uncle Bertie. 'But ... tell me, what do you intend to put in the picture frames?'

Mr Simon and Aunt Cecile gazed at him perplexed.

'What do you mean?' asked Mr Simon, dropping his accent in surprise.

Uncle Bertie glared. 'I mean what sort of pictures will go in them eventually?' Mr Simon looked at Auntie for help.

'My husband is fond of good Art,' explained Aunt Cecile, trying to smooth things over.

'Very creditable, very creditable,' repeated Mr Simon. 'I like to deal with cultured business men.'

'I love *Art*,' said Uncle encouraged. 'Da Vinci, Botticelli, er ... Rembrandt!'

Aunt kicked me under the table by mistake and Uncle rambled on unadmonished.

'I mean a man can sell everything but not his soul,' said Uncle.

'Of course, of course,' said Mr Simon stupidly.

Aunt Cecile, endeavouring to stop him, pretended to have a fit of coughing, but Uncle Bertie was in full flow, waving his hands. 'Art,' he said, 'is the Spice of Life. Art is magnificent.'

'Yes, it is,' said Mr Simon, bewildered.

Uncle, thinking he was making a great impression, worked himself into a fury of love for Art and Aunt Cecile helplessly watched him. It was then the cat, who had jumped up on to the sideboard, unfortunately knocked down some of the Swansea china, shattering it on to the floor. Uncle Bertie stood up dismayed. 'That was great Art,' he choked and suddenly drew his gun out from the holster, shooting the cat dead.

Mr Simon rose from the chair. 'Oh Bertie!' said Aunt. The whole room seemed to spin around, catching expressions of fear and amazement. Dumbfounded, dumbstruck, the company stared at the dead cat. Uncle Bertie stood up, the fulcrum of the room, his gun still smoking in his hand.

'It's dead,' said Clive tonelessly.

'I love Art more than Life, Mr Simon,' explained Bertie, staring around the room belligerently, waving his gun.

Mr Simon, still white in the face, soon afterwards remembered an important appointment and Uncle saw him to the door with the gun still in his hand.

'If you can assure me good painting will go into the frames I'll let you have thousands next to nothing,' we heard Uncle Bertie shouting in the hall.

When the front door slammed, Auntie said, 'He's plain mad and I must be mad to put up with him.'

'The poor cat,' said Clive.

Uncle Bertie came through the door, beaming. 'I'm sorry about the cat,' he said, 'but I certainly impressed Mr Simon.' When nobody answered, he said, like an overgrown boy, all questions in his eyes, 'Let's have another cup of tea, love.'

'Look what you've done,' said Aunt, agitated, overwhelmed.

'What I've done! Look what the cat's done,' he objected.

'Dad, you're mad,' said Clive.

'Shut up!' said Uncle. 'Never mind,' he added, putting his arm around Aunt Cecile. 'Today I saw a beautiful necklace I'm going to buy you for your birthday.'

'What with?' she asked.

'There's going to be a boom soon,' he declared optimistically. 'A boom.'

'There's been one,' said Auntie. And she began to cry.

'You're great Art,' he said hopelessly, trying to console her, 'Very Great Art.'

*   *   *

The mechanical voice of the loudspeaker floated disembodied across the station clock that had stopped long ago in the year 1933. The sinister German voice mingled with the Guards in black uniforms and the sorrowful Alsatian dogs cocked up their ears. The voice over the crackling loudspeaker shouted, 'All change at Auschwitz – Dachau.' The engine gave a shriek of pain and the dogs would not look. Near the Refreshment Room stood a hygienic-looking shed containing a few gas chambers, inside one of which a stray passenger now found himself.

The rest of the passengers sat in the train, their luggage on the rack of pain. These suitcases were labelled Munich, Berlin, Vienna, Madrid, Prague. When the engine gave its plaintive shriek in the still air, no passenger moved, no passenger spoke. They merely sat, the hooked-nosed ones, gazing straight ahead, waiting for the train to move out. Not looking at the pictures lining the carriages. Neither that of Hitler addressing a huge crowd, nor aeroplanes over Barcelona, nor troops goose-marching through Austria. Nobody looked, nobody spoke, nobody waved a last farewell.

A Guard came and opened the door. 'All change!' he screamed. They changed into skeletons. Skeletons row after row sitting bolt upright in the carriages of Time.

The loudspeaker crackled again. The next train to arrive at platform two will be the London train.

The engine pulled in.

'There they are,' said Uncle Bertie.

Leo bundled out of the train, mother and father after him, smiling.

'All change!' a porter shouted.

*   *   *

August. Butterflies staggering across the rockery. Mother pouring boiling water over the ants that had multiplied outside the scullery door. Bluebottles grumbling up and down the window-pane. The sound of Z in the grass and R, like an aeroplane, in the blue lazy skies that drizzled sunlight. Matriculation exams over and hip pip hooray and, luckily, Keith and I had passed, so it was to be holidays at Ogmore, by the sea by the river by the surf by a field of sheep, all day and all night. At the last moment, Lydia couldn't come for she had to accompany her adamant parents to the Gower Coast and Nancy didn't dare camp with us alone.

I dare you!

Really, I can't, father wouldn't let me.

But it didn't matter – with our sleeping bags and tent on our backs, forks in our belts like Sheffield swords, we intended to

128

hitch-hike, thumb a Rolls-Royce or a bony lorry up Tumble Down Dick on to Cowbridge (which has more pubs to the square inch than any place in Great Britain) to rattle down Crack Hill, to fly along the golden mile built straight and classical by the Romans, to side-track Bridgend and follow the clear eel of the river to Ogmore. Ogmore covered by light green turf and dark green ferns. Ogmore by the sand by the river by the sea. A few miles from the shore when the tide was out we would be able to see black Tuska Rock and the mast of the old shipwreck sticking up like a periscope above the corrugated sea. Way and over the other side of the river the sandbanks would swerve and curve past Jack Peterson's house round the eye's horizon, all the way to Porthcawl that would strike out its lion's paw to be seen distantly but distinctly as if through the wrong end of a telescope.

Our first lift was a lorry, bumpy and shivering, that took us only a few miles out of Cardiff. It was like travelling on top of a huge pneumatic drill and as the lorry crept up Tumble Down Dick, the driver, his foot right down on the accelerator, shouted at it, 'Come on, old girl, come on, my sweetie.' At the top he wiped his forehead with a dirty handkerchief and said, 'There's go in the old girl yet.' And we shook down the road, teeth in our mouths, bells and hooters, ringing and clanging. At length he shouted, 'Whoa, whoa,' to the old engine and she, wheezing and smoking, obeyed willingly. 'This is as far as I go,' he said smiling at us and we climbed on to a still road, glad to stretch our legs.

'Have a good time, kiddo,' he called, and turned down a narrow side road, brushing the lorry against brambles, striped wasps and anxious butterflies.

'Darro,' said Keith, 'I thought it was an earthquake.'

'Bet he has to be X-rayed every time he arrives home,' I said.

We sat on a bit of green on the edge of the road, the sun dripping over us as a few cars swished by. Then we stood up, starting to thumb the oncoming automobiles, but without success.

We waited there the best part of an hour, our spirits falling despite the wooded hills beyond and the buttercups in the field and the free and easy of it all.

'Bet you the third car from now stops,' said Keith. Four more

cars passed us by, one or two of the drivers waving to us, smiling.

'Some sense of humour,' I said.

'When I have a car,' said Keith, 'I'll stop for everybody.' Lunch-time arrived and still no driver deigned to halt for us. So we took out our sandwiches and munched away sadly. Few cars seemed to be passing us now.

'They're all having their lunch,' I said.

So we walked for a while, past hedge and gate, stopping now and then to taste the fresh air and to comment on the sun, hills, and chessboard fields.

'Look,' said Keith, 'car coming.'

'It won't stop on a corner,' I said. 'Let's hurry along.' We raced as fast as we could to a propitious part of the road. The car rode on towards us.

'It's a Riley,' said Keith.

'Just the job,' I said. 'An' I don't think anyone's in it except the driver.'

We stared hopefully at the car. As it zoomed up to us we thumbed it crazily. The driver signed to us that he was going towards the right and we stopped thumbing to think for a moment.

'Why, that's the way we're going,' shouted Keith exasperated. But it rushed away and was gone, the sun gleaming on its roof.

'The bloody bastard,' I said. 'He could have stopped.'

'I hope he has four bloody punctures,' said Keith.

'And no spare tyre,' I added.

We walked on gloomily.

'Nobody's goin' to stop,' grumbled Keith.

'More cars seem to be going into Cardiff than away from it,' I said.

'We could go back and catch a train,' said Keith.

'Somebody'll stop,' I said optimistically.

'If we were girls they'd stop, they'd bloody well stop.'

'Look, you lie on the road and pretend you're ill or dead.'

'If we had Nancy with us,' said Keith, 'we could hide behind a hedge and when a car – '

'Here's another one,' I called.

A van crawled towards us and we stared at it belligerently.

130

'You wave it,' Keith said. 'I'm unlucky. I feel unlucky.'

'No, you.'

We both waved it and the driver stared at us curiously.

'Anyway, it's not raining,' I said.

But a hundred yards down the road it stopped. We didn't say anything but started to walk towards it. Then, as if someone had given us a signal, we began to run, our hearts higher than our heads.

'Where you goin'?' the man asked through the window.

'Ogmore.'

'I'm goin' nearly to Cowbridge.'

'Fine,' we said. 'Thanks very much.'

'Well, jump in,' he said.

The driver shifted some packages from the front seat and we squeezed in. At the back of the van was a stack of apples. We moved on again. It was past two o'clock. The man drove in his shirt-sleeves and talked all the time. About everything: he wouldn't fight for Smigly-Ritz, he said, and that it was against our tradition to have conscription in peace-time and he wouldn't let any of his kids do six months in the Army and wasn't it terrible about the brand-new submarine, *Thetis*. As for the Bishop of Chester, he didn't hold with clergymen playing barrel-organs in public, even for charity. It encouraged the IRA to plant time-bombs in suitcases at railway stations or something. And he was going to London for his summer holiday and visit the Zoo to see the Giant Panda. He dropped us the other side of Cowbridge though he hadn't meant to go that far.

'By the way,' he said, 'would you like some apples?'

We stood on the blue dazed road to Bridgend, on a straight bit of road that led out of Cowbridge, still smelling the petrol from the apple van and hearing the monotonous voice of the driver: '*Thetis* . . . Giant Panda . . . Smigly-Ritz . . . Conscription.' We threw the apples' stumps into a field and the silly birds whistled away in a hot tree and the cars floated by, floated by, sunlight dazzling their windscreens. The motorists ignored our desperate gesticulations. A cow came to thrust its heavy head over a nearby hedge to gaze at us mournfully, uncomprehending. Brown eyes,

brown cow, black flies, tail swish, and the cars floating by until four o'clock. Down below us we saw the black Daimler for the first time. It was Keith's turn to go to work. 'Smile sweetly,' I said. Keith quickly combed his carrot-coloured hair into a suggestion of respectability. He was already waving at the car when I saw that the driver wore a sort of black uniform. 'For God's sake stop thumbing it,' I cried, 'it's a taxi.' A young woman sat alone in the back of the car and she stared out at us mildly smiling. We saw her leaning forward to speak to the driver.

'It's not a taxi,' said Keith. 'That was a chauffeur.'

'It's stopped,' I called. 'It's damn well stopped.' We leapt towards it joyfully. 'They must be rich,' I thought, running with my pack now like twenty ton on my back. The chauffeur had already come out of the car when we reached it, and we asked him breathlessly, 'We're going to . . .'

'They're going to Ogmore, madam,' he said.

'That's very fortunate for them.'

And we arranged ourselves in the car, myself at the back with the lady and Keith next to the chauffeur. 'All the way,' I thought. 'All the lovely way in a Daimler.' Down Crack Hill and bearing to the left of the garage. It was slow-going now, for the road to Ogmore from there on was narrow and winding, hardly width enough for two cars to pass. Once we had to stop because of a flock of sheep on the road.

'Why are you going to camp at Ogmore?' the lady asked. 'Porthcawl or Barry is more popular, isn't it?'

'That's why,' I answered. 'Ogmore isn't spoilt, it's much wilder.'

And again she smiled mildly. She must have been about thirty. She wore her black raven hair parted in the middle, with a sort of bun at the back, but not school-marmy at all. Her clear white skin and large dark eyes contrasted strikingly. She looked Spanish but she was a natural Welsh beauty, speaking though without a trace of an accent. She must have been very rich. Or married to one very wealthy – because of the Daimler, the Chauffeur, the expensive rings on her fingers and the quality of her black summer frock. Around her neck she wore a thin silk yellow scarf and on her ears yellow earrings.

132

'Where do you intend camping?' she asked.

'Hardy's field.'

'Oh yes.'

Now on the left, hills covered with ferns, some rusted by the heat, climbed away from the road. To the right, fields slanted abruptly down to the river below. The car purred along smoothly. Around each corner the chauffeur would delicately press his hooter. Then the sea, the sea! The prettiest sight, I swear, in Glamorgan: the mouth of the river and the singing sea. The sandbanks beyond, and in a heat haze, Porthcawl stretching itself out into the water. The tide was in and Tuska Rock could not be seen. Sometimes across the sea one could see the coast of Somerset; but that meant rain. Now on the horizon sat only a ship and the smoke of a summer afternoon. The sun threw down dazzling silver arrows, a rain of arrows into the sea, the sea.

'I'm afraid we turn down here,' she said. 'Shall I drop you or will you come all the way with me?'

'Whatever's convenient,' we said.

Soon we turned into a gravel drive and drew up before a white house which was crowned by a green Moorish undulating roof. On the veranda sat a middle-aged man in a blue blazer and white trousers. He stood up, glass in hand, as we poured out of the car.

'They were hitch-hiking,' she explained.

'My dear, I'm glad you're back,' the man said. She turned her face so that he could kiss her on the cheek. 'For I need the car to go to Cardiff.'

'Why, tonight, Raymond?'

'Yes, tonight.'

We stood there awkwardly waiting to say good-bye and to thank her once again.

'You needn't take the car into the garage,' the man she had called Raymond said to the chauffeur. 'I shall need it in a few hours.'

'Very well, Mr Gregory.'

The chauffeur walked over the gravel towards the back of the house.

Mr Raymond Gregory then looked at us for the first time. He

was running to fat and his face was red as a lobster, which perhaps was his natural colour or may have been the result of the sun. He had grey sparse hair. In a few years' time he would undoubtedly be bald. I decided that he must be an uncle or some sort of relative of the raven-haired lady.

'Where are you camping?' he asked.

'We hope to stay in Hardy's field.'

He threw back his head and laughed sadly. 'I wish I could do that again. It's wonderful to be young. Henrietta, you must be hungry. Boys, will you have tea with us?'

'Oh no,' I began to say but Keith coolly replied, 'Thank you, sir, that would be very nice.'

'There you are, Henrietta, we can have a party. Yesterday you said you would like a party.' And he ushered us into the room behind the veranda. It was one of the largest rooms I'd ever been into and eccentrically painted. The walls white, the woodwork and doors a jasmine yellow. The furniture, which was made of white wood, seemed rough and utilitarian beside the elegant lampshades and *objets d'art*.

'Oh Raymond, what lovely flowers,' the raven-haired lady said.

'I always have to bring my wife yellow flowers to blend with the woodwork,' said Mr Gregory. 'Last Spring it was yellow tulips or daffodils, now it's yellow roses. In the Autumn no doubt it will be yellow chrysanthemums ... eh, Henrietta?'

His young wife smiled vaguely, like a smile behind glass.

'What flowers did you bring last winter, sir?' I asked politely.

He looked at his wife startled and rang a small hand-bell. But his wife insisted, 'We weren't here last winter.'

'The room's very nice and gay,' said Keith.

'It's part of my rehabilitation,' remarked Mrs Gregory.

Her husband rang the bell again and a maid appeared.

'Sadie, these young gentlemen are staying for tea,' said Mr Gregory. 'In the meantime would you show them to the bathroom; I'm sure they'd be glad of a clean-up after their travels, eh?'

Sadie the maid showed us to the lavatory. Next door, clear and white-tiled, waited the bathroom where we washed. Keith put

134

water on his red hair and frantically smoothed it down with his hand.

'She's beautiful,' he said. 'She's the most beautiful woman I've ever seen in my life.'

'Isn't it all fantastic?' I said. 'You never know what's going to happen when you're hitch-hiking.'

'I think I'm in love with her,' said Keith seriously. 'I wish we could stay here, instead of in Hardy's field.'

'Why?' I asked.

Keith stopped messing around with his hair. 'Don't you see,' he said, 'she's unhappy. She's a prisoner here. Married to a man twice her age. Can't you see how unhappy she is? So pale, so withdrawn.'

'She's probably been ill,' I said. 'They said something about rehabilitation.'

'I'd like to rescue her.'

Keith told me to shut up when I laughed. 'I thought you were sensitive,' he said fiercely.

'What do you think you are?' I stang back. 'A knight saving a princess locked in a tower?'

We made our way back down the corridor.

'In here,' shouted Mr Gregory. 'There's more sun this side of the house in the evening.' The garden doors were open, leading into spacious grounds, partly cultivated, partly wild, that rolled down towards the sea. This other room was conventional, though expensively furnished.

'What a wonderful piano,' said Keith to Mrs Gregory. The maid brought in tea on a trolley, and we settled down to eat dainty cheese and tomato sandwiches. It was after tea that Mr Gregory asked us again where we were going to stay.

'In Hardy's field,' I told him.

'Oh yes,' he said. 'Hardy's field . . . I must say it's become very popular this year. There are many campers there, I've noticed.'

'Oh,' said Keith. 'We were hoping to have it more or less to ourselves.'

'I'm afraid you'll find it rather full,' chuckled Mr Gregory.

The maid collected our plates and cups, and wheeled the trolley

out. Keith was right. Henrietta Gregory certainly was beautiful. She sat in the armchair, her profile to us, gazing into the garden. Sunlight lit red sparks in her black hair, above her alabaster forehead.

'I don't suppose . . .' Keith stuttered. 'I don't suppose, you'd allow . . . I mean would it be too much for us to ask if you . . .'

Mr Gregory turned round to him curiously.

'I mean, I wonder if you'd let us camp in your grounds . . . We'd be no trouble at all,' Keith said quickly. 'We'd only want water and . . .' his voice trailed off.

Mr Gregory stared at Henrietta for a moment before answering. 'I don't see why not,' he said. 'Do you, Henrietta? You could use the tennis court too,' he continued. 'Do you play tennis?'

'Oh yes, sir.'

'You'd have to be very good to beat Henrietta.'

'Then we could camp here?' I said.

'Yes. Yes, why not?'

'That's awfully decent of you, sir. We won't be a nuisance at all,' smiled Keith.

'I hope you don't think we're impudent,' I apologized.

'No,' said Mr Gregory, 'not at all. Hardy's field is full. By all means.'

'That's marvellous, that's wonderfully kind of you,' Keith said effusively.

'You'll be careful when you make fires, won't you?' Mr Gregory asked. 'When I come back I still want to see the house in one piece . . . Anyway you can camp beyond the tennis court, a good way down towards the sea.'

Mr Gregory turned his red-beaten face towards his wife, but she just stared into the garden, into the field beyond, as if she hadn't heard a sentence of the conversation.

Mr Gregory took the Daimler and went away that evening and we camped an eighth of a mile from the back of the house. We had put up our tent near a broken-down wall to gain some protection from the sea-winds. Darkness rose out of the turf and earth, and insects clicked in the grass. We made a fire and sat round it whilst above us the sky became tremendous with stars.

After we'd drunk down some Heinz Tomato Soup and cooked our tinned meat and tinned beans, Keith pulled out his pocket Shakespeare and we read sonnets to each other in the firelight. Far away an owl hooted and night-jars shrieked in the muted air. On the sea, the moonlight crawled magically toward the black promontory of Porthcawl.

'This is the life,' I said.

We stopped reading, and sat on our groundsheet (because of the dew) in front of the crackling fire and I thought of Job and the wise men who sat many nights in the dark, in silence, perhaps also listening to a bird suddenly screech in the cowled Night; and then for no reason I remembered waiting in the front seat of my father's motor-car whilst he had gone into some house or another. It was raining and there was the noise of the windscreen-wiper pushing away a pattern of rain to show a perspective of a slummy street beyond. There had been so many days of waiting in empty motor-cars, sitting next to an empty driver's seat. It was sad and meaningless perhaps. But this was different: squatting before a sodium-yellow and red fire and seeing a boy's face opposite me. It was religious in a way that waiting in an empty motor-car was not. Keith's face appeared strange in the firelight. It wasn't his face at all.

'Look,' he said, 'she's going to bed.'

A light had bloomed in one of the upstairs windows of the house, and a shadowy figure pulled fast the curtains.

'It's probably the maid, Sadie.'

'No,' said Keith with certainty. 'It's Henrietta going to bed.'

After stamping on the fire we moved into the tent. The oil lamp flickered, casting huge shadows on the canvas and a moth fluttered around the lamp desperately. As we prepared our sleeping-bags Keith said again, 'She's beautiful, utterly beautiful, I'd like to tell her so.'

'Well, do,' I said unkindly. 'Nobody's stopping you.'

'Isn't he old and ugly?' said Keith.

The string had come out of my pyjama trousers and I couldn't thread it through.

'I could drown myself for a woman like that,' pronounced Keith.

'I wonder if the tide'll be in tomorrow morning,' I remarked. 'It's dangerous to swim if it's right on the rocks.'

Keith turned out the oil lamp.

'When the tide goes out, you have to be careful too,' I continued, 'there's a hell of a current because of the river.' We lay down in the dark. The ground was very hard. Wherever I shifted my sleeping-bag I seemed to find a bump that made my back ache.

'Lots of people have been drowned in Ogmore, Keith.'

Later Keith said, 'I wonder why she married him?'

'Money, I suppose.'

'I bet she hates him.'

'Oh, I dunno.'

'She hates him,' said Keith dogmatically.

'Let's go to sleep,' I yawned.

It must have been an hour later when I awoke and heard a voice muttering in the darkness. At first, I thought my friend was praying and in reverence I lay back in the dark, pretending to be asleep. But after a pause he started again and the words came through to my side of the tent more distinctly:

'Shall I compare thee to a summer's day?
Thou art more lovely and more temperate.
Rough winds do shake the darling buds of May,
And summer's lease hath all too short a date.'

'For God's sake, shut up!' I called out.

The next morning we scrambled into khaki shorts and out into the sun. The sea looked negatively blue, reflecting the clear skies, while the haze over the sea promised another true summer's day. I pumped away at the primus whilst Keith walked over to the house to obtain water. I noticed that Tuska Rock could barely be seen, and there was no sign of the shipwreck at all. That meant the tide was half-way in or half-way out. Eventually the primus burnt properly with its blue flames, but it was some

time before Keith came into sight carrying a bucket of water. I stooped round the tent slackening the ropes and stung my leg on a nettle.

'You've been a long time,' I said.

'I saw her in her dressing-gown,' he said. 'Her hair's awfully long, like a mermaid.'

'She was probably born in a rock-pool,' I said.

'I think you're jealous,' Keith said.

We poured some water into a kettle and put it on the primus.

'She asked if we'd like to go riding with her this morning,' said Keith.

'I can't ride,'

'I know,' said Keith, 'so I apologized for you and said that I should like to – that is if you don't mind.'

I felt cheated, and didn't say anything. After all, I *had* come to Ogmore to camp with Keith.

'You don't mind, do you?' my friend said. 'We'll only be gone for an hour or so . . . It was very nice of her to ask us.'

'I thought this morning we could go for our first swim together,' I said.

The kettle began to boil, its lid rattling, and steam poured out of its snout. Keith emptied tea into the pot and laid out the two mugs.

'Look,' he said. 'You go for a swim. Don't be a spoilsport. I'd love to go for a ride.'

'Sure,' I said reluctantly. 'Go to the devil.'

Keith poured the tea into the mugs and passed the sugar. We cracked a couple of eggs into the frying-pan and they sizzled in the fat.

After breakfast we smoked cigarettes and from the house we saw Henrietta Gregory walking towards us. She was dressed in riding-habit, and her raven-coloured hair was once again tied into a bun. We rose from the ground when she came near to us. She was smiling, perhaps because we were smoking cigarettes.

'You don't ride?' she said to me.

'I'm afraid not.'

'But he doesn't mind if I go,' said Keith.

'Well, are you sure?' she asked me.

I saw Keith staring at me from his poison-blue eyes.

'Not at all,' I conceded. 'I'll go for a swim.'

'I don't like to separate you,' Mrs Gregory said. 'Perhaps you had better both go for a swim.'

'No, really,' I said, trying to present myself in a generous light, 'Really, I don't mind.'

'We could all go for a swim this afternoon,' Keith suggested. Mrs Gregory laughed. 'Well ... we'll see about that ... but if you don't mind,' she said to me.

'No, honestly.'

Later, when Keith went off with Henrietta Gregory, I began to think that perhaps my friend wasn't bad-looking after all. Lydia Pike had once remarked on Keith being attractive. Certainly he was growing tall now and looked older than his age. His blue eyes and red hair and wide-boned face perhaps appealed to a woman. I looked at myself in the little mirror with some disgust. Henrietta Gregory wasn't likely to look at me twice. With a self-righteous self-pity I rolled my bathing costume in a towel and strolled down towards Hardy's Bay. Down between boulders, and sheep branded H, and down along a narrow path bordered by green ferns over which fluttered an occasional nervous white butterfly. There were many rabbit-holes around and about. And then I was on the sea-turf that led down to the sea rocks, over which I climbed to reach the short strip of sand. There before me was the sea, the sea. I had the beach to myself, though the other side of the rocks in Hardy's Bay proper a number of morning swimmers shouted in the waves or played with a football on the firm sand. Tuska Rock lay submerged beneath the sea, two miles out: the tide was coming in. 'I wish Lydia was here,' I said to myself. A seagull floated down in its perfect poise of geometry and art, and I undressed, pulling on my bathing costume.

At the sea's edge I hesitated, warily letting the white tongues of the sea lick my ankles. It was cold. And as I stood on the edge of the world, listening to the dog-chained growling sea scrambling up the beach for a bone, I thought of the vertical death of the

140

drowned, of the white-haired prisoners in the sea, and those others who slept in the feathery fathoms below the watery grey and green eiderdown that was pulled back and fore by the two-time swell.

Then I forgot the catastrophe of the *Thetis*, and like a bull, I suddenly rushed into the sea and the matador waves slapped my belly familiarly and the cold whistled into my shattered breath before I dived into a taller wave, and rose and snorted, and blew my nose, and wee-weed in the water for a joke. I stood on my hands so that anybody on the beach could see how clever I was, but it was lonely and cold. I didn't swim out too far because of the menace of the tide and because nobody would be able to hear me cry 'help' or 'save me'. Seeing my clothes obliquely piled on a mustard-stained rock, I struck for shore deliciously exhilarated. Once more in my depth, I let the procession of waves attack me and I skipped as they rose, as they crashed in my ears. Coming out, I was surprised how warm the water was near the sea's edge and, seeing that the few who had occupied Hardy's Bay had gone, I ran up and down like a crazy animal on the lengths of sand. Teeth chattering, towel rubbing my head to curls, I dressed again and made up tales to tell Keith when I returned to the green-roofed house. 'Funny thing, Keith, I met a mermaid when I went for a swim this morning.' 'How come?' he would ask. 'It was like this – I heard somebody shouting for help and I swam out miles to sea and there she was, almost drowning.' My friend would ask, 'A mermaid drowning?' I could see him doubting me. 'She had cramp,' I'd explain . . .

I shook my head to get water out of my ear and lay down on the sand in the sun. Gradually everything grew calm and there was nothing at all but the sound of the sea. All the noise in my head fell away, crumbled to nothingness, and I lost my identity. I was as much part of the beach as the mustard-tainted rock on which earlier I had piled my clothes. I felt clean inside and strangely elated. It was more than the freedom and beauty of the seas and skies, more than being the last person in the world alive. Something moved across the heart like a benediction. It is hard to explain. It would be easier to describe a colour no one had ever

141

seen. Only I felt a great exultation and a holiness I never sensed before and have only experienced once since. I felt I was given the power to do enormous good. And that delusion stayed with me for the rest of the morning. I stared at the beach, but it was not my eyes that looked out. I moved my hand, but it was not my hand that moved. I was neither up nor down. A seagull glided and swooped to its shadow on the sea. I too floated above the pebbles in a heat haze, integrated with the landscape. I wrote my name in the sand near the sea, and watched the waves erase it, and I knew the significance of things, the meaning of the whole world, its mystery and motion. All the long morning I knew that secret and then, when I returned to the house with the green roof and spoke to the maid, Sadie, I forgot what that angel and message was. Just as one forgets a face only once seen.

In the kitchen there was a lovely smell of cooking.

'Been for a swim?' asked Sadie.

'Yes,' I said. 'Is my friend returned?'

'They're in the back room,' she said. 'You're all 'aving lunch 'ere.'

I opened the door into the corridor and heard the piano being played. The garden doors of the 'back' room were open. Keith played the piano and Mrs Henrietta Gregory sat in the armchair with a cigarette, absently looking out towards the sea, perhaps listening, perhaps not.

I wanted to tell them that something had happened to me on the beach. Something had passed into me, changing me, had made me older and more lonely, but what words could I discover to explain to them? In any case, Keith didn't notice me enter, and the raven-haired lady gazed out at the distant sea, beyond my telling.

The next week I saw less and less of Keith as he accompanied Henrietta Gregory on every possible journey: whether to go shopping, walking, or riding, though Mrs Gregory in no way seemed to encourage him. But there was one advantage in all this: we ate now – except for breakfast – almost always at the Gregory table. Sometimes, of course, I would be the inconspicuous third, which

made me feel a little daft. Thus, when one afternoon we all went swimming together and Keith picked up Mrs Gregory and threw her into the sea – 'Don't Keith, don't be silly – you're incorrigible, Keith, please' – dissolving into laughter and a scream – I stood watching, smiling sickly and embarrassed, particularly as Henrietta (Keith called her Henry) was an eyeful in a bathing costume – and much smaller than one would expect, without her high heels. On her 'stilts' she was my height, a little shorter than Keith. Without shoes, she appeared younger, more vulnerable to Keith's amorous advances! In the evenings Keith played the piano for her, or they listened to records and often I would go out unwanted and glad to walk up to the *Seagull Café* or *Hardy's Café* alone.

One evening I returned after a long walk when the tide was right out, leaving pools of sea-water across the naked sand. The sun was low in the sky and these pools gleamed red and gold in the sunset's tired light. Clouds had piled themselves high in the sky, dark-fringed – thunder clouds, I thought, for the air was still and stuck in invisible gossamer. Keith and Henrietta Gregory were playing tennis in the long shadows and I went in to talk to Sadie.

'The master's coming back the day after tomorrow,' she informed me.

I helped her to dry the dishes.

'Mrs Gregory's been much better the last month,' continued Sadie.

'What's been wrong with her?' I asked.

'She 'ad a breakdown,' said Sadie, touching her forehead with her index finger. 'But she's all right now. I'm glad you boys 'ave come. Mr Gregory do 'ave to go away a lot and she gets miserable and thinking when she's on 'er own. Your friend is a real terror and I do think he tire her; but Mr Gregory don't play tennis and doesn't like riding very much. She needs it, the exercise, I think. She says to me, Sadie, them boys are a real nuisance, but I think she's glad you're 'ere. She was very ill after 'er father died. And the last month she's been much better.'

'We haven't been here a month,' I said.

'She's been on the mend before you came,' Sadie said. 'But

that Keith's 'as finished it off. She needs the flattery and the exercise even if it's only from a little boy.'

'Keith isn't a little boy,' I said, but Sadie just laughed.

'Go away,' she said. 'You 'aven't got your nappies off of you yet. Anyway the master'll be back soon.'

After I finished washing-up with Sadie I strolled over to the tent to collect a book to read. As I passed the tennis court Keith saluted me with his racquet and Mrs Gregory, dressed in white blouse and white shorts, smiled kindly.

'It's getting too dark to see the ball,' I heard Mrs Gregory say.

In the tent I sorted out the two books I had brought with me from Cardiff. One by Llewellyn Powys and the other entitled *Poems for Spain* with its poignant war poems which would almost make me cry to read them.

Mrs Gregory and Keith caught me there, straining my eyes and reading a poem out loud:

> 'Look I am opened, like a wound
> Look, I am drowned, drowned
> in the midst of my people and its ills.
> Wounded I go, wounded and badly wounded
> bleeding through the trenches.'

They laughed and I looked up.

'Henry suggested you might like to have a cold drink with us,' said Keith.

We sat on the veranda drinking iced lemonade. It was very hot indeed. The weather stood sultry and still, presaging a disaster, and the poem kept echoing in my head.

> 'The lament pouring through valleys and balconies
> deluges the stones and works in the stone,
> and there is no room for so much death,
> and there is no wood for so many coffins.'

'Mr Gregory's coming back the day after tomorrow then, Henry?' Keith said.

'Oh yes,' she said. 'He's been away too long.'

*

That night Keith seemed excited.

'Her husband won't stay long,' he said.

I'd already turned in and was waiting to extinguish the oil lamp, but Keith seemed in no hurry to undress.

'He mustn't stay long. I can't bear to know she's sleeping with him,' he said.

'He's coming back soon, isn't he?' I asked.

Keith nodded.

'I love her,' he said dramatically.

'Put a sock in it,' I said.

'You don't understand,' Keith continued. 'You don't know what love is.'

There's father, mother, Wilfred, Leo, I thought – I love them dearly – and maybe Lydia Pike.

'I've kissed her,' said Keith, interrupting my thoughts. He looked at me triumphantly, for I must have looked astonished.

'Really?'

'I'm going to sleep with her.'

'Has she agreed?'

'Not exactly.'

'Have you asked her?'

'You don't ask a woman,' said Keith, 'you just do it.'

'What about babies?' I asked reluctantly.

'What about them?'

'I mean . . .'

'There's such a thing as contraceptives,' said Keith, very old suddenly.

'I know,' I remarked, pretending to yawn. 'Llewellyn Rees showed me one.'

'Well then?'

'How much do they cost?' I asked.

'Not very much . . . I don't think.'

'Where do you get 'em from?'

'The chemist, stupid,' said Keith. 'I'll get some tomorrow.'

'In Ogmore?'

'In Bridgend – you'll come with me?' asked Keith.

'What for?'

'You're my friend, aren't you?'

'Yes, but what's that got to do with it?'

'Well, I'll need some sort of support.'

'What do you do?' I asked.

'One just goes in and asks for a packet of them,' Keith told me.

'Not me,' I said.

'Why not?'

'It's your problem,' I said.

Next morning we climbed up to the *Seagull Café* to catch the green-coloured bus destined for Bridgend. Below us the wind combed the ferns that rolled down to the turf and the sparkling sea. Such a morning it was, clear and clean, with islands of cotton wool in the airy blue sky. The bus chugged down the tarry road, past the Roman wall and the white cottages, to stop outside the *Seagull Café*. It was blue, green and white, as far as the eye could see, and we clambered aboard. The conductor pulled a cord that made a bell croak, and the bus jerked forward again, empty but for Keith and me and a talkative hatchet-faced conductor.

'Boo-ootiful mornin', in' it?' said the conductor. 'On 'oliday are 'u? O, I do wish I 'ad a bit of leisure to do some fishin', see. Un-iv-ersity stoodents are 'u?'

Flattered, we nodded our heads. 'Soon will be,' said Keith.

'Ay,' said the bus conductor. 'Nothin' there is like education. I wish I 'ad it. Couldn't afford it when I was little 'un. They didn't learn me much. But you need it 'ere,' he said tapping his head. 'When you're an old 'un like me, it's 'ard, oh it's 'ard, 'ard to take it in. Mind you, I'm a tidy bugger with the books. I belongs to the Chain Library.'

The bus peeped a horn and shunted over to one side to let another bus pass by. There was just enough room for both of them.

'Shw'mae Dai,' yelled the conductor on the other bus. And Dai, our conductor, waved a friendly hand. We were shifting again quite fast now and Dai said, 'This old bus can fair tamp along when it's got its mind for it.' He rolled a fag, and lit up.

146

'Think there'll be a war?' he asked. 'They've called up the Reservists and making them all try on their gas-masks again. Fat lot of good that'll do, mun; the rubber on my mask perished already. 'E's askin' for it, 'Itler is.'

We smiled agreement. 'If there do come a war, it won't be like the last one. It'll be total,' continued Dai, 'total, total. It's a mean thing, a war is, I can tell 'u. I was in the last, I was.'

'So was my father,' I said.

'My Dad was an officer,' said Keith.

'This war, if it do come, won't be like the last. An' I think it will come,' said Dai prophesying. 'We give our word to the Poles an' we'll 'ave to keep it, I do say.'

'What about the Czechs?' said Keith.

'Ay,' said the conductor. 'My last territorial claim, by damn. 'E's a tidy bastard. I never liked the Germans, I don't like the Germans, an' I never will like 'em, see. There's only one good German an' that's a dead 'un, bachgen. But war's a mean thing. A mean thing. An' now we're fillin' sandbags again and diggin' trenches and trying on gas-masks. Air Raid Precautions, it is. An' the Reservists called up 'cause of that mean bugger 'Itler. It's a tragedy, mun, a foul tragedy.'

'What we want is a Soviet Alliance,' said Keith.

'Ay,' said the conductor. ''Ow the 'ell can we 'elp the Poles without an Alliance? I seen the map. It do look a long way away. Maybe there won't be any war. Germans are bluffers, that's what I do say. Mean bluffers. An' bullies. They do get tough with the small nations, see, but when they do see *our* mailed fist . . .'

'They've got a lot of armaments,' I said.

'Ay, an' we've got our Navy,' said Dai fiercely.

The bus stopped to let an old man climb aboard. The conductor took his stick and hoisted him up, like a flag, and the old man, red-eyed and puffing, sat down on the seat opposite us, clearing his throat. The bus stumbled forward changing gears and the old man spat on the floor.

''Ere, Mr Jenkins,' said the conductor. 'Can't you read that sign there?'

The sign read: Penalty for Spitting five pounds.

'No, Dai – what is it?' the old man asked cunningly.

'You know what it do say, Twm Jenkins. No Gobbin', that's what it do say.'

'An' you're smokin',' the old man said.

The conductor took a last puff at his cigarette before throwing the dibby over a green hedge.

'Well, I'm not smokin' now,' said the conductor.

'An' I'm not gobbin',' said the old man.

The bus continued with silent passengers until the conductor said, 'Some people aren't social, some people aren't.'

Five minutes later the old man started coughing, wheezing and clearing his throat. The conductor watched him suspiciously. The old man paused before spitting again, and said quickly: 'Well, you can't expect me to swallow it, Dai James, can you? It's not 'ealthy. Ask your panel doctor.'

'It's not social,' said the conductor. 'You worse than that bloody 'Itler, putting your fingers up at the law. Five pounds, it'll cost you, I swear to you, mun, if you do spit again.'

'I 'aven't got five pounds,' said the old man mildly.

'Well, then,' said the conductor, 'you can't afford to spit.'

'I thought you were a socialist, Dai James. An' now you're talking about privileges.'

Bridgend is quite a busy town. It hasn't a cathedral of course, but it owns a bus yard, a lunatic asylum and, more important, chemist shops. Keith and I walked out into the cobbled bus yard. Looking back we saw Dai James, the conductor, helping old Mr Jenkins down. 'Easy there, mun, easy there – old dear,' Dai was saying. Once on *terra firma*, Mr Jenkins spat loudly on to the cobbles.

'Five pounds, eh, ten pounds, fifteen pounds,' he shouted, spitting twice, thrice in the bus yard.

We stood for some time outside Ap John's, the chemist in Paradise II Street, staring at the big globes of coloured water in the window.

'You'll come in with me?' said Keith anxiously.

'If you insist,' I said, 'though I'm not sure that they are safe.'

'Why?' asked Keith.

'Llewellyn Rees told me that sometimes the shop girls stick pins in them for fun.'

'Some fun,' said Keith.

'It's probably one of Rees's old tales,' I remarked. We looked through the window but there was a customer inside. We waited until he quitted the shop and then, with a quick look up and down the street, like fugitives, we entered the chemist's. The pharmacist was going through a curtain into the back just as we passed through the door. We waited anxiously inside looking at the rows of coloured fluids in bottles, at the jars of pills and significant boxes. Keith coughed loudly, but nobody appeared. I went to the door and opened and closed it, making a bell ring, but before the pharmacist came through the curtain behind the counter, a middle-aged woman waded into the shop. We looked at each other and made for the door.

Outside, I began to laugh hysterically until Keith said, 'I don't see the joke.'

'If you feel like that,' I said, 'you can go into the next shop yourself.'

'Let's look for one in a side street,' said Keith.

At the corner of Metal Street we found a likely looking shop. It was deserted.

'Are you coming in or not?' said Keith.

'Well, I don't know.'

'Please,' said Keith urgently. 'Please.'

A small carving of a man stood on the counter. The carved figure held up a huge weight that made his brass muscles swell and bulge impressively. Under it the advertisement ran: *Testex gives you strength.* 'You want some of that,' I said to Keith. Eventually a young lady dressed in a white coat appeared, startling us.

'Good morning,' she said.

'Good morning,' said Keith.

'Can I help you?' she asked.

Keith's face matched his red hair and I stood on the weighing machine, pretending I wasn't with my friend.

'Can I have ... er ...' I heard him say tremulously. 'Have

you got some Maclean's toothpaste?' he asked suddenly.

'A small or a large packet, sir?' asked the young lady.

In the street Keith said, 'Well, I couldn't ask a woman – besides, I need toothpaste.'

We went back to Ogmore with two packets of toothpaste, a bar of soap, and some razor blades.

When Mr Raymond Gregory returned, Keith and I saw less and less of Henrietta. We were not invited to eat at the house any more and Keith never joined them riding. Henrietta would say 'Good morning' or 'Good afternoon' to us formally and Mr Gregory would smile, saying, 'Are you enjoying your holiday, boys?' For two days they went away to Porthcawl and Keith mooched around unhappily.

'I hate him. I hate him more than my father.'

'You don't hate your father,' I said, surprised.

'I do,' said Keith quietly. 'I've not told you before, but I despise him. I found him out when I was a kid.'

'What do you mean?' I asked.

Keith sat on the sand throwing pebbles across the waves so that they skimmed and bounced on the water.

'Because he drinks . . .?' I said tentatively.

Keith just rose and walked away and I ran after him.

'What's the matter with you?' I said. 'Your father pays for you to have piano lessons. He's had a hard time considering . . .'

He walked faster.

I looked back, seeing our double footprints in the soft sand.

'Look, Keith, do you want to be alone or something?'

'You can do what you like.'

He stopped on one of the rocks, looking down at a pool of sea-water: the clear water and the green slime.

'Fathers can be very difficult,' I said, 'but we owe them a lot.'

As we came round the pathway through the ferns we saw the black Daimler on the gravel drive, parked outside the house.

'They're back,' I said.

'Let's go in and talk to them,' said Keith.

'What excuse can we make?'

'You don't need an excuse,' Keith said, but he hesitated all the same. 'We can ask them what they think about the Soviet Alliance,' he said.

'I don't understand it,' I said. 'I don't understand it at all. I wonder what Leo thinks of it.'

'You don't have any opinions until Leo gives them to you,' remarked Keith coldly.

'Well, of all the cheek! Where do you get your opinions from?'

'Are you coming or not?' interrupted Keith. 'I've got to speak to her.'

We walked round the back of the house and the garden doors were open. We could hear them talking together clearly. Keith raised his finger to pursed lips, signalling 'Shush', and guiltily we listened to what we should never have heard.

'Well, it's nice to be back again,' Mr Gregory was saying. 'It's a good job that we have this place in Ogmore if there's going to be a war. No bomb will fall here.'

'You're not very optimistic, Bunny,' said Henrietta.

'Some of my friends told me in London that there is a distinct possibility of a war. If Hitler marches into Danzig, public opinion will drive this Government into a war. This Nazi-Soviet pact gives Hitler a free hand almost.'

'You really think so, Raymond?'

'It could be,' he said.

'Well, I'm glad you're here,' said Henrietta. 'I must say, darling, I feel much better now than I did a month ago.'

'It's the fresh air and the sun. That's all you needed,' he replied.

'I must say those boys camping over there are quite sweet. I think one of them is in love with me.'

'I'm not surprised,' he said, and laughed.

I looked at Keith, but his expression showed no sign that he had heard. He stood there as dead. Inside the house Sadie was singing upstairs:

> 'My life one hell you're making
> You know I'm yours for just the taking . . .
> Body and Soul.'

'All the same I'm glad you're back, Bunny. The boy they call

Keith nearly made a scene the other day. He said he had a secret to tell me . . . He stood there gawkily and said that I was very pretty and then asked – did I have brains as well.'

'Good Lord . . . what *did* you say?'

'What could I say? I just laughed out of sheer embarrassment – and he blushed and said that Beauty and Brains seldom go together.'

Each side of the garden doors the sunlight fell across us both, casting our grotesque shadows on the shale wall of the house. Keith stared down at his feet miserably.

'Bunny, you should have seen him. He just walked away; it was either that or he would have tried to kiss me.'

'He's just a child,' said Mr Gregory.

'He lost his mother years ago, but he was becoming too much for me. I'm no good as a mother-substitute,' she said.

Keith moved away from the window and walked quietly towards the tent. They continued talking about Keith and Porthcawl and Stalin and Hitler. There was nothing to do but follow Keith.

When I entered the tent he was lying on the groundsheet, face down. I just sat there beside him, not knowing what to say.

'I wouldn't be upset by that,' I said after a while.

Suddenly he got up and stared out at the grass. His face showed no sign of any emotion.

'Want a fag?' I asked.

He didn't reply.

'I think I'm becoming a chain-smoker,' I said.

As the match spurted in the coolness of the tent he said, 'Fancy calling that fat-arsed old man "Bunny".'

That same night, when we were lying in our sleeping-bags and had turned out the lamplight, Keith said, 'I wish I had the power to know what everybody was doing exactly, without being there.'

'I know what you mean,' I replied. 'If one only had a sort of machine so that we could tune in to somebody's wavelength.'

'Who would you tune in to?' Keith asked.

'Dunno,' I said. 'Maybe Lydia. Maybe home.'

152

We both lay back in the darkness imagining the wonderful invention that could tell us the impossible.

'Wouldn't be any good if everybody had it,' I said.

'No, just us two,' said Keith. 'I'd tune in to *The Bull With One Leg* and see the old man. Listen to his conversation an' everything.'

'Wouldn't you tune in to Henrietta?' I asked.

Keith didn't say anything and it was so quiet I could hear him breathing from the other side of the tent.

'I'd tune in to Hitler,' I said quickly, trying to distract him. But he didn't answer.

'Think what scoops you'd have if you had that instrument,' I said. 'They'd make you a leader writer for the *South Wales Echo*. You could prognosticate everything. Why, you'd be the master-spy. Would be like being God,' I said astonished.

Keith didn't seem to be in the mood for talking any more. Maybe he was still thinking of Henrietta, so I said 'Good night' and he mumbled something. 'What's that?' I said.

'Good night,' he said louder.

Perhaps God's got an instrument sort of like that? I thought.

I woke up later and fumbled for my watch and saw it was past midnight. The phosphorescent figures on my watch jumped out like tigers' eyes in the dark. I had been dreaming of the Instrument. I had been the Saviour of the World because of the marvellous instrument I had invented. But I did not then know that East of Berlin the anonymous lorries, the tractors and the phallic guns pointing at the sky, the rumbling tanks, all rolled forward, division after division, towards the Polish frontier. It was a starry, clear, summer night in Ogmore.

It was dark already as we bundled into the Daimler. The chauffeur closed the door and walked round to the driver's seat. Mr and Mrs Gregory stood on the gravel. Behind them Sadie, dark against the light, waited framed by the front door.

'It's very kind of you,' I said again to Mr Gregory.

The Germans had crossed into Poland and because of the likelihood of war we had to go home. Mr Gregory was sending the

chauffeur to Cardiff on some urgent private business and so he offered us transport. It was the end of the holidays, but we were going home in style.

'Aren't you going to say good-bye?' Henrietta said to Keith.

'Good-bye, Mrs Gregory,' replied Keith mechanically. We shook hands and the engine started up. From the back window I waved to them. I could see them clearly in the starlight. As we turned round the bend they already began to move back into the house. Keith sat grumpily in the front seat with the driver and we flashed by the *Seagull Café* with its electric sign and then we reached the road to Bridgend. The chauffeur stopped for a moment to pull back the sliding roof and I reclined easily, staring at the grandeur of the starry sky. The car made hardly any noise at all. The chauffeur whistled phrases of 'When the Deep Purple Falls' before relapsing into silence. There was only the click of summer insects against the windscreen and in no time at all we were climbing up Crack Hill. It had been a grand holiday and now it was over. Keith would forget about Henrietta. Last night I had said to him: 'Time is a great healer,' but he had only grunted and stared at the distance from dark blue eyes.

The Daimler had been travelling very fast. The headlights flung themselves forward like two soft phosphorescent antennae groping out into the darkness to illuminate here a hedge, there a road sign. The car passed a hitch-hiker who waved desperately – a strange male gesticulating creature momentarily crucified in the glare of the beams before he too, along with the road signs, the gates, the hedges, was swallowed up by the darkness. The headlights gave everything a brief tremendous reality – and afterwards there was nothing, nothing, that is, save an emphasized darkness. Suddenly I imagined we were going nowhere, coming from nowhere, but destined to travel on and on through the countryside forever. It was a revelation: we were doomed to travel irrevocably into the dark, going to no destination, coming from a departure that never existed. The chauffeur and Keith sat as mute shadows in the front seat, figures frozen and damned into silence. Why didn't they speak? There was only the insistent purring of the automobile and the click of summer insects against the wind-

screen. They could not speak, that was it. They were dead! . . . They *were* dead . . . I *was* dead. We were all dead and this was our damnation: to journey on forever through the dark. 'You're damned, little one,' Mr Thomas had said.

In the distance I could see the tiny red rear-light of another car which no doubt contained other passengers committed to this same damnation of ever travelling forward from nowhere to nowhere. Always travelling, pulled by two headlights illuminating hedges, gates, signposts – images of a dead country. And up above, through the open roof, the cruel and indifferent pattern of stars. Now we passed that other automobile of death, and if we had waved to those other occupants it would have been as the lost waving to the lost.

Soon we dipped over Tumble Down Dick and, before us, the lights of Cardiff lay spreadeagled below the hills. We were not dead after all, for we had a destination, and Keith spoke, shattering the illusion completely.

'Home,' he said, 'soon we'll be home.' And then, 'Poor Henrietta.' The chauffeur began to whistle phrases from 'When the Deep Purple Falls'. We were journeying from Ogmore to Cardiff.

The next Sunday we heard Chamberlain saying, 'I have to tell you that no such understanding has been received and that consequently this country is at war with Germany.'

*   *   *

The noise wailed inhumanly over Cardiff. First one siren, then another sounded in the distance like an echo. Sombre, admonitory, the noise fell away into the wind, was carried away with the smoke blown from thousands of chimney-pots, carried forward and away with the paper blown through the night streets. The trees stood at attention on the pavements, waiting, under a moon threading bare the soap-sud clouds. In expectancy, the City stopped for a moment, listening to itself, to its own footsteps. The mood of landscapes abruptly became sinister, the church on the hill, the secretive street leading to the municipal baths, the deserted garage at the crossroads. In the cinemas a notice fell across

155

the screen distracting the audience of flickering, uplifted, tired faces from Bette Davis or Gary Cooper. It read: 'An Air-Raid Warning has sounded. Stay in your seats. Don't panic. Be British.' Soon the film ended in a close-up of a kiss and, as if by magic, out of the dark pit the juke-box organ ascended, gaudy, elephantine, changing colours as it wheezed out the popular tunes:

> 'I'll be seeing you
> In all the old familiar places.'

Outside, the trams, long blue-lit phantoms, jerked to a halt, and motor-cars, wearing slotted masks over their headlights, speeded swiftly down the dark avenues of absence. Somebody was knocking at a door.

'Mr Morris, your curtains aren't properly pulled.' And the chink of electric light leaking from the third-floor window was promptly stopped up. Others hurried through the Black-out with their hand-torches extinguished. Hurried home in the dark, anonymous, nameless.

'Excuse me. I'm sorry. Is that you, Dora? I'm lost. The moon's gone behind the clouds.'

Be British. Don't panic. The organ rode down into the pit again and the audience clapped perfunctorily. A horizontal beam of light splashed on to the screen and the Metro-Goldwyn-Mayer lion roared. Outside searchlights floundered in the sky, spooky and curious. Spiritual cold devices poking the clouds that sailed high over the balloons, high over the patched rooftops. In the distance, like a throb of a dying pulse, the malignant sound of aeroplanes. In the distance, the white fur of fire of the Ack-Ack guns touching and fumbling briefly the hillsides all along the coast.

'Swansea's 'aving it tonight.'
'Barry's 'aving it tonight.'
'Newport's 'aving it tonight.'

My father switched on the wireless. Mother said: 'Where are they both? Running after *shiksehs* on a night like this. Where are they? And it's Leo's last night before he goes back to Camp.

156

They should be home; that's where they should be.' Dad put his ear nearer to the loudspeaker.

'Wilfred's safer out in India,' Mother prattled on. 'He'll be all right. A good batman to look after him, clean his shoes.' My father, exasperated, twiddled with the radio-knobs, wanting to hear Lord Haw-Haw.

'What do you want to listen to that for?' protested mother. 'There's enough noise outside. You, and your Germany calling, Germany calling.'

'Listen,' said Dad, as the needle flickered between four stations, 'Moscow.' Three voices in different languages spoke at once, harshly gyrating behind a background of jazz.

'I don't care if it's Joe Stalin,' said my mother. 'Switch it off.'

'Perhaps you want me to switch the light off too,' argued Dad.

Mother picked up her knitting, pretending that outside it was all a dream, that nothing really was happening, and soon the alarm clock would ring and she would wake up. Dad only fiddled with the knobs of the radio, hoping to hear the voice of God telling him that the war would be over tomorrow, that Hitler and Mussolini were to be placed in cages for display in circuses, and that Wilfred and Leo would be sent home to be demobilized and pursue the lives he had planned for them.

No such voice spoke in the worried room. Dad eventually knocked off the wireless and began to cough. They listened to the noise outside, wondering what had been, what was to be, uncertain and afraid.

'I remember in the last war . . .' began my father.

'You remember. You don't remember anything. Where are the boys?' my mother asked for the tenth time.

'Climbing Snowdon. What do you think?' barked father.

The saddest time of all, thought Leo. Going back after too short a leave to the Unit. Too soon he would be there again, at that point of departure, looking at the empty Station Clock, the cold Refreshment Bar. All too soon he'd be looking out of the carriage, rubbing the window clean of breath to see her fractured face amongst the tale of kitbags and 'Got a light, chum?' Somebody

157

was shooting a line. Flying a Tiger Moth, that's something. Climbing up the slippery air on a clear spring day, that's something to write home about. Up and down the slippery air with the wind howling, rushing, leaping, pushing, pulling – and the whole aluminium and bloody fabric business of bolts and nuts shaking in an epileptic samba. That's flying, boy. Icarus would have appreciated that. Christ, it's fun. The land tilting towards you – the undulating yellow and green draughtboard fields beneath you. And the blasted wind with a bump and a bump and nothing again. Like riding a bicycle airborne, with a flat tyre airborne, high over the fields and miniature towns. Chagall high, over the cardboard rooftops and the silly minute spires – over the fields looking like patched quilts, like eiderdowns. But these other tubular monsters. These are just like riding big buses from here to there – with nothing to do between, except to check the instruments. Just like riding big automatic buses through the air. Nothing to it, except the taking off and the landing. So terribly mechanical and arrogant. Machines too fast, too powerful for pity. These aren't kites at all. They really are aeroplanes. Aeroplanes that are becoming to look more like fish and less like birds every day. Oh, give me the big, noisy, lovely, gawky, stinking birds. Give me the . . .

Leo brought his glass over to the corner of the pub, and Megan winked. The boys started singing. And my brother sat there in a blue uniform, rough to his body as a cat's tongue.

> 'Roll out the barrel,
> We'll have a barrel of fun,
> Roll out the barrel,
> We've got the Blues on the Run.'

'Last year,' said Leo, 'it was "We'll Hang Out the Washing on the Siegfried Line".'
'All together,' somebody shouted.
'I heard that on the Bob Hope programme!' a voice said.
'Be British,' another yelled. 'Don't panic.'
Laughter. Glasses. Singing. Laughter.

*

Uncle Bertie refused to stop the game. Despite the muffled emptiness of stark sound outside, the two players continued the more earnestly. The spectators had fled. Somebody had remarked ten minutes before to Uncle Bertie, 'I understand you're moving to Preston,' and somehow, in between, time had dwindled so that there, in the empty billiard hall, it seemed the question had just that moment been asked. The voice of the questioner still hung in the air. Uncle Bertie chalked his cue as Dafydd Morgan folded himself like a penknife, at right angles, over the green table. Uncle Bertie said, 'When we move to Preston . . .'

The cue made its diminished sound and the ivory balls clicked before the red one dropped out of sight down the far corner pocket.

'Good shot,' said Uncle.

'It's left me on, too.' said Morgan.

'The only thing that makes me hesitate about going to Preston,' continued Uncle Bertie, 'is Clive.'

'What do you mean?' said Morgan, putting the red ball on the spot.

'What do you mean, what do I mean?' growled Bertie. 'Supposing the boy comes back. To an empty house.'

'But Clive's . . . Well,' started Morgan. Then abruptly, impatiently, 'Look, Bertie, you know as well as I do the boy's dead.'

'He's not,' shouted Uncle. 'He's missing, just missing, somewhere near Dunkirk.' Neither player spoke again. Outside the green flares dropped, leaving the streets cut out in wounds of gangrene. The sky, green arson, luminous. But the curtains were drawn and the players continued heedlessly, though Mr Morgan spoilt his 'break' when one explosion rooted itself very near to the Club.

'Bertie,' said Morgan, 'some of the fellows are saying you're ill.'

'What's that?' Uncle asked.

'I mean they think you're not entirely well.'

'If you mean they say I'm mad – why don't you say so, Morgan?'

'No, I didn't say that. Except they think you might see a doctor or somebody.'

'What do I want to see a doctor for?' said Bertie. 'I'm as strong as a bull.'

When the bomb fell across the road into a tree of blazing light, Mr Morgan threw himself dramatically on the floor. Uncle Bertie stood upright, waving his cue, as bits of plaster fell from the ceiling. 'You bloody Germans!' he shouted. 'You bloody Huns!' The lights vacillated across the green table, making swinging shadows all over the billiard room.

'Easy, Bertie,' said Morgan.

'Do you know how old Clive was?' he shouted. 'Eighteen. Just eighteen.'

> 'Roll out the barrel,
> We'll have a barrel of fun,
> Roll out the barrel,
> We've got the Blues on the Run.'

The pub was full of cigarette smoke, and half the lights had been turned off.

'Is that you, Mr Thomas?'

'Hello, Leo,' said Mr Thomas. 'What're you drinking?'

'Not any more, thank you,' said Megan.

'Just came in,' continued Mr Thomas. 'It's as light as day outside. But I couldn't bear to be in the house. Keith is quite fearless. He just plays the piano and I feel so alone.'

'How is Keith?' asked Leo.

'He's a difficult boy,' said Mr Thomas. 'I find it difficult to get on with him these days. Whatever I do seems to be wrong as far as he's concerned.'

'It's just a phase,' said Leo.

'Maybe,' said Mr Thomas. 'Now what did you say you're having? Oh, come on. You're not on leave every day.'

'That was shrapnel,' said Ennis Aaronowich. It had made a crumbly, tinny noise as it pierced the lid of the dustbin. The three of them, and the baby, sat in the shelter at the bottom of the garden. Dr Aaronowich took out a red pill from a little white box and

Ennis stared down at the baby sleeping in the shadow of the shawl. It was dark and silent in the shelter, and it was pervaded with the acrid smell of autumn leaves and earth.

'Are you comfortable, Sarah?' asked Dr Aaronowich.

'I'd rather be in the house,' she replied.

When the flares dropped, turning the darkness into a ghastly green luminosity, old Mrs Aaronowich began to shake. 'I can't help it,' she said. 'I'm not afraid, but I can't help it.'

The Rev. Aaronowich sat quiet, thinking: this is the Age of the Victim. 'In the old days,' he started to say, 'the Romantic Hero was the Martyr. All the heroes in tragedy, real or literary, were Martyrs – Martyrs because they knew why they were dying and chose to die rather than surrender their faith. But for our world' – he nodded at the desperate livid sky and the fires above the rooftops – 'the symbol is the Victim. It is the quality of the Victim to be unaware and to have no choice. Like the Jews of Europe who went into the gas chambers asking ''why? why?'' because they had disinherited themselves from their faith. The symbol of our Age is the train that's gone off the rails, the mangled accident, the catastrophe – the passengers flung across the tracks or drowning at sea whispering ''why? why?'' And in wartime it is the bombed, or those majorities in uniform who kill and are killed without even understanding words like ''Democracy'', ''Communism'', ''Fascism''. Victims not Martyrs: those Jews of Europe, Passengers, Soldiers, Civilians – because they did not choose and do not understand why they are dying.'

'Jack is not a Victim,' said Ennis. 'He and millions of others know why they are fighting.'

'We are all Victims,' replied the old man. 'All of us. The Age of the Martyr is over; the Age of the Victim has begun. This is our world where the heroes are Victims, not Martyrs. What a subject for tragedy. Who apart from Kafka will make a Romantic Hero of the Victim?'

'What are you babbling about?' complained his wife. 'Look, you've woken up the baby.'

The baby began to cry and Ennis hummed, rocking the child gently.

161

'I hope when Jack comes on leave there won't be any air-raids,' said Sarah Aaronowich. 'When we're in the house again, will you read me his letter, Ennis?'

My mother had nearly finished knitting the Balaclava helmet.

Father said, 'He's got a head on him.'

Mother said, 'So has Wilfred.'

Father said, 'But Leo'll get on. He's clever. The trouble is he's a bit like your family.'

'Like my family,' mother exclaimed. 'Well, he's a charming boy.'

'What I don't like about him is the part that resembles your family,' insisted father.

'Well, Wilfred is like your family,' said mother.

'Well, he's a clever boy,' said my father. 'A psychiatrist.'

'A dreamer,' said mother.

'There's a bit of my family in Wilfred and a bit of my family in Leo,' said Dad. 'But the youngest one is all your family.'

'Like your family,' said mother.

'What are we goin' to do with him?' said father. 'He can't earn a living by poetry.'

'It's a disease with him,' said mother.

'What's that?' said father in a different tone of voice.

'Just a bomb,' said mother. 'He's like Uncle Isidore,' she said, returning to the old conversation.

'Exactly like Uncle Isidore,' repeated my father.

Phyllis came into the room and stood there watching Keith playing the piano. She called his name but he just went on playing. His shoulders hunched over the keyboard and his hands never for a moment still.

'Keith,' the maid called. 'Keith.'

The boy brought his two fists down again and again on the keyboard, transforming the music into a sort of gunfire, before swivelling round on the piano-stool to face Phyllis.

'Well?' he asked.

She just looked down at her feet.

'Don't be worried,' said Keith more gently. 'The raid's nearly over, I'm sure, and we're all right unless a bomb's got our names written on it.'

'Where's your father?' she asked.

Keith sighed and began to turn round to play again.

'I'm worried about him,' she cried.

'Why?' Keith replied coldly. 'He can look after himself.'

'He drank half a bottle of rum before he went out.'

'That won't affect . . .' Keith stopped speaking, and they both waited, listening to the curious whine coming nearer. Afterwards, Keith turned back to the piano.

'Come under the stairs,' Phyllis said. 'It's safer there.'

'Go there, then.'

'Won't you come?'

'It's easier playing the piano. Go on,' he added.

'Shall I make you a cup of tea?'

'No, you go and sit under the stairs. Presently I'll bring you a cup.'

And the boy turned over the music sheets. Phyllis stood watching him for a while. As she closed the door she could hear Keith playing, and the music reassured her as it sounded muffled from the room. The music seemed so sad and emotional. She felt foolish, sitting alone under the staircase, but the aeroplanes appeared to be immediately overhead. Explosions and gunfire seemed only next door, and frantically she pinned up a mackintosh over the window in the hall, to prevent glass spraying over her should a bomb fall. The drone of the aeroplanes receded as she first heard the thin whistle of the bomb dropping. It grew into a whine coming nearer and nearer. She held her breath and ducked, but the sound increased. It would never stop. There was a final rushing sound before the terrific explosion, and the lights went out and the whole house shook. She believed she hit her head on something as she fell, but even only half-conscious she knew she was shivering. It was dark and silent and the sound of the music from the drawing-room had stopped. Everything seemed to have collapsed around her. In the distance there was the sound of gun-

fire again. In the dark, she tried to rise to her feet, but then she felt the quiet pain in her leg. 'Keith,' she called 'Keith, Keith.'

Tensely she waited for an answer before calling out the boy's name again and again. 'Keith, KEITH.' There was something warm and wet and sticky on her leg. In the dark she smelt something burning. 'Help!' she cried. 'Help, help!' She was sobbing.

Mr Thomas brought over another two pints and a gin-and-lime for Megan.

'I'm beginning to feel fuzzy,' said Leo.

'Drink up,' said Thomas.

Megan was giggling when the pub fell silent as they listened to the All Clear.

'About time,' said Leo, rising from the chair. 'Come on, Megan.'

'Don't go yet,' said Mr Thomas, plucking at his sleeve. 'There's plenty of time.'

'Air-raids are timeless,' said Leo. 'It's getting late.'

'The clock's always fast,' said Mr Thomas. 'What'll you have? Same again?'

'No, no,' replied Leo. 'We must go really.'

Mr Thomas looked lost, aimless, as the young couple went out into the night. Resigned, he pushed himself through the khaki and blue to reach the bar.

Across the screen they signalled *The All Clear has sounded*. The film continued as if nothing had happened. Inside the cinema no indication of the severity of the raid could be guessed. Lydia and I didn't leave until the programme ended. We stood to attention as they played God Save the King. Then I helped Lydia into her coat and we walked out into the Black-out.

'Burr,' she remarked. 'It's quite cold.'

I began to hum, 'I've got my love to keep me warm', which was our secret signature tune. Now I would take her home and kiss her good night in the telephone-box opposite her house. Throughout the film we had held hands. I had rested my arm on her knee and

put my leg next to hers, just touching, as if by accident. We walked through the dark streets, her arm linked through mine and my hands deep in my pockets.

'What time's your lecture tomorrow morning?' she asked for no reason.

'Ten o'clock,' I answered absently.

We waited at the tram stop along with some land-girls and, soon, the long blue ghost of a vehicle drew up, and we climbed on the tram sitting close together, very close together, in the back seat upstairs.

At the White Wall where we alighted, we saw the flames for the first time and we started to run. It was coming from Keith's street and as we came nearer we saw it was from Keith's house. They had cordoned off the road and a fire-engine stood by. An ambulance drew up. We stood silently with the crowd watching the firemen. The St John's men were carrying two stretchers towards the flames.

'Anyone killed?' somebody asked.

Nobody knew.

We tried to get nearer but the policeman held us back. 'My friend's in there,' I said.

They were bringing two stretchers towards us, towards the ambulance. We glimpsed the pale face of Phyllis. Over the other one a blanket was drawn.

'He's not . . .' I said.

'Out of the way, laddie,' cried one of the policemen.

The crowd stood around muttering. They opened the back door of the ambulance. A man said: 'Can I help? I'm a doctor.'

'The girl's broken her leg,' said one of the St John's Ambulance men. 'I'm afraid you can't do anything for the boy. Come this way, Doctor.'

'You heard what he said?' asked Lydia stupidly, but I couldn't say anything. I wanted to say 'Keith' as they drove the ambulance away. The crowd remained there watching the hoses working on the fire. We started to walk back towards the White Wall. There was nothing else to do. It was the way the ambulance had gone. 'I've known Keith all my life,' I thought. 'All my life.'

'I can't believe it,' said Lydia, almost whispering.

'Shut up,' I wanted to say. 'Shut up.' But she didn't say more anyway.

A tram stopped near the White Wall and a figure climbed down, nearly falling on the pavement. He walked a few paces before seeing us. 'I'm damned,' he said simply. 'An' I'm drunk. So I can see the truth. I'm damned an' I'm drunk. I know what God is, so I know what sin is. Thy kingdom come. Don't laugh at me,' he shouted. 'You have power if you laugh at me. I'm not a stupid man ... I'm ... I am ... a happy man.' He gave us a little bow and passed us. We didn't say anything. We heard him begin to whistle 'Roll out the Barrel' as he walked into the dark.

* * *

I didn't go home because Leo had just been posted overseas and my parents would be saying the same things all over again. 'Both boys abroad. Wilfred in India will be comfortable. A good batman. But Leo. It's not safe there. There's a big battle going on there. Soon Dan will be called up.'

It had been raining, but now the sun, aware that it was my birthday, rubbed its way through the clouds, transforming their edges into a silver splendour. I sat down on a wooden bench that was still wet and I thought for a moment of my mother who would have said, 'You'll get piles or rheumatism.' But I sat there alone in the wonder of watching, my breath steaming out of my mouth. In the distance, a nun passed through the gate but otherwise the park was empty. 'Perhaps it wasn't a nun,' I thought, 'but a German spy.' And I laughed until I stopped laughing. It seemed less like a park since they had taken down the iron railings to use as war material. Near the brook a few air-raid shelters (which had hurriedly been constructed some years before) and a concrete turret camouflaged with autumn colours, stood convalescent in the weak sunlight. I had ducked out from a lecture at the University to celebrate my birthday with a cup of tea and synthetic cream cakes at the Kardomah. Now I sat in the park, emperor of my eighteen years, king of the tall fading trees,

big boss of the grass that was covered with a net of leaves. For the leaves were falling. Some branches already leaned nakedly into the scant oxygen – grim, wintry, and dead looking. Other trees were but lightly dressed and, minute after minute, another leaf would drop silently to the damp earth. The breeze would catch one sometimes and, instead of descending like a dead bird perpendicular to the grass, it would float in the air blown this and that way, like a child's paper aeroplane thrown, before descending unwillingly to the ground below. This was the death of leaves. Their falling was their dying. Those that came down unhindered, straight down the vertical rope of air were lucky, falling as they did, without protestation, a quick, easy, silent journey to death everlasting. But those that danced so gracefully, so lightly, so sadly to earth shouted in their untranslatable leaf-vocabulary. I was one who heard, that late autumn afternoon, their death agony. They fought against falling, even as some of us might, at night, struggle against falling in our most vivid dreams. Their descent was a cry of longing; they looked up yearningly at the branches from which they fell – not wishing to go. Like hands they dropped, yellow khaki hands, cold red hands, sinking in the air, waving good-bye, good-bye, to the branches that, already in our war weather, ached with their absence.

Near the air-raid shelters I heard, also, the waterfall crashing down into its disaster and saw, in the harp of wind, pools of rainwater trembling on the gravel pathway, reflecting shuddering fragments of sky. Pieces of sky, water, leaves, hands all fallen, falling in the convalescent sunlight. I stood up and walked out of the park, crossing the brook over the toy bridge, only stopping when I reached the street to gaze back at the distant summerhouse, at the nearer tall trees, at one more leaf, like a coloured minute, poised between high branch and grass – and I heard not one lingering cry of a child playing in that park which was made for children. I lit a cigarette, turned up the collar of my mackintosh, and strolled home that was never to be home again.

Discover more about our forthcoming books through Penguin's FREE newspaper...

Penguin Quarterly

It's packed with:

- exciting features
- author interviews
- previews & reviews
- books from your favourite films & TV series
- exclusive competitions & much, much more...

Write off for your free copy today to:
Dept JC
Penguin Books Ltd
FREEPOST
West Drayton
Middlesex
UB7 0BR
NO STAMP REQUIRED